Praise for *Spin* and *Axis* by Robert Charles Wilson

"Outstanding . . . The various science and thriller plot elements are successful, but this is first and foremost a novel of character. Turk and Lise, who might well be played by Bogart and Bacall, are powerfully drawn protagonists, and their strong presence in the novel makes the wonders provided all the more satisfying."
—*Publishers Weekly* (starred review) on *Axis*

"The long-anticipated marriage between the hard SF novel and the literary novel, resulting in an offspring possessing the robust ideational vigor of the former with the graceful narrative subtleties of the latter, might finally have occurred in the form of Robert Charles Wilson's *Spin*. Here's a book that features speculative conceits as brash and thrilling as those found in any space opera, along with insights into the human condition as rich as those contained within any mainstream mimetic fiction, with both its conceits and insights beautifully embedded in crystalline prose. . . . Wilson does so many fine things, it's hard to know where to begin to praise him."
—*The Washington Post*

"*Spin* is many things: psychological novel, technological thriller, apocalyptic picaresque, cosmological meditation. But it is, foremost, the first major SF novel of 2005, another triumph for Robert Charles Wilson in a long string of triumphs."
—*Locus*

**By Robert Charles Wilson
from Tom Doherty Associates**

A Hidden Place
A Bridge of Years
Mysterium
Darwinia
Bios
The Perseids and Other Stories
The Chronoliths
Blind Lake
Spin
Axis
*Julian Comstock: A Story of
    22nd-Century America*
Vortex
Burning Paradise
The Affinities
Last Year

VORTEX

**Robert
Charles
Wilson**

A TOM DOHERTY ASSOCIATES BOOK
NEW YORK

VORTEX

Copyright © 2011 by Robert Charles Wilson

All rights reserved.

Edited by Teresa Nielsen Hayden

A Tor Book
Published by Tom Doherty Associates
175 Fifth Avenue
New York, NY 10010

www.tor-forge.com

Tor® is a registered trademark of Macmillan Publishing Group, LLC.

ISBN 978-0-7653-6320-6

Our books may be purchased in bulk for promotional, educational, or business use. Please contact your local bookseller or the Macmillan Corporate and Premium Sales Department at 1-800-221-7945, extension 5442, or by e-mail at MacmillanSpecialMarkets@macmillan.com.

First Edition: July 2011
First Mass Market Edition: March 2012

Printed in the United States of America

0 9 8 7 6 5 4 3 2

VORTEX

CHAPTER ONE

SANDRA AND BOSE

No more, Sandra Cole thought when she woke up in her sweltering apartment. Today was the last day she would drive to work and spend her day in the company of emaciated prostitutes, addicts in the first sweaty stages of withdrawal, chronic liars, petty criminals. Today was the day she would hand in her resignation.

She woke every weekday morning with the same thought. It hadn't been true yesterday. It wasn't true today. But someday it would be true. *No more.* She savored the idea as she showered and dressed. It kept her going through her first cup of coffee and a quick breakfast of yogurt and buttered toast. By then she had mustered the courage to face the day. To face the knowledge that nothing, after all, would change.

o   o   o

She happened to be passing the reception area at State Care when the cop brought in the boy to be registered for evaluation.

The boy would be her responsibility for the next week: his folder had already been attached to her morning case list. His name was Orrin Mather, and he was supposed to be nonviolent. In fact he looked terrified. His eyes were wide and moist and he darted his head left and right like a sparrow scouting for predators.

Sandra didn't recognize the cop who brought him in—he wasn't one of the regulars. In itself that wasn't unusual; delivering minor arrests to the Texas State Care intake facility wasn't high-prestige duty at the Houston Police Department. Oddly, though, this particular cop seemed personally concerned with his charge. The boy didn't cringe away but pressed close to him, as if for protection. The cop kept a steady hand on his shoulder and said something Sandra couldn't hear but which seemed to soothe the boy's anxiety.

They were a study in contrasts. The cop was tall, big-bodied but not fat, with a dark complexion, dark hair, dark eyes. The boy was six inches shorter, dressed in a prison-issue jumper that sagged over his skinny body. He was so pale he looked like he'd been living in a cave for the past six months.

The orderly on reception duty at State was Jack Geddes, a man plausibly rumored to moonlight as a bouncer in a downtown bar. Geddes was often rough with patients—too rough, in Sandra's opinion. He sprang forward from his place behind the reception desk as soon as he registered Orrin Mather's agitation, quickly followed by the duty nurse with her armamentarium of sedatives and needles.

The cop—and this was *very* unusual—placed himself squarely between Orrin and the orderly. "None of that ought to be necessary," he said. His voice was Texas with a hint of something foreign. "I can escort Mr. Mather wherever you need him to go."

Sandra stepped forward, slightly embarrassed that she hadn't spoken first. She introduced herself as Dr. Cole and said, "The first thing we'll need to do is an intake interview. Do you understand, Mr. Mather? That happens in a room down the corridor. I'll ask you some questions and take down your information. Then we'll assign you a room of your own. Do you understand?"

Orrin Mather took a steadying breath and nodded. Geddes and the nurse backed off, Geddes looking a little annoyed. The cop gave Sandra an evaluative look.

"I'm Officer Bose," he said. "Dr. Cole, can I have a word with you once you get Orrin settled?"

"That might take some time."

"I'll wait," Bose said. "If you don't mind."

And that was the most unusual thing of all.

Daytime temperatures in the city had topped 100 degrees Fahrenheit for ten consecutive days now. The State Care evaluation facility was air-conditioned, often to the point of absurdity (Sandra kept a sweater in her office), but only a trickle of cool air forced its way through a ceiling grate into the room that was reserved for intake interviews. Orrin Mather was already sweating when Sandra took the chair across the table from him. "Morning, Mr. Mather," she said.

He relaxed a little at the sound of her voice. "You can call me Orrin, ma'am." His eyes were blue and his big lashes looked incongruous in his angular face. A gash in his right cheek was healing into a scar. "Most everybody does."

"Thank you, Orrin. I'm Dr. Cole, and we'll be talking together over the next few days."

"You're the one who decides who keeps me."

"In a way, that's true. I'll be doing your psychiatric evaluation. But I'm not here to judge you, do you understand? I'm here to find out what kind of help you need and whether we can give it to you."

Orrin nodded once, ducking his chin to his chest. "You decide whether I go to a State Care camp."

"Not just me. The whole staff is involved, one way or another."

"But you're the one I talk to?"

"For now, yes."

"Okay," he said. "I get it."

There were four security cameras in the room, one in each corner where the walls met the ceiling. Sandra had seen recordings of her own and other sessions and knew how she would look on the monitors in the adjoining room: foreshortened and prim in a blue blouse and skirt, her ID badge dangling on a lanyard around her neck as she leaned across the plain pine table. The boy would be reduced by the alchemy of closed-circuit video to a generic interviewee. Though she really ought to stop thinking of Orrin Mather as a boy, as young as he looked. He was nineteen, according to his file. Old enough to know better, as Sandra's mother used to say. "You're originally from North Carolina, Orrin, is that right?"

"I guess it says so in those papers you're looking at."

"Do the papers have it right?"

"Born in Raleigh and lived there, yes, ma'am, all my life till I came to Texas."

"We'll talk about that later on. For now I just need to be sure I have the basics right. Do you know why the police took you into custody?"

He lowered his gaze. "Yes."

"Can you tell me about it?"

"Vagrancy."

"That's the legal word. What would you call it?"

"I don't know. Sleeping in an alley, I guess. And getting beat up by those men."

"It's not a crime to get beaten up. The police took you into custody for your own protection, didn't they?"

"I suppose they did. I was pretty bloody when they found me. I didn't do anything to provoke those fellas. They just set on me because they were drunk. They tried to get my satchel, but I didn't let them. I wish the police had come along a little earlier."

A police patrol had found Orrin Mather semiconscious and bleeding on a sidewalk in southwest Houston. No address, no identification, and no apparent means of support. Under the vagrancy laws written in the aftermath of the Spin, Orrin had been taken into custody for evaluation. His physical injuries had been easy enough to treat. His mental state was an open question, however, one which Sandra was expected to resolve over the course of the next seven days. "You have family, Orrin?"

"Just my sister Ariel back in Raleigh."

"And the police have contacted her?"

"They say so, yes, ma'am. Officer Bose says she's coming by bus, to get me. That's a long trip, that bus trip. Hot this time of year I expect. Ariel don't care for hot weather."

She would have to ask Bose about that. Usually, if a family member was willing to assume responsibility, there was no need for a vag case to end up in State Care. There were no violent acts in Orrin's arrest record, and he was clearly aware of his situation, not obviously delusional. At least not at the moment. Though there *was* something uncanny about him, Sandra thought. (An unprofessional observation, which she would not record in her notes.)

She began with the standard interview from the Diagnostic and Statistical Manual. Did he know the date and so forth. Most of his answers were straightforward and coherent. But when she asked him whether he heard voices, Orrin hesitated. "Guess I don't," he said at last.

"Are you sure? It's okay to talk about these things. If there's a problem, we want to help you with it."

He nodded earnestly. "I know that. It's a hard question, though. I don't hear voices, ma'am, no, not exactly . . . but I write things sometimes."

"What kind of things?"

"Things I don't always understand."

Here, then, was the entry point.

Sandra added a note to Orrin's file—*poss. delusions, written*—for later exploration. Then, because the subject was obviously distressing to him, she smiled and said, "Well, that's enough for now." Half an hour had passed. "We'll talk again soon. I'll have an orderly escort you to the room where you'll be staying over the next few days."

"I'm sure it's very nice."

Compared to the back alleys of urban Houston, maybe it would be. "The first day at State can be hard for some people, but trust me, it's not as bad as it seems. Evening meals are at six in the commissary."

Orrin looked doubtful. "Is that like a cafeteria?"

"Yes."

"Can I ask you, is it loud in there? I don't care for noise when I eat."

The patient commissary was a zoo and generally sounded like one, though the staff made sure it was safe. *Sensitivity to noise,* Sandra added to her notes. "It can get a little loud, yes. Do you think you can deal with it?"

He gave her a downcast look but nodded. "I'll try. Thank you for warning me up front—I appreciate it."

One more lost soul, more fragile and less combative than most. Sandra hoped a week in State would do Orrin Mather more good than harm. But she wouldn't have cared to lay odds on it.

The remanding officer was still waiting when she left the interview room, much to Sandra's surprise. It was customary for cops to dump a case and walk away. State Care had begun its institutional existence as a means of relieving the overloaded prison system during the worst years of the Spin and after. That emergency had ended a quarter of a century ago, but State still served as a dumping ground for trivial offenders with obvious head issues. It was a convenient arrangement

for the police, less so for the overextended and underfunded State Care staff. There was seldom any follow-
up from law enforcement. As far as the police were
concerned, a transfer was a closed file—or worse, a
flushed toilet.

Bose's HPD uniform was crisp despite the heat. He
started to ask her about her impressions of Orrin
Mather, but because it was past time for lunch, and
her afternoon schedule was heavily booked, Sandra
invited him to join her in the cafeteria—the staff cafeteria, not the patient commissary Orrin Mather would
almost certainly find distressing.

She took her usual Monday soup and salad and
waited while Bose did the same. It was late enough
that they had no trouble finding a free table. "I want
to do some follow-up on Orrin," Bose said.

"That's a new one."

"Excuse me?"

"We don't generally get a whole lot of follow-up
from HPD."

"I guess not. But there are some unanswered questions in Orrin's case."

It was "Orrin," she noticed, not "the prisoner" or
"the patient." Clearly, Officer Bose had taken a personal interest. "I didn't see anything too unusual in his
file."

"His name came up in connection with another
case. I can't talk about that in any detail, but I wanted
to ask . . . did he mention anything about his writing?"

Sandra's interest ticked up a notch. "Very briefly,
yes."

"When he was taken into custody Orrin was carrying a leather satchel with a dozen lined notebooks

inside, all of them filled with writing. That's what he was defending when he was attacked. Orrin's generally a cooperative guy, but we had to struggle to get the notebooks away from him. He needed to be reassured that we'd keep them safe and give them back as soon as his case was resolved."

"And did you? Give them back, I mean?"

"Not yet, no."

"Because if Orrin is so concerned with those notebooks they might be pertinent to my evaluation."

"I understand that, Dr. Cole. That's why I wanted to talk to you. The thing is, the contents are relevant to another case HPD is dealing with. I'm having them transcribed, but it's a slow process—Orrin's handwriting isn't easy to decipher."

"Can I see the transcripts?"

"That's what I came here to suggest. But I need to ask a favor of you in return. Until you've looked at the whole document, can we keep this matter out of official channels?"

It was an odd request and she hesitated before answering. "I'm not sure what you mean by official channels. Any pertinent observation goes into Orrin's evaluation. That's nonnegotiable."

"You can make any observation you like, as long as you don't copy or quote directly from the notebooks. Just until we resolve certain issues."

"Orrin's under my care for just seven days, Officer Bose. At the end of that time I have to submit a recommendation." A recommendation that would change Orrin Mather's life drastically, she did not add.

"I understand, and I'm not trying to interfere. Your evaluation is what I'm interested in. What I'd like to get from you, informally, is your opinion of what Orrin wrote. Specifically the reliability of it."

At last Sandra began to understand. Something Orrin had written was potential evidence in a pending case, and Bose needed to know how trustworthy it (or its author) was. "If you're asking me for testimony in a legal proceeding—"

"No, nothing like that. Just a back-channel opinion. Anything you can tell me that doesn't violate patient confidentiality or any other professional concerns you have."

"I'm not sure—"

"You might understand a little better once you've read the document."

It was Bose's earnestness that finally persuaded her to agree, at least tentatively. And she was genuinely curious about the notebooks and Orrin's attachment to them. If she discovered something clinically relevant she would feel no compunction about disregarding any promise she made to Bose. Her first loyalty was to her patient, and she made sure he understood that.

He accepted her conditions without complaint. Then he stood up. He had left his salad unfinished, a bed of lettuce from which he had systematically extracted all the cherry tomatoes. "Thanks, Dr. Cole. I appreciate your help. I'll email you the first pages tonight."

He gave her an HPD card with his phone and an e-mail address and his full name: Jefferson Amrit Bose. She repeated it to herself as she watched him disappear into a throng of white-clad clinicians at the commissary door.

o   o   o

After a day of routine consultations Sandra drove home under the long light of the setting sun.

Sunset often made her think of the Spin. The sun had aged and expanded during the radically foreshortened years of the Spin, and although it looked prosaic enough in the western sky, that was an engineered illusion. The real sun was an aged and bloated monster, furiously dying at the heart of the solar system. What she saw on the horizon was what remained of its lethal radiation after it had been filtered and regulated by the inconceivably powerful technology of the Hypotheticals. For years now—for all of Sandra's adult life—humanity had been living on the sufferance of those alien and voiceless beings.

The sky was a hard blue, obscured to the southeast by clouds like glassy coral growths. One hundred five degrees Fahrenheit in downtown Houston according to the weather report, just as it had been yesterday and the day before. The talk on the newscasts was all about the ongoing White Sands launches, rockets that injected sulfur aerosols into the upper atmosphere in an attempt to slow global warming. Against *that* pending apocalypse (which was none of their doing) the Hypotheticals had offered no defense. They would protect the Earth from the swollen sun, but the CO_2 content of the atmosphere, apparently, was none of their business. It was, self-evidently, mankind's business. And yet the tankers continued creeping up the Houston Ship Channel with their cargoes of oil, plentiful and cheap now that Equatorian crude had begun to flow from the new world beyond the Arch. Two planets' worth of fossil fuels to cook ourselves with, Sandra thought. The car's laboring air conditioner hummed a rebuke to her hypocrisy, but she couldn't bring herself to forego the rush of cool air.

Ever since she finished her internship at UCSF and went to work for State Care, Sandra had spent her days rendering pass/fail verdicts over troubled minds, applying tests most functional adults easily passed. Is the subject oriented to time and place? Does the subject understand the consequences of his actions? But if she could give the same test to humanity as a whole, Sandra thought, the outcome would be very much in doubt. *Subject is confused and often self-destructive. Subject pursues short-term gratification at the expense of his own well-being.*

By the time she reached her apartment in Clear Lake night had fallen and the temperature had dropped a trivial degree or two. She microwaved dinner, opened a bottle of red wine, and checked to see if Bose's e-mail had reached her yet.

It had. A few dozen pages. Pages Orrin Mather had supposedly written, but she saw at once how unlikely that was.

She printed the pages and settled down in a comfortable chair to read them.

My name is Turk Findley, the document began.

CHAPTER TWO

TURK FINDLEY'S STORY

1.

My name is Turk Findley, and this is the story of the life I lived long after everything I knew and loved was dead and gone. It begins in the desert of a planet we used to call Equatoria, and it ends—well, that's hard to say.

These are my memories. This is what happened.

2.

Ten thousand years, more or less, is how long I was away from the world. That was a terrible thing to know, and for a span of time it was nearly all I knew.

I woke up dizzy and naked in the open air. The sun was hammering out of an empty blue sky. I was radically, painfully thirsty. My body ached and my tongue felt thick and dead in my mouth. I tried to sit up and nearly toppled over. My vision was blurred. I didn't know where I was or how I had gotten here. Nor could I really remember where I had come from. All I had of knowledge was the sickening conviction that almost ten thousand years (but who had counted them?) had passed.

I forced myself to sit absolutely still, eyes closed, until the worst of the vertigo passed. Then I raised my head and tried to make sense of what I saw.

I was outdoors in what appeared to be a desert. There was no one on the ground for miles, as far as I could tell, but I wasn't exactly alone: a number of aircraft were passing overhead at low speed. The aircraft were peculiarly shaped and it wasn't obvious what was keeping them aloft, since they seemed to have no wings or rotors.

I ignored them for the time being. The first thing I needed to do was to get out of the sunlight—my skin was burned red and there was no telling how long I'd been exposed.

The desert was hardpacked sand all the way to the horizon, but it was littered with fragments of what looked like gigantic broken toys: a smoothly curved half-eggshell, at least ten feet tall and dusty green, a few yards away; and in the distance other similar shapes in bright but fading colors, as if a giant's tea party had come to grief. Beyond all this there was a range of mountains like a blackened jawbone. The air smelled of mineral dust and hot rock.

I crawled a few yards into the shadow of the fractured eggshell, where the shade was blissfully cool. What I needed next was water. And maybe something to cover myself up. But the effort of moving had made me dizzy again. One of the strange aircraft seemed to be hovering overhead; I tried to wave my arms to attract its attention but my strength had deserted me, and I closed my eyes and passed out.

3.

The next time I woke I was being lifted into some kind of stretcher.

The bearers were dressed in yellow uniforms and wore dust masks over their mouths and noses. A woman in the same yellow clothing walked beside me. When our eyes met she said, "Please try to stay calm. I know you're frightened. We have to hurry, but trust me, we'll get you to a safe place."

Several of the aircraft had landed, and I was carried into one of them. The woman in yellow said a few words to her companions in a language I didn't recognize. My captors or saviors set me on my feet and I discovered I could stand without falling. A door came down, cutting off the view of the desert and the sky. Softer light suffused the interior of the aircraft.

Men and women in yellow jumpers bustled around me, but I kept my eye on the woman who had spoken English. "Steady," she said, taking my arm. She wasn't much taller than five feet and change, and when she pulled off her mask she looked reassuringly human. Her skin was brown, her features were vaguely Asian, her dark hair was cut short. "How do you feel?"

That was a complicated question. I managed to shrug.

We were in a large room and she escorted me to one corner of it. A surface like a bed slid out of the wall, along with a rack of what might have been medical equipment. The woman in yellow told me to lie down.

The other soldiers or airmen—I didn't know how to think of them—ignored us and went about their business, working control surfaces along the walls or hurrying off to other chambers of the aircraft. I felt a rising-elevator sensation and I guessed we had lifted off, though there was no noise apart from the sound of voices speaking a language I didn't recognize. No bounce, no chop, no turbulence.

The woman in yellow pressed a blunt metallic tube against my forearm and then against my rib cage, and I felt my anxiety ease into numbness. I guessed I had been drugged but I didn't really mind. My thirst had vanished. "Can you tell me your name?" the woman asked.

I croaked out the fact that I was Turk Findley. I told her I was an American by birth but that I had been living in Equatoria lately. I asked her who she was and where she was from. She smiled and said, "My name is Treya, and the place I'm from is called Vox."

"Is that where we're going now?"

"Yes. We'll be there soon. Try to sleep, if you can."

So I closed my eyes and tried to take inventory of myself.

My name is Turk Findley.

Turk Findley, born in the last years of the Spin. Variously a day laborer, sailor, small-plane pilot. Worked my way across the Arch to Equatoria on a coastal freighter and lived in Port Magellan some years. Met a woman named Lise Adams who was searching for her father, a search that took us among the kind of people who liked to experiment with Martian drugs—took us deep into the oil lands of the Equatorian desert at a time when ash began to fall from the sky and strange things grew out of the ground. I had loved Lise Adams well enough to know I wasn't good for her. We had been separated in the desert . . . and I believed it was then that the Hypotheticals had taken me. Had picked me up and carried me the way a wave carries a grain of sand. And dropped me on this beach, this shoal, this sandbar, ten thousand years downcurrent.

That was my history, as much as I could reconstruct of it.

When I came to myself again I was in a smaller and more private cabin of the aircraft. Treya, my guard or my doctor (I didn't know exactly how to think of her), was sitting at my bedside humming a tune in a minor key. She or someone else had dressed me in a simple tunic and trousers.

Night had fallen. A narrow window to the left of me showed scattered stars that turned like points on a wheel whenever the aircraft made a banking turn. The small Equatorian moon was on the horizon (which meant I was still in Equatoria, however much it might have changed). Down below, whitecapped waves glistened with phosphorescence. We were flying over the sea, far from land.

"What's that song you're humming?" I asked.

Treya gave a little start, surprised to find me awake. She was young—I guessed twenty or twenty-five years old. Her eyes were attentive but cautious, as if she were subtly afraid of me. But she smiled at the question. "Just a tune . . ."

A familiar tune. It was one of those lamentations in waltz time that had been so popular in the aftermath of the Spin. "Reminds me of a song I used to know. It was called . . ."

" 'Après Nous.' "

Yes. I had heard it in a bar in Venezuela when I was young and alone in the world. Not a bad tune, but I couldn't imagine how it had survived one hundred centuries. "How do you know it?"

"Well, that's not easy to explain. In a way, I grew up with that song."

"Really? How old *are* you exactly?"

Another smile. "Not as old as you, Turk Findley. I have some memories, though. That's why they assigned me to you. I'm not just your nurse. I'm your translator, your guide."

"Then maybe you can explain—"

"I can explain a lot, but not right now. You need to rest. I can give you something to make you sleep."

"I've *been* asleep."

"Is that how it felt when you were with the Hypotheticals—like sleep?"

The question startled me. I knew I had been "with the Hypotheticals" in some sense, but I had no real memory of it. She appeared to know more about the subject than I did.

"Perhaps the memories will come back," she said.

"Do you want to tell me what we're running from?"

She frowned. "I don't understand."

"You all seemed in a hurry to get away from the desert."

"Well . . . this world has changed since you were taken up. Wars were fought here. The planet was radically depopulated and has never really recovered. In a way, a war is *still* being fought here."

As if to confirm this statement, the aircraft banked sharply. Treya gave the window a nervous glance. A burst of white light obscured the stars and lit the rolling waves below. I sat up to get a better view and I thought I saw something on the horizon as the flash faded, something like a distant continent or (because it was almost geometrically flat) an enormous ship. Then it was gone in the darkness.

"Stay down," she said. The aircraft went into an even steeper curve. She ducked into a chair attached to the nearest wall. More light bloomed in the window. "We're out of range of their seagoing vessels, but their aircraft . . . It took us time to find you," she said. "The others should be safe by now. The room will protect you if our vehicle is damaged, but you need to lie down."

It happened almost before the words were out of her mouth.

There were five aircraft (I learned later) in our formation. We were the last flight out of the Equatorian desert. The attack came sooner and more powerfully than expected: four escort craft went down protecting us, and after that we were defenseless.

I remember Treya reaching for my hand. I wanted

to ask her what kind of war this was; I wanted to ask her what she meant by "the others." But there wasn't time. Her grip was fiercely tight and her skin was cold. Then there was sudden heat and a blinding light, and we began to fall.

4.

A combination of programmed emergency maneuvers and sheer luck carried our piece of the broken aircraft as far as the nearest island of Vox.

Vox was a seagoing vessel—a *ship,* in the broadest sense—but it was much more than that word implies. Vox was an archipelago of floating islands, vastly larger than anything that had ever put to sea in my lifetime. It was a culture and a nation, a history and a religion. For nearly five hundred years it had sailed the oceans of the Ring of Worlds—Treya's name for the planets that had been linked together by the Archways of the Hypotheticals. Its enemies were powerful, Treya explained, and they were close. Equatoria was an empty world now, but "an alliance of cortical democracies" had sent pursuit vessels. They were determined to prevent Vox from reaching the Arch that connected Equatoria to Earth.

She didn't believe they could succeed. But the latest attack had been crippling, and one of the casualties had been the aircraft in which we were traveling.

We survived because the compartment in which Treya was treating me had been rigged with elaborate survival mechanisms: aerogels to cushion us from catastrophic deceleration, deployable wing surfaces to glide us to a landing place. We had come to rest on one of the out-islands of the Vox archipelago, currently uninhabited and far from the city Treya called Vox Core.

Vox Core was the hub of the Vox Archipelago, and it had been the primary target of the attack. By the light of dawn we could see a pillar of smoke rising from below the windward horizon. "There," Treya said in a traumatized voice. "That smoke . . . that must be from Vox Core."

We left the smoldering lifeship and stood in a grassy meadow as the sun cleared the horizon. "The Network is silent," she said. It wasn't clear to me what this meant or how she knew it. Her face was rigid with grief. Apart from our survival compartment, the rest of the aircraft must have fallen into the sea. Everyone aboard had died except us. I asked Treya how it happened that we had been singled out to survive.

"Not *us*," she said. "*You*. The aircraft acted to preserve you. I just happened to be nearby."

"Why me?"

"We waited centuries for you. For you and the others like you."

I didn't understand. But she was dazed and bruised and I didn't press the question. Rescue would come, she said. Her people would find us. They would send out aircraft, even if Vox Core had been damaged. They wouldn't leave us in the wilderness.

She was wrong about that, as it turned out.

The exterior wall of the downed survival chamber was still steaming—it had scorched the meadow grass it landed on—and the interior was too hot to use even as a temporary shelter. Treya and I ferried out a few armloads of salvageable material. The survival room had been liberally stocked with what I guessed were pharmaceuticals and medical supplies, less generously with packages Treya identified as food. I grabbed any box she pointed at and we stacked the salvage under a nearby tree (not a species I recognized). The tree was all we needed for shelter at the moment. The air outside was warm, the sky clear.

Despite all this physical effort I felt reasonably good, much better than I had when I first woke up in the desert. I wasn't tired or even especially anxious, no doubt because of the drugs Treya had pumped into me. I didn't feel sedated, just calm and energetic and not inclined to dwell on the dangers at hand. Treya dabbed some sort of ointment on her cuts and scratches, which closed immediately. Then she applied a blue glass tube to the inside of her arm. A few minutes later she appeared to be as functional as I felt, though she still wore her grief like a mask.

As the sun cleared the horizon it was possible to see more of the place where we had landed. It was a sumptuous landscape. When I was little my mother used to read to me from an illustrated children's Bible, and the island reminded me of watercolor pictures of Eden before the Fall. Rolling meadows carpeted with small cloverlike plants merged into thickets of fruit-bearing trees in every direction. No lambs or lions, though. Or people or roads. Not even a path.

"It would help," I said, "if you could explain a little of what's going on."

"That's what I was trained for—to help you understand. But without the Network it's hard to know where to start."

"Just tell me what a complete stranger might like to know."

She looked up at the sky, at the ominous pillar of smoke to windward. Her eyes reflected clouds.

"All right," she said. "I'll tell you what I can. While we wait to be rescued."

Vox had been built and populated by a community of men and women who believed it was their destiny to travel to Earth and enter into direct communication with the Hypotheticals.

That was four worlds and five centuries ago, Treya said. Since then Vox had held steadfastly to her purpose. She had traversed three Arches, making temporary alliances, fighting her declared enemies, accreting new communities and new artificial out-islands, until she reached her current configuration as the Vox Archipelago.

Her enemies ("the cortical democracies") believed any attempt to attract the attention of the Hypotheticals was not only doomed but suicidally dangerous, and not just for Vox itself. The disagreement had occasionally escalated to the point of open warfare, and twice in the last five hundred years Vox had nearly been destroyed. But her population had proven to be more disciplined and clever than her enemies. Or so Treya declared.

When Treya's slightly breathless narrative began to

slow down I said, "How did you come to pluck me out of the desert?"

"That was planned from the beginning, long before I was born."

"You expected to find me there?"

"We know from experience and observation how the body of the Hypotheticals repairs and restores itself. We know from geological evidence that the cycle repeats every nine thousand eight hundred and seventy-five years. And we knew from historical records that certain people had been taken up into the renewal cycle in the Equatorian desert—including you. What goes in comes out. It was predicted almost to the hour." Her voice became reverent. "You've been in the presence of the Hypotheticals. That makes you special. That's why we need you."

"Need me for what?"

"The Arch that joins Equatoria to Earth stopped functioning centuries ago. No one has been to Earth in all that time. But we believe we can make the transit, as long as you and the others are with us. Do you understand?"

No—but I let it pass. "You said 'the others'—what others?"

"The others who were taken up into the Hypothetical renewal cycle. You were there, Turk Findley. You must have seen it, even if you don't remember it. An Arch, smaller than the ones that connect the worlds but still very large, rising out of the desert."

I remembered it the way you might remember a nightmare by the light of morning. The earthquakes it caused had been deadly. Hypothetical machines had been drawn to it from across the solar system, falling from the sky like toxic ash. It had killed friends of mine. Treya called it "a temporal Arch" and implied that it was part of some cycle in the life of the Hypotheticals. But we hadn't known that at the time.

I shivered, despite the warm air and the comforting pharmaceuticals coursing through my bloodstream.

"It took you up," she said, "and held you in stasis for almost ten thousand years. It *marked* you, Turk Findley. The Hypotheticals *know* you. That's why you're important. You and the others."

"Tell me their names."

"I don't know their names. I was assigned to you in particular. If the Network were working properly . . . but it's not." She hesitated. "They were probably in Vox Core at the time of the attack. You might be the only survivor. So someone *has* to come for us. They'll come as soon as they can. They'll find us and they'll take us home."

So she said, though the sky remained blue and vacant.

That afternoon I scouted the area where we'd landed, keeping within sight of camp and collecting kindling for a fire. Many of the trees on this island of the Vox Archipelago produced edible fruit, Treya had said, and I collected some of that, too. I bundled together the kindling with a length of ribbony twine salvaged from the lifeship, and I tucked the fruit—yellow pods the size of bell peppers—into a cloth sack, also salvaged. It felt good to be doing something useful. Apart from an occasional bird call and the rustling of leaves, the only sound was the rhythm of my breathing, my feet moving through the meadow grass. The rolling landscape would have been soothing if not for the column of smoke still smudging the horizon.

The smoke was on my mind when I came back to camp. I asked Treya whether the attack had been nuclear and whether we ought to worry about fallout or radiation. She didn't know about that—there hadn't been a thermonuclear attack on Vox "since the First Orthodoxy Wars," more than two hundred years before she was born. The history she had learned hadn't discussed the effects.

"I guess it doesn't matter," I said. "It's not like we can do anything about it. And it looks like the wind is favoring us." The plume of smoke had begun to feather out parallel to our position.

Treya frowned, shielding her eyes and looking to windward. "Vox is a ship under power," she said. "We're at the stern of it—we *should* be downwind of Vox Core."

"What's that mean?"

"We may be rudderless."

I didn't know what that might imply (or what might constitute a "rudder" on a vessel the size of a small continent), but it was confirmation that the damage to Vox Core had been extensive and that help might not reach us as soon as Treya hoped. I guessed she had come to the same conclusion. She helped me dig a shallow pit for the fire, but she was moody and uncommunicative.

We didn't have a clock to count the hours of the day. I slept a little when the stimulants wore off, and when

I woke the sun was just touching the horizon. The air was cooler now. Treya showed me how to use one of the salvaged tools to light the kindling I had gathered.

Once the fire was crackling I gave some thought to our position—that is, the physical position of Vox relative to the coast of Equatoria. In my day Equatoria had been a settled outpost in the New World, the planet you reached when you sailed from Sumatra through the Arch of the Hypotheticals. If Vox was making for Earth she would have been headed toward the Equatorian side of that same Arch, aiming to make the transverse journey. So I wasn't surprised when the peak of the Arch began to glitter in the darkening sky just after sunset.

The Arch was a Hypothetical construct, built to their incomprehensible scale. Back home, its legs were embedded in the floor of the Indian Ocean and its apex extended beyond the atmosphere of the Earth. Its Equatorian twin was the same size and may even have been, in some sense, the same physical object. One Arch, two worlds. Long after sunset the peak of it still reflected the light of the sun, a thread of silver high overhead. Ten thousand years hadn't changed it. Treya looked up steadily and whispered something quiet in her own language. When she had finished I asked her whether the words had been a song or a prayer.

"Maybe both. You might call it a poem."

"Can you translate it?"

"It's about the cycles of the sky, the life of the Hypotheticals. The poem says there's no such thing as a beginning or an ending."

"I don't know anything about that."

"I'm afraid there's a lot you don't know."

The unhappiness in her face was unmistakable. I told her I didn't understand what had happened to Vox Core but I was sorry for her loss.

She gave me back a sad smile. "And I'm sorry for *your* loss."

I hadn't thought of what had happened to me that way—as a loss, something to be mourned. It was true: I was ten irrevocable centuries away from home. Everything known and familiar was gone.

But I had been trying for most of my life to put a wall between myself and my past, and I hadn't succeeded yet. Some things are taken away from you, some you leave behind—and some you carry with you, world without end.

Come morning Treya gave me another hit from the apparently inexhaustible supply of pharmaceuticals she carried. It was all the consolation she could offer, and I accepted it gladly.

5.

"If help were coming it would have come by now. We can't wait forever. We have to walk."

To Vox Core, she meant: to the burning capital of her floating nation.

"Is that possible?"

"I think so."

"We have all the food we need right here. And if we stay close to the wreckage we'll be easier to find."

"No, Turk. We have to get to Core before Vox

crosses the Arch. But it's not just that. The Network is still down."

"How is that a problem?"

She frowned in a way I had begun to recognize, struggling to find English words for an unfamiliar concept. "The Network isn't just a passive connection. There are parts of my body and mind that depend on it."

"Depend on it for what? You seem to be doing okay."

"The drugs I've been giving myself are helpful. But they won't last forever. I need to get back to Vox Core—take my word for it."

So she insisted, and I was in no position to argue with her. It was probably true about the drugs. She had dosed herself twice that morning, and it was obvious she was getting less mileage out of the pharmaceuticals than she had the day before. So we bundled up all the useful salvage we could carry and began to walk.

We settled into a steady rhythm as the morning unfolded. If the war was still going on, there was no sign of it. (The enemy had no permanent bases in Equatoria, Treya said, and the attack had been a flailing last-ditch attempt to keep us from attempting to cross the Arch. Vox had launched a retaliatory strike before her defenses went down; the empty blue sky was probably a sign that the counterattack had been successful.) The rolling land offered no real obstacles, and we aimed ourselves at the pillar of smoke still rising from beyond the horizon. Around noon we crested a small hill that allowed a view to the margins of the island—ocean on three sides, and to windward a hump of land that must have been the next island in the chain.

More interestingly, four towers rose above the canopy of the forest ahead of us—man-made structures, windowless and black, maybe twenty or thirty stories tall. The towers were separated from one another by many miles, and heading for any one of them would have required a serious detour—but if there were people there, I suggested, maybe we could get some help.

"No!" Treya shook her head fiercely. "No, there's no one inside. The towers are machines, not places where people live. They collect ambient radiation and pump it down below."

"Below?"

"Down to the hollow part of the island, where the farms are."

"You keep your farms underground?" There was plenty of fertile land up here, not to mention sunlight.

But no, she said; Vox was designed to travel through inhospitable or changing environments all along the Ring of Worlds. All the worlds in the Ring were habitable, but conditions varied from planet to planet; the archipelago's food sources had to be protected from changes in the length of days or seasons, wild variations in temperature, greater or lesser degrees of sunlight or ultraviolet radiation. Over the long term, aboveground agriculture would have been as impossible as raising crops on the deck of an aircraft carrier. The forest here was lush, but that was because Vox had been anchored in hospitable climates for most of the last hundred years. ("That might change,"

Treya said, "if we cross to Earth.") Originally these islands had been bare slabs of artificial granite; the topsoil had accumulated over centuries and had been colonized by escaped cultivars and windblown seed from islands and continents on two neighboring worlds.

"Can we get down to the farmland?"

"Possibly. But it wouldn't be wise."

"Why—are the farmers dangerous?"

"Without the Network, they might be. It's difficult to explain, but the Network also functions as a social control mechanism. Until it's restored we should avoid untutored mobs."

"The farm folk get rowdy when they're off their leash?"

She gave me a disdainful look. "Please don't make facile judgments about things you don't understand." She adjusted her pack and walked a few paces ahead of me, cutting short the conversation. I followed her down the hillside, back into the shadow of the forest. I tried to gauge our progress by marking the relative positions of the black towers whenever we crossed an open ridge. I calculated that we might reach the windward shore in a day or two.

The weather turned sour that afternoon. Heavy clouds rolled in, followed by erratic winds and bursts of rain. We marched on grimly until we began to lose daylight; then we found a sheltering grove and stretched a sheet of waterproof cloth between the closely woven branches to serve as a shelter. I succeeded in getting a small fire going.

As night fell we huddled under the tarp. The air reeked of woodsmoke and wet earth. Treya hummed to herself while I heated rations. It was the same song she had been humming in the aircraft before it was destroyed. I asked her again how she had come to know a ten-thousand-year-old popular song.

"It was part of my training. I'm sorry, I didn't realize it was bothering you."

"It's not. I know that song. First time I heard it I was in Venezuela, waiting for a tanker assignment. Little bar there that played American tunes. Where'd you hear it?"

She looked past the fire, out into the dark of the forest. "On a file server in my bedroom. My parents were out, so I cranked it up and danced." Her voice was faint.

"Where was this?"

"Champlain," she said.

"Champlain?"

"New York State. Up by the Canadian border."

"Champlain on *Earth*?"

She looked at me strangely. Then her eyes widened. She put her hand to her mouth.

"Treya? Are you all right?"

Apparently not. She grabbed her rucksack, fumbled through it, then pulled out the pharmaceutical dispenser and pressed it against her arm.

As soon as she was breathing normally she said, "I'm sorry. That was a mistake. Please don't ask me about these things."

"Maybe I can help, if you tell me what's going on."

"Not now."

She curled closer to the fire and closed her eyes.

o   o   o

By morning the rain had turned to mist and fog. The wind had calmed, but during the night it had blown down a bounty of ripe fruit, an easy breakfast.

The column of smoke from Vox Core was invisible in the overcast, but two of the dark towers were close enough to serve as landmarks. By midmorning the fog had thinned and by noon the clouds had lifted and we could hear the sound of the sea.

Treya was talkative by daylight, probably because she was fairly heavily medicated. (She had applied the ampoule to her arm twice already.) Obviously she was leaning on the drug as a way of compensating for the loss of "the Network," whatever that meant to her. And just as obviously, her problem was getting worse. She started talking almost as soon as we broke camp, and it wasn't a conversation but a nervy, absent-minded monologue—a cocaine monologue, I would have thought in another time and place. I listened closely and didn't interrupt, though half of what she said made no sense. In the odd moments when she paused, the wind in the trees seemed suddenly loud.

She told me she had been born to a family of workers in the far leeward quarter of Vox Core. Both her father and her mother had been equipped with neural interfaces that allowed them to perform any of dozens of skilled jobs, "overseeing infrastructure or implementing novel instrumentalities." They were a lower caste than "the managers" but they were proud of their versatility. Treya herself had been trained from birth to join a group of therapists, scholars, and medics whose sole purpose was to interact with the survivors plucked from the Equatorian desert. As a "liaison therapist" assigned specifically to me (knowing only as much about me as had been preserved in historical records: my name and date of birth and the fact that I had vanished into the temporal Arch), she needed to speak colloquial English as it had been spoken one hundred centuries ago.

She had learned it from the Network. But the Network had given her more than a vocabulary: it had given her an entire secondary identity—a set of implanted memories synthesized from twenty-first-century documents and channeled through the interactive node that had been attached to her spinal cord at birth. She called this secondary personality an "impersona"—not just a lexicon but a life, with all its context of places and people, thoughts and feelings.

The primary source from which her impersona had been constructed was a woman named Allison Pearl. Allison Pearl was born in Champlain, New York, a little after the end of the Spin. Allison's diary had survived as an historical document, and the Network had synthesized Treya's impersona from those diary entries. "When I need an English word I get it from Allison. She loved words. She loved writing them. Words like 'orange,' the fruit. A fruit I've never seen or tasted. Allison loved oranges. What I have from her is the word and the concept, the roundness and brightness and the color of an orange, though not the *qualia,* the taste . . . But memories like that are dangerous. They have to be kept within boundaries. Without the Network's neurological constraints, Allison's personality is beginning to metastasize. I reach for my memories and I come up with hers. It's . . . confusing. And it will only get worse. The drugs, the drugs help, but only temporarily . . ."

Treya said all that and more. Insofar as I understood it, I believed she was telling the truth. I believed her because her voice had taken on an American twang, colored with phrases that might have been lifted directly from Allison Pearl's diary. It explained the song she had been compulsively humming, her fits of absentmindedness, the way she stared into space with her head cocked as if she were listening to a voice I couldn't hear.

"I know these memories aren't real, they're made of Network inferences and collations of ancient data, but even talking about it this way feels strange, as if—"

"As if what?"

She turned and stared at me. Probably she hadn't realized she was talking out loud. I shouldn't have interrupted her.

"As if I don't belong here. As if this is all some peculiar *future*." She scuffed her heel into the damp earth. "As if I'm a stranger here. Like you."

Not long before sunset we reached the edge of the island. *Edge*, not *shore*. Here the island's artificiality was obvious. The forest gave way to a slope of scrub grass and exposed rock that fell away almost vertically, a drop of some few hundred feet to the sea. Across that gap was the next island in the Vox archipelago, separated from this one by a chasm half a mile wide. "Pity there isn't a bridge," I said.

"There is," Treya said tersely. "A sort of bridge. We ought to be able to see it from here."

She got down on her belly and scooted to the edge

of the cliff, motioning for me to do the same. Heights don't bother me particularly—I had flown airplanes for a living in the world before this one—but inching over that vertical drop wasn't the most comfortable thing I had ever done. "Down there," Treya said, pointing. "Do you see it?"

The sun was sinking and the chasm was already in shadow. Seabirds nested where centuries of wind and rain had carved hollows in the obdurate, artificial rock. Far to the left, I could see what she was pointing at. An enclosed tunnel connected this artificial island to the next, though only the far end of it was visible around the precise curvature of the island's wall. The tunnel was a salt-rimed shade of black, the same color as the sea below. Vertigo and the odd perspective made it hard to judge its true size, but I guessed you could have put a dozen semi trucks abreast and driven them from one end to the other with room to spare. Even so, there were no spars, ropes, wires, or girders supporting it—somehow the structure carried its own weight. Each island in the archipelago contained its own drive system, slaved to a central controller at Vox Core. Still, I couldn't help wondering about the physical stress born by the link between these two enormous floating masses, even if the tunnel itself was bearing only a fraction of the load.

"Automated freight carriers pass through the tunnel carrying raw biomass to Vox Core and refined goods back to the farmers," Treya said. "It's not meant to be crossed on foot, but it'll have to do."

"How do we get inside?"

"We don't. We might be able to do that from down

in the farmholds, but not from here. We'll have to cross on the outside."

I held that thought for a moment, trying to keep it at a reassuring distance.

"There are stairs carved into the cliff," she added. "You can't see them from this angle. But they were cut during the original construction, so they're probably somewhat eroded." Even the foamed-granite composite the islands were made of couldn't resist wind and salt water indefinitely. "It won't be an easy climb."

"The top of the tunnel is a curved surface, and it looks pretty slick."

"It may be wider than you think."

"Or it may *not*."

"We don't have a choice."

But it was too late to begin the attempt, with only a couple of hours of daylight left.

We set up a fresh camp back in the forest. I watched Treya take another hit from her drug syringe. I said, "Is that thing bottomless?"

"It refills itself. It has its own metabolism. It draws a little blood during the injections and uses that as raw material to catalyze active molecules. It runs on body heat and ambient light. For you, it fabricated a drug to suppress anxiety. What it gives me is something different."

I had stopped taking doses when she offered them—I had decided to live with my anxiety, for better or worse. "How does it know what to synthesize?"

She frowned the way she did whenever she tripped over a concept for which her ghostly tutor Allison

Pearl didn't have a ready word. "It samples blood chemistry and makes an educated guess. But no, it isn't bottomless. It needs to be refreshed, and this one is getting tired." She added, "If you want to use it, though, that's all right."

"No. What's it giving you?"

"A kind of . . . you could call it a cognitive enhancer. It helps maintain the boundary between my real and my virtual memories. But it's only a temporary solution." She shivered in the firelight. "What I really need is the Network."

"Tell me about the Network. It's what, some kind of internal wireless interface?"

"Not exactly what you mean by that, but yes, in a sense. Except that the signals I receive are expressed as biological and neurological regulators. Everybody on Vox wears a node, and we're all linked by the Network. The Network helps us formulate a limbic consensus. I don't know why it hasn't been repaired. Even if the transponders at Vox Core were destroyed, workers should have been able to restore basic functionality by now. Unless the processors themselves were damaged . . . but they were built to sustain anything short of a direct hit from a high-yield weapon."

"Maybe that's what happened—a direct hit."

She shrugged unhappily by way of response.

"Which means there's a good chance we're marching toward a radioactive ruin."

"We don't have a choice," she said.

I sat up after she fell asleep, nursing the fire.

Without the calming drugs, my own recent memories had begun to firm up. Just days ago I had been trying to survive a series of earthquakes generated by the temporal Arch as it rose from its dormant state in the Equatorian desert. Now I was here on Vox. You can't really comprehend events like that, I thought. You can only endure them.

I let the fire burn down to a glow of embers. The Arch of the Hypotheticals glimmered overhead, an ironic smile among the stars, and the rush of the sea was amplified by the echo from the nearby cliffs. I wondered about the people who had nuked Vox Core, the "cortical democracies," and why they had done it, and whether their reasons were as superficial as Treya had suggested.

I was a neutral in the conflict, insofar as that was possible. It wasn't my fight. And I wondered whether Allison Pearl, the Champlain Ghost, might be similarly neutral. Maybe that was what Treya found so disconcerting: "Allison" and I were both shades of a disinterested past, both potentially disloyal to Vox Core.

6.

We broke camp at dawn and followed the curving cliff until we came to what Treya had called "stairs," broad declivities cut into the face of the granite. Time had beveled the steps into sloping ledges separated by giddy ten-foot drops. Every surface was slick with mossy growths and bird dung, and the deeper we descended the louder the roar of the ocean became. Eventually the high edges of the two adjoining islands closed off all of the sky apart from a few slanting rays of sunlight. We made slow progress, and twice we paused while Treya took hits from her high-tech syringe. Her expression was grim and, under that, terrified. She kept glancing backward and up, as if she was afraid we were being followed.

By the angle of the light I guessed it was past noon when I helped her down the last vertical gap to the roof of the tunnel itself. The roof of the tunnel was broader than it had looked from above and we were able to stand on it safely enough, though it was unnerving to walk on a surface that rounded away on both sides to a sheer drop. It was maybe a half mile to the opposite anchor point, now concealed by mist, where we would have to do another round of serious climbing, with any luck before darkness set in. Night would come fast down here.

For the sake of distraction I asked Treya what she (or Allison Pearl) remembered about Champlain.

"I'm not sure it's safe to answer that question." But she sighed and went on: "Champlain. Cold winters. Hot summers. Swimming in the lake at Catfish Point. My family was broke most of the time. Those were the years after the Spin, when everybody was talking about how the Hypotheticals might actually be benevolent, protecting us. But I never believed that. Walking down those Champlain sidewalks, you know the way concrete glitters in the summer sun? I couldn't have been more than ten years old but I remember thinking that was how we must look to the Hypotheticals—not just us but our whole planet, just a glimmer underfoot, something you notice and then forget."

"That's not how Treya talks about the Hypotheticals."

She gave me an angry look. "I *am* Treya." And walked a few paces more. "Allison was wrong. The

Hypotheticals—they're gods by any reasonable definition, but they're not *indifferent*." She stopped and squinted at me, wiping salt mist from her eyes. "You ought to know that!"

Maybe so. Before long we reached the midpoint of the transit, where the wind came roaring between the chasm walls in a focused gale and we had to crawl on our hands and knees like ants clinging to a rainy clothesline. Conversation was impossible. Intermittent vibrations came through the palms of my hands from the tunnel, as of metal groaning under incalculable stress. I wondered what it would take to tear this damaged archipelago apart—another nuclear attack? Or something as simple as a high sea and a strong wind, given what had already happened? I pictured cables the size of subway trains snapping, island-ships like battered piñatas spilling their contents into the sea. It wasn't a reassuring thought. If not for Treya I might have turned back. But if not for Treya I wouldn't have been here in the first place.

Finally we came into the shadow of the opposing cliff wall, where the wind eased to a low moan and we could stand upright again. The stairs that had been cut into the granite cliff were identical to those across the gorge: eroded and mossy, steep and stinking of the sea. We had climbed about a dozen of them when Treya gasped and came to a dead halt.

The ledge above us was full of people.

They must have seen us coming, must have hidden until they were ready to show themselves. It didn't look like a welcoming committee.

"*Farmers,*" Treya whispered.

There were thirty or so of them, male and female, all staring at us with grim expressions. Many of them carried implements that might have been weapons. Treya cast a quick look back at the bridge we had just crossed. But it was too late and too dark to run. We were outnumbered and effectively cornered.

She reached for my hand and took it. Her skin was cold. I felt the beat of her pulse. "Let me talk to them," she said.

I boosted her up the next ledge and she pulled me after and then we were level with the crowd. The farmers surrounded us. Treya held out her hands in a conciliatory gesture. Then the head man stepped up.

At least I guessed he was the head man. He wasn't wearing any insignia to mark his rank, but no one appeared to question his authority. He carried a metallic rod the length of a walking stick, tapered at the end to a fine point. Like the people behind him, he was tall. His dark skin was finely wrinkled.

Before he could open his mouth Treya said something in her native language. He listened impatiently. In English Treya whispered, "I told him you're one of the Uptaken. If that matters to him at all—"

But it didn't. He barked a few words at Treya. She said something hesitant in return. He barked again. She bowed her head and trembled.

"Whatever happens," she whispered, "don't interfere."

The head man put his hands on her shoulders. He pushed her down to the slick surface of the granite tier and gave her a shove so that she sprawled onto her stomach. Her cheekbone grazed the rock and began to bleed. She closed her eyes in pain.

I had been in my share of fights. I wasn't a particularly good fighter. But I couldn't stand passively and watch. I lunged at the farmer. Before I could reach him his friends had their hands on me, holding me back. They forced me to my knees.

The boss farmer put his foot on Treya's shoulder, holding her down. Then he raised his weapon and slowly lowered it.

The sharp end touched a knob of Treya's spine just below the neck. Her body stiffened at the pressure of it.

Then the farmer drove the point down hard.

CHAPTER THREE

SANDRA AND BOSE

Sandra went to bed convinced the document was a fake—a bad joke, though it was too late to call Bose and accuse him of it. Although, if it *was* a joke, it was a pointlessly elaborate one. She couldn't believe that Orrin Mather, the shy and inarticulate young man she had interviewed at State, had written any of this. Her best guess was that he had copied the text from some science fiction novel and pretended it was his own work . . . though she couldn't imagine why.

So she tried to shrug off the unanswerable questions and get a decent night's rest.

Come dawn she had managed, she reckoned, at most three hours of useful sleep, which meant she would go through the day sandy-eyed and irritable. And the day would be another hot one, judging by the haze tinting the view from her living room window. The kind of smog only August in Houston could brew up.

She tried to call Bose from the dashboard phone in her car but the number bounced to voice mail. She left her name and work number and added, "Is it possible you sent me the wrong file? Or maybe I ought to be interviewing *you* for State Care. Please call as soon as you can and clear this up."

Sandra had been employed at the Greater Houston Area State Care facility long enough to have a feeling for the place—the flow of its internal politics, the rhythm of daily business. She could tell, in other words, when something was up. This morning, something was up.

The work she did had a certain moral ambiguity even at the best of times. The State Care system had been mandated by Congress in the messy aftermath of the Spin, when homelessness and mental illness had risen to epidemic levels. The legislation had been well intended, and it was still true that for anyone with a full-blown psychiatric disorder State Care was better than life on the street. The doctors were sincere, the pharmaceutical protocols were finely tuned, and the communal housing, while basic, was reasonably clean and well policed.

Too often, however, people were swept into State Care who didn't belong there: petty criminals, the belligerent poor, ordinary folks who had been driven to chronic bewilderment by economic hardship. And State Care, once you were given involuntary

commitment status, wasn't easy to leave. A generation of local pols had campaigned against inmates
being "dumped back on the street," and State's halfway house program was forever under attack from
NIMBY activists. Which meant the State Care population was continually rising while its budget remained fixed. Which led in turn to underpaid staff,
overpopulated residential camps, and periodic scan-
dals in the press.

As an intake physician it was Sandra's job to short-
circuit those problems at the front end, to admit the
genuinely needy while turning away (or referring to
other social welfare agencies) the merely confused. In
theory it was as simple as checking off a patient's
symptoms and writing a recommendation. In fact her
work involved a great deal of surmise and many painful judgment calls. Turn away too many cases and the
police or the courts would get testy; accept too many
and management began to complain about "overin-
clusiveness." Worse, her cases weren't abstractions but
people: wounded, weary, angry, sad, and occasionally
violent people; people who too often saw State Care
as a kind of prison sentence, which in a real sense it
was.

So there was a certain inevitable tension, a balance
to be maintained, and within the institution itself
there were invisible wires that vibrated to the right or
wrong notes. Coming into the wing where she had
her office, Sandra noticed the nurse at the reception
station giving her covert looks. A vibrating wire.
Wary now, she paused at the warren of plastic cubby-
holes where staff kept paperwork on pending cases.
The nurse, whose name was Wattmore, said, "Don't

bother looking for the Mather chart, Dr. Cole—Dr. Congreve has it."

"I don't understand. Dr. Congreve took Orrin Mather's case file?"

"Isn't that what I just said?"

"Why would he do that?"

"I guess you'll have to ask him." Nurse Wattmore turned back to her monitor and clicked a few keys dismissively.

Sandra went to her office and put in a call to Congreve. Arthur Congreve was her superior at State. He supervised all the intake staff. Sandra didn't like him—he struck her as aloof, professionally indifferent, and far too concerned with producing a smoothly trending flow of statistics that would impress the budget committees. Since he had been appointed last year, two of the facility's best intake physicians had elected to quit rather than submit to his patient quotas. Sandra couldn't imagine why he might have pulled the Mather file without warning her. Individual cases were usually far below Congreve's personal radar.

Congreve started talking as soon as he picked up. "Help you, Sandra? I'm in B Wing, by the way, about to go into a meeting, so let's make this quick."

"Nurse Wattmore tells me you took the Orrin Mather file."

"Yeah . . . I thought I saw her beady little eyes light up. Look, I'm sorry I didn't talk to you beforehand. It's only that we have a new intake person—Dr. Abe Fein, I'll be introducing him at the next general meeting—and I thought I should walk him through a safe case. Mather's the least troublesome candidate we've got on hand, and I didn't want to start out the new guy with a hostile subject. Don't worry, I'll be backstopping Fein all the way."

"I didn't know we had a new hire."

"Check your memos. Fein did his internship at Baylor in Dallas, very promising, and as I say, I'll keep him on a short leash until he gets a handle on what we do here."

"Thing is, I already put in the preliminaries with Orrin Mather. I think I established a little bit of rapport with him."

"I assume everything pertinent is in the file. Is there anything else, Sandra? I don't mean to be rude, but I have people waiting."

She knew it would be useless to push. Despite his medical degree, Congreve had been hired by the board of directors for his managerial talents. As far as he was concerned, the intake psychiatrists were nothing more than hired help. "No, nothing else."

"Okay. We'll talk later."

Threat or promise?

Sandra settled behind her desk. She was disappointed, obviously, and a little angry with Congreve for his preemptive behavior, not that it was uncharacteristic.

She thought about the file on Orrin Mather. She hadn't entered anything into her notes about Officer Bose's interest in the case. She'd promised Bose she would be discreet about the sci-fi narrative Mather had allegedly written. Was that promise still binding, under the circumstances?

She was ethically required to divulge to Congreve (or the new guy, Dr. Fein) anything that might be relevant to the evaluation. But intake evaluation was a weeklong process, and she guessed there was no need for full disclosure just yet. At least not until she had a better sense of why Bose was interested and whether the document she had been reading had in fact been written by Orrin Mather. She'd have to ask Bose about that, and as soon as possible.

As for Orrin himself . . . there was no rule against paying him a social visit, was there? Even if he was no longer her patient.

Nonviolent patients awaiting assessment were encouraged to socialize in the supervised lounge, but Orrin wasn't the sociable type. Sandra guessed he would be alone in his room, which proved to be the case. She found him sitting cross-legged on his matttress like a bony Buddha, staring at the cinderblock wall opposite the window. These small rooms were pleasant enough, if you ignored the evidence that they were effectively prison cells: the shatterproof window panes threaded with fiberglass, the conspicuous absence of all hooks, hangers, and sharp edges. This one had been recently repainted, disguising the generations of obscene graffiti scratched into the walls.

Orrin smiled when he saw her. His face was guileless, transparent to every emotion. Big head, high cheekbones, eyes pleasant but open too wide. He looked like he would be easy to lie to. "Dr. Cole, hi! They told me I wouldn't be seeing you again."

"Another intake physician has been assigned to your case, Orrin. But we can still talk, if you like."

"Okay," he said. "That's fine."

"I spoke to Officer Bose yesterday. Do you remember Officer Bose?"

"Yes, ma'am, of course I do. Officer Bose is the only policeman who took an interest in me." Poe-*lease*-man, in Orrin's trailer-park accent. "He's the one who called my sister, Ariel. Is she in town yet, have you heard?"

"I don't know, but I'll be talking to Officer Bose later—I can ask." She added, not knowing how to approach the subject except bluntly, "He mentioned the notebooks you were carrying when the police picked you up."

Orrin seemed neither surprised nor upset that Sandra knew about the notebooks, though his sunny expression dimmed a little. "Officer Bose says the police have to keep them for now but I can have them back sooner or later." He frowned, buckling a V under his high hairline. "That's true, isn't it? No matter what they decide about me here?"

"If Officer Bose says so, I think it's probably true. Are the notebooks important to you?"

"Yes, ma'am, I suppose they are."

"May I ask you what's written in them?"

"Well, that's hard to say."

"Is it a story?"

"You could call it that I guess."

"What's the story about, Orrin?"

"Well, it's hard for me to keep in my mind. That's why I like to have the notebooks, so I can refresh my memory. It has to do with a certain man and a certain woman. More than that. It's about . . . you could say God? Or at least the Hypotheticals." Hah-poe-*thet*-ickles.

"Did you write the story yourself?"

Peculiarly, Orrin blushed.

"I *wrote it down*," he said finally, "but I don't know I can say for sure I *wrote* it. I'm not much of a writer. Never was. A teacher at Park Valley school—that's back in North Carolina—told me I don't know a noun from a verb and never will. And I guess that's true. Words don't come easy to me, except—"

"Except what, Orrin?"

"Except *those* words."

Sandra didn't want to push it any harder. "I understand," she said, though she didn't. One more stab at it: "Turk Findley . . . is that someone in your story, or is he a real person?"

Orrin's blush deepened. "I don't guess he exists, ma'am. I guess I made him up."

It was obvious he was lying. But Sandra left it at that. She smiled and nodded.

When she stood up to leave, Orrin asked her about the flowers growing in the small garden outside the window of his cinderblock room: did she know by what name they were called?

"Those? They're called 'bird of paradise.'"

His eyes widened; he grinned. "That's their real name?"

"Mm-hm."

"Huh! Because those flowers surely do look like birds, don't they?"

The yellow beak, the rounded head, the single drop of crystalline sap that glinted like an eye. "Yes, they do."

"It's like a flower that has the idea of a bird inside

it. Only nobody put it there. Unless you could say God did."

"God or nature."

"Maybe comes to the same thing. You have a nice day, Dr. Cole."

"Thank you, Orrin. You, too."

Bose finally returned her call midafternoon, though his voice was hard to hear, coming through a background of what sounded like mass chanting. "Sorry," he said. "I'm down at the ship channel. It's some kind of environmental demonstration. We have about fifty people sitting on the railroad tracks in front of a string of tanker cars."

"More power to them." Sandra's sympathies were entirely with the demonstrators. The environmentalists wanted to ban the import of fossil fuels from beyond the Arch of the Hypotheticals, in an attempt to keep global warming under five degrees Celsius. Sufficient unto the planet are the carbon resources thereof, they believed, and to Sandra it was ridiculously obvious that they were right. As far as she could tell, the exploitation of the vast oil reserves under the Equatorian desert was a disaster in progress, enabling a mad prosperity purchased at the price of redoubled CO_2 emissions. The generation that had grown up in the wake of the Spin wanted cheap gas and boom times and no cavilling voices at the table, and the whole world was (or would be) paying the piper.

Bose said, "I'm not sure having an activist crushed by a freight train would be absolutely helpful. You got the document I sent?"

"Yes," she said, wondering how to proceed.

"You read it?"

"Yes. Officer Bose—"

"You can just call me Bose. My friends do."

"Okay, but look, I still don't know what you want from me. Do you honestly believe Orrin Mather wrote the text you sent me?"

"I know, it hardly seems plausible. Even Orrin is reluctant to take credit for it."

"I asked him about that. He told me he wrote it down, but he wasn't sure he actually *wrote* it. As if somebody dictated it to him. Which I guess would explain a few things. Anyway, what do you want from me exactly? Literary criticism? Because I'm not much of a science fiction fan."

"There's more to the document than what you've seen. I'm hoping I can send you another batch of pages today and maybe we can get together face-to-face, like say lunch tomorrow, to talk about the details."

Was she willing to take another step into this strangeness? Oddly, she discovered she was. Put it down to curiosity. And maybe compassion for the bashful childman she had discovered in Orrin Mather. And the fact that she had found Bose to be reasonably pleasant company. She told him he could send along more pages but she felt compelled to add, "There's a complication you ought to know about. I'm not Orrin's case physician anymore. My boss turned him over to a trainee."

Now it was Bose's turn to pause. Sandra tried to make out the chanting in the background. Somethingsomething *our children's children*. "Well, damn," Bose said.

"And I doubt my boss would be willing to take you into his confidence, no offense. He's—"

"You're talking about Congreve? People at HPD say he's a bureaucratic prick."

"No comment."

"Okay . . . but you still have access to Orrin?"

"I can talk to him, if that's what you mean. What I don't have is any kind of decision-making authority."

"Complicates things," Bose admitted. "But I'd still like your opinion."

"Again, it would help if I knew what's so important to you about Orrin and these notebooks of his."

"Better if we discuss it tomorrow."

Sandra negotiated the lunch details, a place reasonably close to State Care but slightly more upscale than the strip mall alternatives; then Bose said, "Gotta go. Thanks, Dr. Cole."

"Sandra," she said.

CHAPTER FOUR

TREYA'S STORY / ALLISON'S STORY

1.

You want to know what it was like, what happened to Vox and afterward?

Well, here it is.

Something to leave behind, you might say.

Something for the wind and the stars to read.

2.

I was born to the name Treya and a five-syllable suffix I won't repeat here, but it might be better to think of me as Allison Pearl Mark II. I had a ten-year gestation, a painful eight-day labor, and a traumatic birth. From my first full day of life I knew I was a fraud, and I knew just as truly that I had no choice in the matter.

I was born seven days before Vox was due to cross

the Arch to ancient Earth. I was born into the custody
of rebel Farmers, born with my own blood weeping
down my back. By the time I remembered how to
speak the blood had mostly dried.

The Farmers had crushed and carved out of my
body and subsequently destroyed my personal limbic
implant, my Network interface, my node. Because the
node had been attached to my spine at the third ver-
tebra almost since birth, the pain was intense. I woke
up from the trauma with waves of agony sparking up
my neck and into my skull, but the worst part was
what I *didn't* feel, which was the rest of my body. I
was numb from the shoulders down—numb, helpless, hurt and frightened beyond thought. Eventually
the Farmers poked me with some kind of crude anesthetic from their primitive pharmacopoeia . . . not
out of kindness, I suspect, but simply because they
were tired of hearing me scream.

The next time I came to myself my body was tin-
gling and itching unbearably, but that was okay because it meant I was recovering my physical functions.
Even without the node, my augmented body systems
were busy splicing damaged nerves and repairing
bone. Which meant I would eventually be able to sit
up, stand up, even walk. So I began to take a greater
interest in my surroundings.

I was in the back of a cart, lying on a sort of bed of
dried vegetable matter. The cart was moving along at
a brisk pace. The walls of the cart were too high to
see over, but it was open to daylight. I could see the
cloud-flecked sky and the occasional treetop swaying
past. There was no way of knowing how much time

had passed since I was captured, and that was the question that preyed on my mind above all others. How close were we to Vox Core, and how close was Vox to the Arch of the Hypotheticals?

My mouth was dry but my voice worked well enough. "Hey!" I called out a couple of times before I realized I was speaking English. So I switched to Voxish: *"Vech-e! Vech-e mi!"*

All that yelling was painful, and I shut up when I realized nobody was paying attention.

It was dusk when the cart finally jostled to a stop. The first stars were coming out. The sky was a shade of blue that reminded me of the stained glass in the church back in Champlain. I'm not a big fan of churches but I always liked stained glass, the way it looked when the Sunday morning sun lit it up. I could hear the sound of Farmer voices. Farmers speak Voxish with an accent, as if they all went around carrying stones in their mouths. I could smell their cooking, which was torture because I hadn't been given anything to eat.

Eventually a face appeared above the side of the cart. It was a man's face. His skin was dark and wrinkly, but that was true of all the Farmers. He was bald except for his bushy eyebrows. His eyes were yellow around the iris and he looked at me with undisguised distaste.

"You," he said. "Can you sit up?"

"I need to eat."

"If you can sit up you can eat."

I spent the next few minutes forcing my still-unwieldy body into a sitting position. The Farmer didn't offer to help. He watched me with a kind of clinical disinterest. When I finally had my back braced against the wall of the cart, I said, "I did what you wanted. Please feed me."

He glowered and went away. I didn't really expect to see him again. But he came back with a bowl of something green and glutinous, which he put down next to me. "If you can use your hands," he said, "it's yours."

He turned away.

"Wait!"

He sighed and looked back. "Well?"

"Tell me your name."

"Why, what does it matter?"

"It doesn't matter. I just want to know."

He said his name was Choi. He said his family was Digger, Level Three, Harvest Quarter. In my head I translated it into English as Digger Choi.

"And you're Treya, Worker, Outrider Therapeutics." Sneering at the Core honorifics.

I heard myself say, "My name is Allison Pearl."

"We read your internal tags. You can't lie."

"Allison," I insisted. "Pearl."

"Call yourself whatever you want."

I put my disobedient hand into the bowl of food and cupped it to my mouth. It was a globby green muck that tasted like mown grass, and I lost about half of every handful, but my body accepted it hungrily. Digger Choi stuck around until I was finished, then took the bowl. I was still hungry. Digger Choi refused my request for seconds.

"Is this how you treat your prisoners?"

"We don't take prisoners."

"What am I, then?"

"A hostage."

"You think I'm that valuable?"

"You might be. If not, it will be simple enough to kill you."

Because I could move my body again, the Farmers took the precaution of tying my arms behind me. They left me like that all night—in some ways it was worse that being paralyzed. And in the morning they pulled me out of the cart and frog-marched me to another one, identical in all ways except that it contained Turk Findley.

During the transfer I was able to survey the Farmers' encampment. We had reached the island that contained Vox Core, but here at the periphery it still looked like an out-island—an uncultivated wilderness. Locally, all the fruit-bearing trees had been stripped to feed the marching Farmers.

There were a lot of them. An army of them. I estimated maybe a thousand warm bodies in this meadow alone, and I could see the smoke from other encampments. The Farmers were armed with makeshift blades and machine parts filched from harvesters and threshing machines . . . weapons that would have been laughable in the face of a fully Networked Core militia; but under the present circumstances who could say? The Farmers themselves were all dark and wrinkled, descendents of the long-ago Martian diaspora. Digger Choi escorted me through a mob of his Farmer compatriots, who gave me hard looks and shouted a few hard words.

The cart he dragged me to was larger than the one I'd been dumped in. From the outside it was basically a box on two wheels, with long poles out front so an animal or a robot or an able-bodied Farmer could drag it. Simple tech, but not as primitive as it appeared. The Farmers' carts were made of a smart material that transformed random bounces into forward momentum. They were self-balancing and could adapt to rough terrain. They also made a suitable prison, if your prisoners were securely bound.

Turk was securely bound and so was I. Digger Choi lowered the rear wall of the cart, pushed me inside, and locked the barricade behind me. I rolled up against Turk Findley, whose hands were also tied behind his back, and we spent an awkward moment sorting ourselves out and bracing our legs so we could face each other. Turk was badly bruised—he had put up a serious fight when the Farmers took him. The skin over his left cheekbone was cloudy black, fading to green. His left eye was swollen shut. He looked at me sidelong and with unconcealed astonishment. Probably he had thought I was dead, killed when they tore out my limbic implant.

I wanted to say something reassuring but I wasn't sure where to start. He remembered me as Treya of Vox Core. And that was true enough: I continued to be Treya, in a sense. But only *in a sense*.

I had two histories. Treya had described Allison Pearl as the virtual mentor who had acculturated her to twenty-first-century American customs and language. "Allison Pearl" wasn't real, the way most people use that word. But I was Allison now, fully installed, fully functional; it was Allison who was running the show—I was, as the Managers used to say, *psychologically annealed.*

And anyway that wasn't the biggest problem we were facing.

"You're alive," he said.

"Obviously."

He gave me a curious look, probably because it wasn't the kind of thing Treya would have said.

"I thought they killed you. All that blood." It had dried to a brown bib on my tunic.

"It wasn't me they killed, it was my Network interface. The node sits over my spine so it can talk to my brain. The Farmers have implants too, but they must have disabled theirs as soon as the Network failed. They hate the nodes because the nodes keep them docile and useful."

"So they're, what, slaves? This is a slave rebellion?"

"No—it's not as simple as that." Being Allison Pearl, I held no brief for the social structure of Vox. But I had a powerful secondary memory of Treya's fierce loyalty. Treya wasn't a bad person, even if she was a drone. I didn't want him thinking of her as some kind of slave overseer. "These people's ancestors were taken captive centuries ago. They were radical bionormatives, part of the Martian diaspora. They refused to be assimilated, so they made a bargain, their lives in exchange for agricultural labor."

Turk was still giving me uneasy looks—the blood on my clothes, the way I was talking—and I figured it would be best to explain as bluntly as possible. "They cut out my node," I said. "Treya was a translator, right? For years she accessed Allison Pearl as a secondary personality. She ran me like a junior mind, if you understand what I'm saying. And a lot of her own memories and personality got sourced out to the Network. We were all tangled up, me and Treya, but the node always made sure Treya was the controlling entity. But now the node's gone and I'm dominant. She must have ceded a whole bunch of neural real estate to me over the last decade. Big mistake, from her point of view, though she could hardly have expected a tribe of insurgent Farmers to cut out her Network interface."

"Excuse me," Turk said slowly, "but who am I talking to again?"

"Allison. I'm Allison Pearl now."

"Allison," he said. "And Treya's, what, dead?"

"The Network can still embody her if it wants to. She's *potential,* but she's not *incarnate.*" Technical terms, crudely translated.

Turk thought this over. "The future seems like a pretty fucked-up place sometimes."

"If you can just take it on faith that I'm Allison now, maybe we can get on with the business of trying to save ourselves."

"You know how to do that?"

"The point is, we'll die unless we get somewhere safe before Vox crosses the Arch."

"That might not be possible. You saw the sky before dawn? The Arch is at zenith, a straight line across the meridian. That means—"

"I know what it means." It meant we were dangerously close to the crossing.

"So what's safe, Allison Pearl, and how do we get there?"

The Farmers had eaten their breakfast and gathered their gear, and now they were ready to resume their march on Vox Core. A couple of men picked up the draw-poles of the cart, which had the effect of rolling us around like peas in a skillet. It made conversation awkward. But I told Turk what he needed to know. He was almost up to speed by the time we caught our first glimpse of the ruins of Vox Core.

3.

Turk was a quick learner, though the ten thousand years he had spent among the Hypotheticals hadn't taught him much. Well, how could it have? In fact he had never really been "among" them, even though it was conventional to talk about the people who passed through the temporal Arch as if they had been touched by vast hyperintelligent powers. Treya believed he had spent those years in glorious communion with the Hypotheticals, whether he remembered it or not, but now that I was Allison Pearl it sounded like so much quasi-religious BS. If you've traveled through any of the Arches that connect the Eight Worlds you've been "among the Hypotheticals" to just the same degree as Turk had been. Lots of people even in my day (Allison's day) crossed the Arch from the Indian Ocean to Equatoria, which meant they had been taken up and carried across the stars by Hypothetical forces. That didn't make them gods or even godlike—it didn't make them anything at all, except unusually well traveled. But time is a different dimension, supposedly. Spookier.

There were temporal Arches elsewhere in the Worlds, of course. They're a common Hypothetical construct. We knew from geological evidence that temporal

Arches appeared and disappeared every ten thousand or so years. They were part of some Hypothetical feedback mechanism, storing and dispensing information. But the first temporal Arch to engulf living human beings was the one that had popped up in the Equatorian desert and swallowed, among others, Turk Findley. Which meant it would be the first to *disgorge* its human cargo . . . which it had done, precisely on schedule, a couple of weeks ago.

So Turk was one of the first people to exit a temporal Arch alive. But oh, the bullshit that had accrued around that simple fact! It was an article of Voxish faith that the survivors would emerge transformed, conduits between mere humanity and the forces that had engineered the Ring of Worlds. And that those survivors would be able to shepherd us through a dysfunctional Arch back to Old Earth.

Treya had never questioned that dogma, and maybe it was even true, to some degree. But if we did successfully manage the transit to Earth, that was liable to be more a problem than a solution. Because in all likelihood Earth was no longer a habitable planet.

I said some of this to Turk. He asked me whether the people of Vox were entirely sane, believing what they did. I felt the ghost of Treya take offense at the question. "Sane compared to what? Vox has been a functioning community for hundreds of years. It's survived a lot of battles. It's a limbic democracy modulated by the Network, and all this stuff about the Hypotheticals and Old Earth is written into the code. Might even be some truth in it, I don't know."

"But Vox has enemies," Turk pointed out, "who went to the trouble of bombing it."

"They would have finished us by now, if they had anything left to throw."

"So we'll pass under the Arch, one way or another?"

"Two possible outcomes," I told him. "If nothing happens we'll be left adrift and defenseless on the Equatorian ocean. Probably invaded and occupied by the bionormatives, if they get their act together."

"And if we *do* make it to Earth?"

"No way of knowing, but Earth was barely habitable when the Arch stopped working, and that was a thousand years ago, give or take. The oceans were going bad, huge bacterial blooms emitting massive amounts of hydrogen sulfide into the air. We have to assume an atmosphere poisonous enough to kill any unprotected living thing. Which is why it would be a very bad idea to be out of doors if we cross."

"So where do we find protection?"

"The only real safe place is Vox Core. It can seal itself and recycle its air. That's where the Farmers are heading. With the Network and other systems down, they can't count on protection for the out-islands. They want to get inside the walls before the transit. But there isn't room in Core for every outlier community in the Archipelago. The Farmers will have to fight their way in."

4.

At the end of another day's march the Farmer militia halted for the night. Digger Choi lowered the gate of the cart, pushed two bowls of green gruel inside, and untied our hands so we could eat. Turk stood up for the first time today, rubbing his wrists and legs. He balanced himself against the wall of the cart and turned his head to see where we were. That was when he got his first look at Vox Core.

The expression on his face was interesting—awe and fear, mixed together.

Vox Core was mostly underground, but the fraction of it that showed was impressive enough. The Farmers had camped in the lee of a low hill, and from this angle Vox Core looked like a jewelry box abandoned by a spendthrift god. Its half-mile-high defensive walls were the box; the jewels were the hundreds of faceted towers still standing: communications and energy-distribution points, light-gathering surfaces, aircraft bays, managerial residences. To Turk I suppose it looked improbably gaudy, but I knew (because Treya had known) that every material and every surface served a purpose—black or white facades to sink or radiate heat, blue-green panels doing photosynthetic work, ruby-red or smoky indigo windows to block or enhance particular frequencies of visible light. The setting sun gave it all a soft, seductive sheen.

The part of it that was intact, at least. There was enough of Treya in me to ache at the damage that had been done.

Most of what I recognized as the starboard quadrant of the city was gone. That was bad, because what lay beneath that part of the visible city was some of Vox Core's essential infrastructure. Vox was complexly interconnected, and in the past it had sustained major damage without loss of function. But even the most decentralized network will fail if it loses too much connectivity, and that was what must have happened when the nuke penetrated our defenses. It was as if Vox's brain had suffered a massive stroke, the damage spreading and compounding itself until the whole organism lost function. Tendrils of smoke still wafted up from the impact point. A hole had been punched in the starboard wall of the city, which might have provided an entry point for Farmer forces, except that radioactive and still-smoldering rubble had barred the gap.

Treya had spent the whole of her life in this city, and her shock welled up in me and made my eyes water.

Turk—once he made sure Digger Choi was out of earshot—said, "Tell me about the people who did this."

"Built the city or dropped the bomb?"

"Dropped the bomb."

"An alliance of cortical democracies and radical bio-normatives. They were determined not to let us cross the Arch. Scared we'll call down some kind of doom by attracting the attention of the Hypotheticals."

"You think that might happen?"

It was a question Treya would never have entertained. Treya had been a good Voxish citizen, blithely convinced that the Hypotheticals were benevolent and that human beings could aspire to some kind of intercourse with them. But as Allison I could be agnostic about it. "I don't actually know."

"Sooner or later we might have to pick sides in one of these fights."

That would be a luxury, I thought, to *pick* a side.

But for now the question was moot. We ate the pea-green gunk we had been given and stood up for a last look around before Digger Choi came to tie us up for the night. The sky had gotten darker and the

peak of the Arch shimmered almost directly overhead. Vox Core itself had filled with shadows.

That was the saddest thing of all, it seemed to me:
the darkness of Vox Core. All my life (*Treya's* life) the
Core had been ablaze with light. It leaked light like a
glorious sieve. Its light was its heartbeat. And now it
was gone. Not even a twinkle.

The Farmer attack, if it was going to happen at all,
would have to happen soon. Until then there was
nothing to do but look at the sky, and it was obvious
from the dire angle of the Arch that we were at the
critical point of the passage. The Vox Archipelago
was big enough that some of it must already be past
the midway point. But that didn't matter—Vox would
transit all at once or not at all. An Arch—and this
truth had been established many centuries ago—was
more like an intelligent filter than a door. Back when
this Arch was working it had been able to distinguish
between a bird in flight and a boat in the water: send
the boat from Earth to Equatoria but leave the bird
behind. That's not a simple decision. The Arch had to
be able to identify human beings and their works
while ignoring the countless other living creatures
who inhabited (or had once inhabited) both worlds.
Crossing an Arch, in other words, wasn't a mechanis-
tic process. The Arch looked at you, evaluated you,
accepted you or rejected you.

The most likely outcome was that we wouldn't be
admitted to Old Earth at all. But I was more afraid of
the other possibility. Even before the Arch stopped
working, the Earth had changed beyond anything
Turk would have recognized. The last refugees from
the polar cities had described drastic shifts in the

oceanic chemocline, H_2S boiling out of hopelessly eutrophied offshore dead zones, massive and sudden dry-land extinctions.

I closed my eyes and drifted into the dazed semi-consciousness that passes for sleep when you're exhausted and hungry and in pain. Periodically I opened my eyes and looked at Turk where he lay in the shadows with his arms bound behind him. He was nothing like what Treya had once pictured as an emissary from the Hypotheticals. He looked exactly like what he was—a rootless drifter, no longer young, and worn almost beyond endurance.

I guessed he was dreaming, because he moaned from time to time.

Maybe I dreamed, too.

What woke me next—still deep in that long night—was a sound so loud it cut the darkness like a knife. It was a deep-throated hooting, continuous and inhuman but familiar, familiar . . . dazed, I couldn't place it at first; but when I recognized it I felt what I had not felt for many days: *hope*.

I kicked at Turk to rouse him. He opened his eyes and rolled upright, blinking.

"Listen!" I said. "You know what that is? It's the *alarm*, Turk, it's the *call-in*, the *come-to-shelter*," struggling to translate Voxish words into ancient English, "it's the fucking *air-raid siren*!"

The wailing was broadcast from the highest towers of Vox Core. It was a signal to get inside the walls, that some kind of attack was imminent, and surely that was true. But here was the important thing: *if Vox Core was able to sound the siren, at least some of its power must have been restored.*

Vox Core was alive!

"Means what?" asked Turk, still fighting sleep.

"It means we have a chance of getting out of this!" I managed to wiggle upright so I could have a look. Vox Core was still mainly dark . . . but even as I registered that fact a searchlight rayed from the nearest watchtower and swept over the treeless meadows, lighting up the Farmers as they doused their fires and hurried to suit up for war. Then there were more lights: tower by tower, block by block, Vox Core began to reclaim itself from the darkness. Smaller lights like fireflies scattered from the high aerodromes, and those were aircraft, armed and lethal.

It made me giddy. I heard myself shouting into the noise: *Here we are! Come and get us!* Something stupid like that. Treya's old loyalties bursting out of my throat.

Then the weapons rained down, and the Farmers began to die.

CHAPTER FIVE

SANDRA AND BOSE

Sandra booked off two hours for lunch, making creative use of a free hour she had originally scheduled for her next consultation with Orrin Mather. The restaurant where she had arranged to meet Bose was crowded with employees from the carpet wholesaler across the highway, but the table she snagged was out of the way and screened from the worst of the noise by a hedge of plastic ficus. Quiet enough for conversation. Bose nodded approvingly when he arrived.

He wasn't in uniform. He looked better out of police drag, Sandra thought. Jeans and a white shirt that set off his complexion. She asked him whether he was on duty today.

He said he was. "But I don't always wear the blues. I work out of Robbery/Homicide."

"Really?"

"That's not as impressive as it sounds. HPD went

through massive reorganization after the Spin. Departments were dismantled and put back together like Lego blocks. I'm not a detective. I just do grunt work. I'm relatively new in the division."

"So how does that connect you to Orrin Mather?"

He frowned. "I'll explain, but can we talk about the document first?"

"I notice you call it 'the document.' Not 'Orrin's document.' So you don't believe he wrote it?"

"I'm not saying that."

"You want to hear my opinion before you give me yours, in other words. Okay, well, let's start with the obvious. The pages you sent me appear to constitute an adventure story set in the future. The vocabulary is way beyond anything I've heard from Orrin. The story isn't especially sophisticated but it displays a grasp of human behavior more nuanced than anything Orrin demonstrated in the short time I had to speak with him. And unless it was corrected in transcription, the grammar and punctuation are a big notch up on Orrin's verbal skills."

Bose nodded at this. "But you're still reserving judgment?"

She considered the question. "To a degree, yes."

"Why?"

"Two reasons. One is circumstantial. It seems obvious Orrin isn't the author, but then why is he being cagey about that, and why are you asking for my opinion? The second reason is professional. I've talked to a lot of people with personality disorders of various kinds and I've learned not to trust first impressions. Psychopaths can be charming and paranoiacs can appear sweetly reasonable. It's possible Orrin's mannerisms are a learned reflex or even a deliberate deception. He may want us to think he's less intelligent than he really is."

Now Bose was giving her a peculiar and annoyingly cryptic smile. "Good. Excellent. What about the text itself? What did you make of it?'

"I don't pretend to be a literary critic. Looking at it as a patient's production, however, I can't help noticing how concerned it is with identity, especially mixed identities. There are two first-person narrators—more like three, since the girl can't decide who she really is. And even the male narrator is essentially stripped of his past. Beyond that, there's the grandiosity of the story's concern with the Hypotheticals and the possibility of interaction with them. In real life, when people claim they can talk to the Hypotheticals, it's a diagnostic indicator for schizophrenia."

"You're saying Orrin—if he wrote this—might be schizophrenic?"

"No, not at all; I'm just saying it's possible to read the document that way. Actually, my first impression of Orrin is that he might be somewhere on the autistic spectrum. Which is another reason why I can't entirely dismiss him as the author of the text. High-functioning autistics are often eloquent and precise writers even though they're profoundly inhibited in social interactions."

"Okay," Bose said thoughtfully. "Good, that's useful."

Lunch arrived. Bose had ordered a club sandwich and fries. Sandra's Cobb salad was limp and disappointing and she slowed down after a few bites. She waited for Bose to say something more enlightening than "okay."

He polished a dab of mayonnaise off his upper lip. "I like what you said. It makes sense. It's not all psychiatric jargon."

"Great. Thanks. But—*quid pro quo*. You owe me an explanation."

"First let me give you this." He pushed a manila envelope across the table. "It's another installment of the document. Not a transcript this time. A photocopy of the original. A little hard to read but maybe more revealing."

The envelope was dismayingly thick. Not that Sandra was reluctant to take it. Her professional curiosity had been piqued. What she resented was that Bose was still being cagey about what he wanted from her. "Thank you," she said, "but—"

"We can talk more freely later on. Say maybe tonight? If you're free?"

"I'm free now. I haven't finished my salad yet."

Bose lowered his voice: "The problem is, we're being watched."

"Excuse me?"

"Woman in the booth behind the plastic plants."

Sandra canted her head and nearly laughed out loud. "Oh, god!" Whispering now herself: "That's Mrs. Wattmore. From State. One of the ward nurses."

"She followed you here?"

"She's a hopeless busybody, but I'm sure it's a coincidence."

"Well, she's been taking a pretty deep interest in our conversation." He mimed a cupped-hand-to-ear.

"Typical . . ."

"So—tonight?"

Or we could move to a different table, Sandra thought. Or just keep our voices down. She didn't suggest it, however, because it was possible Bose was using this as an excuse to see her again. And she wasn't sure how to interpret that. Was Bose a colleague, a collaborator, a potential friend, maybe even (as Mrs. Wattmore no doubt suspected) a potential lover? The situation was ambiguous. Perhaps exciting for that reason. Sandra hadn't been involved with a man since she broke up with Andy Beauton, another State physician who had been fired in last year's downsizing. Since then, her work had eaten her alive. "Okay," she said. "Tonight." She was reassured by the smile he gave her. "But I still have an hour on lunch."

"So let's talk about something else."

About each other, as it turned out.

They laid out their life stories for inspection. Bose: Born in Mumbai during his mother's ill-fated marriage to an Indian wind turbine engineer, raised there until the age of five. (Which explained the ghost of an accent and his manners, just a touch more genteel than the Texas average.) Brought back to Houston for grade school and subsequently imbued with what he called his mother's "well-honed sense of injustice," he had eventually qualified for police training at a time when HPD was in a hiring frenzy. He talked about himself with a sense of humor that struck Sandra as unusual in a cop. Or maybe she had been meeting the wrong cops. In return she gave him the pocket version—to be honest, the carefully edited version—of Sandra Cole: her family in Boston, med school, her job at State. When Bose asked about her choice of career she mentioned a desire to help people; she didn't mention her father's suicide or what had happened to her brother Kyle.

The conversation evolved toward triviality as they lingered over coffee, and Sandra left the restaurant still unsure whether she ought to treat this as a professional exchange or a boy-girl size-up. Or which she wanted it to be. She found Bose at least superficially attractive. It wasn't just his blue eyes and teak-colored skin. It was the way he talked, as if he was speaking from some calm and happily reasonable place deep inside himself. And he seemed equally interested in her, unless she was overinterpreting. Still . . . did she *need* this in her life?

Not to mention the inevitable gossip that would ensue in the parched social universe of the State Care staff. Nurse Wattmore beat her back to work by half an hour, time enough to spread the word that Sandra had been lunching with a cop. She got a set of knowing glances and half-smiles from the nurses at Reception. Bad luck—but Wattmore was a force of nature, as unstoppable as the tides.

Of course, the tide of gossip flowed both ways. Sandra knew that Mrs. Wattmore, a widow, forty-four years of age, had slept with three of the four former ward supervisors. "That woman lives in a glass house," one of the nurses confided in Sandra when they crossed paths in the staff commissary. "You know? Lately she's been taking her breaks with Dr. Congreve."

Sandra hurried to her office and closed the door. She had two case summaries that needed writing up. She gave the folders a guilty look and pushed them aside. Then she took the envelope Bose had given her

from her purse and tugged out the sheaf of closely
written pages and began to read.

She was brimming with fresh questions when she
met Bose that evening.

This time he had picked the restaurant, a Northside
theme pub, shepherd's pie and Guinness and green
paper napkins embossed with pictures of harps. He
was waiting when she arrived. She was surprised to
find another woman sitting at the table with him.

The woman wore a blue flower-print dress that
was neither fresh nor in good repair. She was skinny
to the point of emaciation and she seemed both nervous and angry. When Sandra approached the table
the woman looked at her warily.

Bose stood hastily. "Sandra, I'd like you to meet
Ariel Mather—Orrin's sister."

CHAPTER SIX

TURK FINDLEY'S STORY

1.

There had been moments during my captivity when I wasn't sure whether I wanted to live or die. If there was any sense or meaning in the life I had lived—from the unforgivable act that had caused me to leave Houston many years ago to the moment I woke up in the Equatorian desert—I couldn't see it. But now the mindless urge to live came roaring back. I watched as swarms of Voxish aircraft began the systematic slaughter of the Farmer rebels, and all I wanted was to get to a safe place.

2.

From the cart on its hillside we were able to see the treeless plain surrounding Vox Core as it became the scene of a rolling apocalypse. The Farmer armies had already begun to retreat as soon as the sirens sounded.

At the first sight of the approaching aircraft they dropped their makeshift pikes and broke formation, but the Voxish warplanes came on relentlessly, skimming over the ranks of their enemies like hunting birds. The weapon they used was new to me: the aircraft projected fiery wave fronts that rolled across the landscape and then vanished like summer lightning, leaving cone-shaped swathes of smoldering soil and charred bodies in their wake. The sound they made was a seismic exhalation, powerful enough that I felt it in my rib cage. The war sirens went on wailing like mournful giants.

Briefly, it seemed as if we might be safe up here on the hill. Then one of the warplanes banked nearby, as if considering us, and the wind carried up the stench of smoke and burning flesh. Our guard detail evaporated, running for the woods, with the exception of Digger Choi, who seemed immobilized. I caught his eye. He was clearly terrified. I held out my bound hands to him, hoping he could interpret the gesture: *Don't leave us tied up like hogs at a slaughter.* Allison added a few pleading words in Voxish, barely audible under the general roar.

Digger Choi turned his back.

I called out, "*Cut us loose, you cowardly fuck!*" And although he surely didn't understand English he stopped and turned back, glowering through his fear. He dropped the latch on the cart's gate and cut us free with the knife he carried, two hasty slashes, first Allison, then me. The blade bit my wrist but I didn't care. I was cravenly grateful.

Allison muttered a Voxish word that might have meant "Thanks." I couldn't translate the Farmer's response, but the go-to-hell tone of it was unmistake-able.

Down on the plain the carnage continued. The stink of frying human flesh became nauseatingly dense. Digger Choi turned to follow his friends in their dash for the treeline, but stopped in his tracks when a shadow eclipsed the distant lights of Vox Core. It was one of the Voxish aircraft, directly overhead, flying slow and low. Suddenly there was light all around us, so bright the air itself seemed whitewashed. An amplified voice called out incomprehensible orders in Voxish. "Stay still," Allison said, putting her hand on my arm. "Don't move."

It was our clothing that saved us—our greasy, blood-stained, road-worn yellow tunics.

The Network had been restored, and if Allison's limbic implant had been intact it would have alerted the Voxish forces to our presence. But the Farmers had destroyed her node, and I had never worn one to begin with, so we should have been indistinguishable from anyone else on this killing ground.

Except for our clothes. Microscopic radio-frequency tags were embedded in the coarse weave, identifying us (or at least what we wore) as survivors of the Equatorian recovery mission. That was enough to buy us a reprieve. The aircraft bellied down to land. A door sprang open and soldiers in military gear vaulted out and formed a cordon around us, weapons aimed.

Digger Choi was caught inside the cordon. He seemed to understand that surrender was his only option. He dropped to his knees and put his hands over his head in a gesture that would have been familiar on any battlefield ten thousand (or twenty thousand) years ago. The Voxish soldiers kept their weapons trained as Allison stammered out an explanation or a demand.

After a quick consultation the soldiers gestured to their aircraft. "They're taking us to Vox Core," Allison said, and the relief in her voice was palpable. "They don't know for sure that I'm telling the truth, but they know we're not Farmers."

They knew with equal certainty that Digger Choi *was* a Farmer, and one of the soldiers aimed a weapon at his head.

I said, "I'm not going anywhere until that man puts his gun down. Tell him so."

Given the slaughter that was taking place on every side of us, maybe the summary execution of Digger Choi was a small bone to choke on. But he had risked his life to set us free, even if he had been sullen about it. I didn't feel like watching his execution.

Allison gave me a peculiar look but she gauged my temperament correctly. She barked out a translation.

The soldier hesitated. I stepped forward, grabbed the Farmer's forearm and pulled him upright. I could feel him trembling under my hand. "Run," I told him.

Allison translated the single word. Digger Choi didn't need to be told twice. He darted toward a part of the forest not yet burning. The soldiers shrugged and let him go.

He lived a little longer because of what I had done. But only a little.

o   o   o

The aircraft carried us over the killing fields and across the city wall to a landing bay on one of the towers of Vox Core. During the brief flight the Voxish soldiers appeared to have received confirmation of our identities: after a quiet mutual consultation they began to treat me with deference and spoke to Allison in what sounded like sympathetic voices. Even before the aircraft docked we were given fresh clothing (crisp new jumpers, this time in a shade of blue). One of the soldiers, evidently a medic, slathered a soothing balm on my wrist where Digger Choi had slashed it in the process of cutting me loose. The same soldier attempted to examine the wound where Allison's node had been removed, but she pulled away from him and snarled. We were given water to drink: clean, cool, heavenly.

The landing dock was a windy rooftop. We left the aircraft and the soldiers escorted us to an enormous elevator housing, but Allison balked at the entrance and asked the soldier in charge a question. Her eyes widened at his answer. She spoke again, he answered curtly; the discussion began to sound like an argument, until at last the soldier gave her an exasperated nod.

"We're almost exactly at the midpoint in the passage of the Arch," she said to me. "The Network estimates twenty minutes or so to the transit, assuming it happens. I'm staying here until it does."

I didn't see the point. Vox would make the crossing to Earth or not, whether we were out here on this ledge or in some more comfortable space below.

"I don't care." She added in a lower voice, "I want to *see* it. I told them you did, too. What I want doesn't matter, but you're Uptaken—they have to pay attention."

So we were escorted to an enclosed balcony a single level below the landing docks, still high above the city, and we stood there like two grimy and slightly bloodstained scarecrows, gazing out at the island of Vox and the far sea shimmering under the small Equatorian moon. Smoke rose from the fields where the Farmers were dying (or had, by this time, surely died), but it trailed abaft of us and the sky ahead was starry and clear. The warplanes were already circling back to their bases.

Allison spoke to the nearest soldier in our escort, then translated her questions and his answers for me. Did the soldier think Vox would actually achieve a transit to Earth? Yes, he was certain of it; the prophecies were being fulfilled; the Uptaken were among us. What about the Uptaken who had already been taken to Vox Core when the city was bombed? Bad luck, the soldier said. Bad luck that a missile had penetrated the Voxish defenses, bad luck that the strike had damaged Vox Core's essential infrastructure— and *very* bad luck that the rescued Uptaken had been situated so close to ground zero.

It wasn't clear to me how many "others" had been collected in the Equatorian desert, but I believed that would have included the hybrid boy Isaac Dvali, possibly his mother, maybe a few unlucky civilians who happened to be nearby. Had the missile killed them all?

"All but one," Allison translated.

"Who's the survivor?"

More translation.

"The youngest one."

The boy, then. Isaac.

"But he was badly hurt," Allison added. "He's only barely alive."

"And that's enough to get the attention of the Hypotheticals? You think they'll really open a closed Arch and carry us to Earth just because they recognize one injured boy and a confused ex-sailor?"

It was a question she didn't have to answer. The answer came out of the sky in a blush of green light.

3.

It had been night on the Equatorian ocean. It was daylight on Earth.

The transition was as sudden and as unnervingly simple as it had been the first time I rode a rusty freighter from Sumatra to Equatoria. I felt a little heavier—Earth is a slightly more massive planet than Equatoria—but it was a sensation no more alarming than the feeling you get in a rising elevator. The other changes were less subtle.

We blinked at murky daylight. Beyond the shores of Vox, the sea was flat and oily to every horizon. The sky was a nasty-looking shade of green.

"God, *no,*" Allison whispered.

The soldiers gawked.

"Poison," she said. "It's all poison . . ."

The war sirens stopped wailing. In the silence the Voxish soldiers stood with abstracted expressions, as if they were listening to voices I couldn't hear—and probably that's what they were doing, consulting their Network or their superiors.

Then one of them addressed Allison. She told me,

"We're ordered below, no exceptions this time. The city's being sealed."

Before we turned away I took a last look at the open land beyond the walls. The corpses of Farmers lay motionless in charred meadowland, bathed in sour green daylight. A few survivors moved among them, but even from this height they looked shocked and aimless. I asked Allison whether at least some of them could be brought inside as prisoners.

"No," she said.

"But if the air's poisonous—"

"Just be grateful *we* were rescued."

"There might be hundreds of people out there. You're talking about abandoning them to die." She nodded blankly. I said, "Whoever's in charge here, do they really want that on their conscience?"

She gave me a peculiar look. "Vox is a limbic democracy," she said. "There's only one conscience. It's called the Coryphaeus. And it doesn't give a shit how many Farmers die."

CHAPTER SEVEN

SANDRA AND BOSE

This is Sandra Cole," Bose said, "Orrin's doctor over at State Care."

"Well, I'm not his doctor exactly," Sandra began, feeling more than a little ambushed. Ariel Mather gave her a look so steely and unwavering that her voice dried up in midsentence. Ariel was skinny but she was tall; even though she was sitting down her head was almost level with Sandra's. She would have towered over Orrin. She had Orrin's bony facial structure and similarly lustrous brown eyes. But there was nothing of Orrin's baleful tentativeness about her. Her glare could have blinded a cat.

"You got my brother locked up?"

"No, not exactly . . . he's being evaluated for admission to the Texas State Care Adult Custodial Program."

"What's that mean? Is he free to go or isn't he?"

Clearly, the woman wanted a blunt answer. Sandra sat down and gave her one. "No, he's not free to go. Not yet, anyway."

"Take it easy, Ariel," Bose said. "Sandra's on our side."

Were there *sides*? Apparently there were, and apparently Sandra had been recruited to one.

An intimidated waiter dropped off a basket of rolls and scurried away.

"All's I know," Ariel said, "is that I got a call from *this* man telling me Orrin was in jail for getting beat up, which I guess is a crime in Texas—"

"He was taken into custody," Bose said, "for his own protection."

"*Custody,* then, and would I come and get him. Well, he's my little brother. I took care of him all his life and half mine. Course I'll come get him. Now I find out Orrin's not in jail anymore, he's in something called *State Care.* That's your business, you said, Dr. Cole?"

Sandra took a moment to compose her thoughts, deliberately buttering a roll under Ariel's flinty scrutiny. "I'm an intake psychiatrist. I work for State, yes. I spoke to Orrin when Officer Bose first brought him in. Do you know how State Care works? It's a little different in North Carolina, I believe."

"Officer Bose says it's some kind of lock-up for crazy people."

Sandra hoped Bose had not said exactly that. "The way it works is, when indigent people, people with no fixed address or income, have trouble with the police, they can be remanded to State Care even if they haven't committed a crime—especially if the police believe the person can't be safely abandoned back on the street. State Care isn't a lock-up, Ms. Mather. And it's not a mental hospital. There's an evaluation period of seven days, during which we determine whether an individual is a candidate for full-time care in what we call a custodial guided-living environment. At the end of that time the person in question is either released or accorded dependency status." She was conscious of using words Ariel probably wouldn't understand—worse, the same words printed in State Care's three-page pamphlet for concerned families. But what other words were there?

"Orrin's not crazy."

"I interviewed him myself, and I'm inclined to agree with you. In any case, nonviolent candidates can always be released into the custody of a willing family member with an income and a legal address." She spared a glance for Bose, who should have explained all this. "If you can prove you're Orrin's sister—just a driver's license and a social security card will do—and if you're verifiably employed and willing to sign the forms, we can release Orrin to you more or less immediately."

"I told Ariel the same thing," Bose said. "In fact I called State to say we were submitting the paperwork. But there's a problem. Your supervisor, Dr. Congreve, claims Orrin had a violent spell this afternoon. He assaulted an orderly, Congreve says."

Sandra blinked. "Seriously? I didn't hear anything about a violent incident. If Orrin assaulted anyone, it's news to me."

"It's *bullshit* is what it *is*," Ariel said. "You talked to Orrin even a little, you'd *know* it's bullshit. Orrin never assaulted nobody in his life. Can't crush a bug without apologizing to it first."

"The accusation may not be true," Bose said, "but it makes it more difficult to release him."

Sandra was still struggling with the idea. "Certainly it doesn't sound like behavior I would expect from Orrin." Though how well did she really know him, after a single interview and a follow-up conversation? "But what are you saying—that Congreve is lying? Why would he do that?"

"To keep Orrin locked up," Ariel said.

"Yes, but why? We're underfunded and overloaded as it is. Usually, if we can remand a patient to family, that's a best-case outcome. Good for the patient, good for us. In fact it's my impression Congreve was hired because the board of directors believed he would reduce the number of people going on State lists." Ethically or not, she added silently.

"Maybe," Ariel said, "you don't know as much as you think you know about what goes on where you work."

Bose cleared his throat. "Keep in mind that Sandra's here to help us. She's our best shot at getting Orrin a fair deal."

"I'll see what I can find out about this incident. I don't know whether I *can* help, but I'll do my best. Ms. Mather, would you mind if I asked you a couple of questions about Orrin? The more I know about his background, the easier it'll be for me to move the case forward."

"I told Officer Bose everything already."

"But if you don't mind repeating yourself? My interest in Orrin is a little different from Officer Bose's."

Or a lot different. Clearly Sandra hadn't yet taken the full measure of Jefferson Amrit Bose. "Has Orrin lived with you all his life?"

"Up till the day he got on the bus to Houston, yes."

"You're his sister—what about your parents?"

"Me and Orrin had different daddies and neither one of 'em stuck around. Mama was Danela Mather and she died when I was just sixteen. She looked after us as best as she could but she got distracted pretty easy. And she had trouble with drugs toward the end. Meth and the wrong men, if you know what I mean. After that it was only me there to take care of Orrin."

"Did he need a lot of taking care of?"

"Yes and no. He never asked for much in the way of attention. Orrin was always happy to be by himself, looking at picture books or whatever. Even when he was little he didn't cry much at all. But he was pretty useless at school and he cried plenty when Mama took him to class, so he just mostly stayed home. And he wasn't good at feeding himself. You didn't put food in front of him twice a day, he'd blink and go hungry. That's just how he was."

"Different from other children, in other words?"

"Different he surely was, but if you mean is he retarded I have to say no he is not. He can write letters and read words. He's smart enough to hold a job if anybody'd hire him. He worked a night watchman job a while back in Raleigh—and here, too, Officer Bose tells me, until he got fired."

"Does Orrin ever hear voices or see things that aren't there?"

Ariel Mather crossed her arms and glared. "I already told you he's not crazy. He just has a good imagination. That was obvious even when he was little, the way he'd make up stories about his toy animals or whatnot. Sometimes I'd find him staring at the TV when it wasn't even turned on, like what he saw in that empty screen was just as interesting as any show on cable. Or at the sky, watching clouds go by. Windows on a rainy day, he liked to look at those. That don't make him crazy, I don't think."

"I don't think so either."

"And what's it matter? All's you have to do is get him out of that place he's locked up in."

"The only way I can do that—*if* I can do that—is to convince my colleagues Orrin isn't in danger of going back to the streets and getting hurt. What you're telling me is helpful. Which I have to assume is why Officer Bose brought us together." Sandra gave Bose another sidelong look. "You said Orrin was never aggressive?"

"Orrin'd run from an argument with his hands over his ears. He's *shy,* not *violent.* It was always hard for him when Mama came home with a man. He hid out, mostly, times like that. Especially if there was any kind of disagreement or unpleasantness."

"And I'm sorry I have to ask this, but was your mother ever aggressive toward Orrin?"

"She had her meth fits sometimes, especially toward the end. Some scenes. Nothing serious."

"You mentioned that Orrin liked to tell stories. Does he ever write them down? Did he keep a journal?"

Ariel seemed surprised at the question. "No, nothing like that. His printing is neat but he don't practice it much."

"Did he have a girlfriend back in Raleigh?"

"He's bashful around women, so no."

"Did he worry about that? Resent it?"

Ariel Mather shrugged.

"Okay. Thank you for your patience, Ariel. I don't believe Orrin needs to go into custodial care, and what you've said tends to confirm that." Though it raised other questions, Sandra thought.

"You can get him out?"

"It's not that simple. We'll have to sort out whatever happened this afternoon that led Dr. Congreve to believe he's violent—but I'll do everything I can." A thought occurred to her. "One more question. What was it that caused Orrin to leave Raleigh, and why did he come to Houston?"

Ariel hesitated. Her posture remained stiff as a spindle, as if her sense of dignity had settled into the knobs of her spine. "He has moods sometimes. . . ."

"What kind of moods?"

"Well . . . most of the time Orrin seems young for his age, I guess you noticed that. Every once in a while, though, a mood takes him . . . and when Orrin's in a mood he don't seem young at all. He'll give you a look like he sees right through you, make you think he's older than the moon and the stars put together. Like a wind blows through him from somewhere far away. That's what Mama used to say when Orrin was like that."

"And does that have something to do with why he came to Houston?"

"The mood was on him at the time. I don't know for sure he even meant to go to Texas in particular. He never said anything to me, just took the five hundred dollars I was saving toward a new car, took it from my dresser drawer when I was out at work. He asked our neighbor, Mrs. Bostick, to drive him to the bus station. He didn't pack a bag or nothing. He wasn't carrying nothing but an old pad of paper and a pen, Mrs. Bostick said. She guessed he was meeting somebody at the depot. Orrin didn't deny it. But once she left him there he must've bought himself a ticket and got on an interstate bus. The mood was on him for some days before that, him all quiet and far-eyed." She gave Sandra a calculating look. "I hope that don't change your opinion of him."

Complicates it, Sandra thought. But she shook her head: no.

Ariel Mather had arrived in town early that morning. Bose had helped her check into a motel before their aborted visit to State, but she had barely had time to unpack her suitcase. She was tired, and she told Bose she wanted to get a decent night's sleep. "But thank you for the dinner and all."

"I still need to discuss a few things with Sandra," Bose said. He asked the waiter to call a cab for her. "While we're waiting, Ariel, one more question?"

"Go ahead."

"Did Orrin contact you after he arrived here in Houston?"

"One phone call to let me know he was all right. I was mad enough to light into him for leaving but that just made him hang up, and I was sorry afterward. I should've known better. Yelling at him never does any good. A week later I had a letter to say he was working steady and he hoped I wasn't too mad at him. I would've wrote back but he didn't put down any return address."

"Did he say anything about where he was working here in town?"

"Not as I recall."

"Nothing about a warehouse? A man named Findley?"

"No, sir. Does it matter?"

"Probably not. Thank you again, Ariel."

Bose said he'd call her tomorrow to let her know how things were progressing. She stood up and made her way to the door of the restaurant with her chin thrust forward.

"Well?" Bose asked. "What's your reaction?"

Sandra shook her head firmly. "Oh, no. No. You don't get anything more from me until *you* answer a question or two."

"I guess that's fair. Listen, I need a ride home—I came in a cab with Ariel. Can I beg a lift from you?"

"I guess so . . . but if you bullshit me, Bose, I swear I'll leave you by the side of the road."

"Deal," he said.

It turned out he lived in a new development off the West Belt, a longish drive and out of her way, but Sandra didn't object: it gave her time to assemble her thoughts. Bose was patient in the passenger seat, hands in his lap, quietly attentive as she pulled into traffic. It was another mercilessly hot night. The car's air conditioner struggled gamely.

She said, "This is obviously not standard police work."

"How so?"

"Well, I'm no expert. But your interest in Orrin seemed unusual from the day you escorted him into State. And I saw you slip the cab fare to Ariel—don't you need some kind of receipt? For that matter, shouldn't you be interviewing her downtown?"

"Downtown?"

"At police headquarters or whatever. In the movies they always call it 'downtown' . . ."

"Oh. *That* downtown."

She felt herself blushing but persisted: "Another thing. At State we talk to HPD referrals every day. A lot of them are considerably less tractable than Orrin, but some are just as scared and just as vulnerable. As a professional I have to behave like a clinician no matter who I'm dealing with. The cops who drop these cases at State, on the other hand . . . for them it's the end of a tedious necessity. Their interest in the individuals they remand to us is less than nil. Except on legal business, no cop *ever* does follow-up. Until you walked in. You acted like you cared about Orrin. So explain that to me, before we get into the question of Orrin's writing or my opinion of his sister. Tell me what your stake in the matter is."

"Maybe I happen to like him. Maybe I think he's being railroaded."

"Railroaded by who?"

"I'm not sure. And if I haven't been entirely frank, it's because I don't want to involve you in something potentially dangerous."

"Your chivalry is noted, but I'm already involved."

"If we handle this badly, you could be putting your job at risk."

Sandra laughed despite herself. "There hasn't been a day in the last year I didn't half hope to be fired. My résumé is out at hospitals all over the country." This was true.

"Any takers?"

No. "Not yet."

Bose looked down the highway into the simmering night. "Well, you're right. What you said. This isn't standard police work."

The Spin had been a difficult time for police and security forces the world over—especially the frightening finale of it, when the stars had reappeared in the night sky and the sun, four billion years older than it had been five years ago, crossed the meridian like a bloody banner of the apocalypse. It had seemed like the end of the world. A great many police personnel had abandoned their duties and joined their families for the final hours. And when it became obvious that the world would *not* end—that the Hypotheticals would filter the radiation reaching the Earth to a tolerable level, giving the planet at least a probationary future—many of those deserters had stayed home despite a general amnesty. Lives had changed beyond recognition or restoration.

New bodies were recruited, some with only marginal qualifications. Bose had joined the force two decades later, at a time when many of those marginal recruits had become senior staff. He had found himself in an HPD rife with internal conflicts and generational rivalries. His own career, such as it was, had advanced at a glacial pace.

The problem, he told Sandra, was an endemic corruption, born out of the years when vice had spent freely and virtue went begging. The incoming tide of Equatorian oil had only compounded the problem. On the surface Houston was a clean enough city: the HPD was good at keeping a lid on property crimes and petty violence. And if, under the city's polished exterior, a river of illicit goods and undocumented cash flowed freely . . . well, it was the job of the HPD to make sure nobody paid too much attention.

Bose had been careful not to skirt too close to the shady side. He had volunteered for drudge work rather than accept dubious assignments, had even turned down offers of promotion. As a result he was considered unimaginative and even, in a certain sense, stupid. But because he never passed judgment on his peers he was also considered useful, an officer whose dogged attention to small matters freed up more ambitious men for more lucrative work.

"So you kept your hands clean," Sandra said, offering it as an observation but withholding her approval.

"Up to a point. I'm not a saint."

"You could have gone to some, uh, higher authority, exposed the corruption—"

He smiled. "Respectfully, no, I couldn't. In this town the money and the power hold hands. The higher authorities are the people taking the biggest dip. Turn right at the intersection. My building's the second left at the light. If you want to hear the rest of this you can come up to my place. I don't entertain much but I can probably crack a bottle of wine." This time his look was almost sheepish. "If you're interested."

She agreed. And not just because she was curious.

Or rather, her curiosity wasn't limited to Orrin Mather and the HPD. She was increasingly curious about Jefferson Bose himself.

Clearly he wasn't a wine person. He produced a dusty bottle of some off-brand Shiraz, probably a gift, long neglected in a kitchen cupboard. Sandra told him beer would do fine. His refrigerator was amply stocked with Corona.

Bose's single-bedroom apartment was conventionally furnished and relatively neat, as if it had been cleaned recently if not enthusiastically. It was only three stories up but it was situated with a partial view of the Houston skyline, all the gaudy towers that had shot up in the aftermath of the Spin like gigantic pixelboards of randomly lit windows.

"It's the money that drives the corruption," Bose said, putting a chilled bottle into her hand and sitting opposite her in a recliner that had seen better days. "Money, and the one thing more valuable than money."

"What's that?"

"Life. Longevity."

He was talking about the trade in Martian pharmaceuticals.

Back in med school, Sandra had roomed with a biochemistry major who had been obsessively curious about the Martian longevity treatment brought to Earth by Wun Ngo Wen—she had suspected that its life-prolonging effects could be teased away from the neurological modifications the Martians had engineered into it, if only the government would free up samples for analysis. That hadn't happened. The drug was deemed too dangerous for general release, and Sandra's roommate had gone on to a perfectly conventional career, but her intuition about the Martian drug had been correct. Samples had leaked out of the NIH labs onto the black market.

The Martians had believed longevity should confer both wisdom and certain moral obligations, and they had designed their pharmaceuticals that way. The famous "fourth stage of life," the adulthood after adulthood, had entailed changes to the brain that modified aggressiveness and promoted sympathy for others. Not a bad idea, Sandra thought, but hardly commercial. The black-marketers had hacked the biochemical combination lock and evolved a better product. Nowadays—assuming you had serious money and the right contacts—you could buy yourself an extra twenty or thirty years of life while avoiding that awkward surge of human sympathy.

All illegal, of course, and massively profitable. Just last week the FBI had shut down a distribution ring in Boca Raton that was processing more cash on an annual basis than most top-fifty corporations, and that was only a fraction of the market. Bose was right: in the end, for some people, life was worth anything you had to pay for it.

"The longevity drug isn't easy to cultivate," Bose was saying. "It's as much an organism as a molecule. You need genetic seed stock, you need a decent-sized bioreactor, and you need a lot of closely watched chemicals and catalysts. Which means you have to buy a lot of look-the-other-way."

"Including some in HPD?"

"That would be a reasonable conclusion to draw."

"And you're aware of this?"

He shrugged.

"But there must be somebody you could talk to—I don't know, the FBI, the DEA . . ."

"I believe the federal agencies have their hands full at the moment," Bose said.

"Okay," Sandra said, "but what does all this have to do with Orrin Mather?"

"It's not Orrin so much as the place he used to work. As soon as he got off the bus from Raleigh, Orrin was hired by a man named Findley. Findley operates a warehouse that holds and forwards imported goods, mainly cheap plastic crap from manufacturers in Turkey, Lebanon, Syria. Most of his hires are transients or immigrants without papers. He doesn't ask for social security numbers and his guys get paid in cash. He put Orrin to work doing the usual lift-and-carry jobs. But Orrin turned out to be an unusual employee by Findley's standards, which means he came in on time and sober, he was bright enough to follow orders, he never complained and he didn't care about finding a better job as long his pay was regular. So after a while Findley took him off day work and made him night watchman. Most nights between midnight and dawn Orrin was locked in the warehouse with a phone and a patrol schedule, and all he had to do was conduct an hourly walk-through and call a certain number if he noticed anything unusual."

"A certain number? Not the police?"

"Definitely not the police, because what passes through the warehouse, along with a lot of die-stamped toys and plastic kitchenware, are shipments of precursor chemicals bound for black-market bioreactors."

"Orrin knew about this?"

"That's unclear. Maybe he had some suspicions. In any case, Findley fired him a couple of months back, possibly because Orrin was getting a little too familiar with the details of the operation. Some of Findley's black-market material comes in or goes out after hours, so Orrin would have seen a few transfers. The firing was pretty traumatic for Orrin—I guess he thought he was being punished for something."

"He talked to you about it?"

"A little, reluctantly. All he says is that he didn't do anything wrong and that it wasn't time for him to leave."

Sandra asked Bose for another Corona, which gave her time to think about all this. What he had said seemed to make everything murkier. She decided to focus on the only part of this she really understood or could affect: Orrin's assessment at State Care.

Bose came back with a bottle, which she accepted but set down immediately on Bose's ring-stained coffee table. He needed new furniture, she thought. Or at least a set of coasters.

"You think Orrin might have information that would be damaging to a criminal smuggling operation."

Bose nodded. "None of this would matter if Orrin had been just another one of Findley's hired drifters. Orrin would have left town or found other work or otherwise disappeared into povertyland, end of story. The trouble is that Orrin surfaced again when we took him into custody. Worse, when we asked him about his employment record, he piped right up about his six months at the warehouse. Mention of the name set off alarms in certain quarters, and I guess word worked its way up."

"So what are the smugglers afraid of, that Orrin will reveal some secret?"

"I said the federal agencies are too busy to take on corruption in HPD, and that's true. But there are ongoing investigations related to longevity-drug rings. Findley—and the people Findley works for—are nervous about Orrin as a potential witness, now that his name and history are in the database. You see where this is going?"

She nodded slowly. "His psychological condition."

"Exactly. If Orrin's admitted to State Care, that constitutes a formal declaration of incompetence. Any testimony he might give would be fatally compromised."

"Which is where I come in." She sipped her beer. She seldom drank beer. She thought it tasted the way old socks smell. But it was gratifyingly cold, and she welcomed the slight buzz, that oddly clarifying wisp of intoxication. "Except I'm not on Orrin's case anymore. I can't do anything to help him."

"I don't expect you to. I probably shouldn't have told you what I did, but—like you said, *quid pro quo*. And I'm still interested in your opinion of Orrin's writing."

"So you think his document is what, some kind of coded confession?"

"I honestly don't know what Orrin's document is. And although it mentions the warehouse—"

"It does?"

"In a section you haven't read. But it's hardly the kind of evidence you can take to court. I'm just . . ."

He seemed to struggle for a word. "You could say, professionally curious."

You could say that, Sandra thought, but you'd only be telling a fraction of the truth. "Bose, I saw the way you acted when you brought him in. You're more than curious. You actually appear to give a shit about him. As a human being, I mean."

"By the time Orrin was remanded to State I'd got to know him a little bit. He's being railroaded, and he doesn't deserve it. He's . . . well, you know how he is."

"Vulnerable. Innocent." But a lot of the people Sandra dealt with were both vulnerable and innocent; it was commonplace. "Endearing, in a kind of spooky way."

Bose nodded. "That thing his sister said back at the restaurant. 'A wind blows through him.' I'm not exactly sure what she meant by that. But it sounds about right."

Sandra couldn't say at what point she decided to stay the night. Probably there was no single point of decision; that wasn't how it worked. In her relatively limited experience, intimacy was a slow glide orchestrated not by words but by gestures: eye contact, the first touch (as she put a hand on Bose's arm to make some conversational point), the easy way he came and sat beside her, thigh to thigh, as if they had known each other for half an eternity. Strange, she thought, how familiar it began to seem, and then how inevitable that she would go to bed with him. There was no first-time awkwardness about it. He was as sweet in bed as she had suspected he would be.

She fell asleep beside him, one hand draped across his hip. She wasn't aware of him when he slipped away from her. But she was dimly awake when he came back from the bathroom, caught for a moment in the amber glow of city light through the bedroom window. She saw the scar she had already felt with her fingertips, a pale ridge that began below his navel and meandered like a mountain road along his rib cage and up toward his right shoulder.

She wanted to ask him about it. But he turned away hastily when he saw her looking, and the moment passed.

In the morning Bose made French toast and coffee even though there wasn't time to linger over it. He moved around the kitchen, heating butter in a skillet, breaking eggs, with a confidence and ease she found pleasant to watch.

A thought had come to her during the night. "You're not working for the federal agencies," she said, "and you're barely working for HPD. But you're not alone in all this. You're working for *somebody*. Isn't that right?"

"Everybody works for somebody."

"An NGO? A charitable organization? A detective agency?"

"I guess we'd better talk about that," he said.

CHAPTER EIGHT

ALLISON'S STORY

1.

Once we'd made the transit to Earth, the managers put us in adjoining medical care suites and we slept for most of two days. A team of nurses hovered over me at all times, and at intervals I asked them about Turk. They said he was doing well and that I could talk to him soon. They wouldn't say more than that.

I needed the rest, for obvious reasons, and it was pleasant to wake, sleep, dream, and wake again without fearing for my life. Obviously, there were problems I would have to face sooner or later. Big ones. But the meds I was swallowing washed away all urgency.

My wounds were minor and they healed nicely. Eventually I woke feeling fit and hungry and for the first time impatient, and I asked the bedside nurse—a male worker with big eyes and a fixed smile—when I could have something more substantial than protein paste to eat.

"After the surgery," he said blandly.

"What surgery?"

"To replace your node," he said, in a tone of voice that suggested he thought he was talking to a slow-witted child. "I know how hard it must have been for you, surviving in the wild without it. When the Network went down it was hard for all of us. Like being alone in the dark." He shuddered at the memory. "But we'll have you repaired before the end of the day."

"No," I said instantly.

"Excuse me?"

"I don't want surgery. I don't want my node back."

He frowned for a moment, then turned his maddening smile back on. "It's perfectly natural to experience anxiety at a time like this. I can adjust your medication—would you like that?"

I told him my medication was fine and that I was simply and explicitly refusing surgery, as was my right under established Voxish medical protocols.

"But it's not an invasive surgery. It's just a repair! I've seen your history. You were implanted at birth like everyone else. We're not *changing* you in any way, Treya. We're *restoring* you."

I argued with him at length and fiercely. I used words I shouldn't have, both Voxish and English. He was shocked at first, then silent. He left the room with moist eyes and a perplexed expression, and I figured I'd won a victory, or at least gained a reprieve.

Ten minutes later they wheeled in the prep cart and the knives. That was when I started to scream. I was too weak to make much noise, but I was loud enough to be heard in the adjoining rooms.

The medical workers were about to strap me down when Turk came bulling through the doorway. Turk was wearing a patient's gown cinched at the waist, and he didn't look intimidating—our sojourn in the wilderness had left him skinny and brown as a nut. But the med staff must have seen the ferocity in his eyes, not to mention his balled fists. More than that, he was Uptaken, touched by the Hypotheticals: in Voxish theology that made him something next door to a god.

I told him in a few words that the medics were trying to re-install my limbic implant and turn me back into Treya.

"Tell them to stop," he said. "Tell them to take their fucking knives away or I will personally call down the wrath of the Hypotheticals on Vox and all its works."

I translated, with embellishments. The medical staff hastened out of the room with eyes averted, abandoning their surgical tools. But this, too, was only a reprieve. The medics were almost instantly replaced by a man in a gray jumpsuit, an administrator, a manager—a man I recognized from Treya's training sessions. He had been one of my teachers, not one of my favorites.

Apparently he and Turk had already met. "Stay out of this, Oscar," Turk said in English.

The administrator's Voxish name was long and decorated with honorifics, but "Oscar" was a decent approximation of the patrilineal fraction of it. Oscar spoke English, of course. His English wasn't as nuanced as mine—he had learned it mainly from ancient textbooks and legal documents—but it was functional, and unlike me he was empowered to speak on behalf of the managerial class.

"Please calm down, Mr. Findley," he said in his reedy voice. He was a small man, pale-skinned, yellow-haired, a couple of years past young.

"Fuck you, Oscar. Your people were about to force a surgical procedure on a friend of mine. I don't take that lightly."

"The woman you describe as your 'friend' was badly injured in the Farmer rebellion. You witnessed that injury, didn't you? In fact you tried to stop it."

It figured that Oscar would attempt some kind of legalistic argument, schooled as he was in ancient writs and warrants. Turk ignored him and turned to me. "Are you all right?"

"I'm okay for the time being. I won't be, if they put my node back in."

"That's irrational," Oscar said. "Surely you must see that, Treya."

"My name isn't Treya."

"Of course it is. Your denial is a symptom of your disorder. You're suffering from a pathological cognitive dissociation that cries out for repair."

"Oscar, *shut the fuck up*," Turk said. "I need to speak to Allison privately."

"There is no 'Allison,' Mr. Findley. 'Allison' is a tutelary construct, and the longer we allow Treya to sustain this delusion the harder it will be to cure her."

Treya herself would have deferred to Oscar without question, and I could still feel that old and craven impulse. But now it was hateful to me. "Oscar," I said in a quieter voice.

He shot me a hard look and repeated his Voxish name with all its status markers: I was a worker, and it was an insolence to call him by his short name. "Oscar," I repeated. "Are you hard of hearing? Turk asked you to shut the fuck up."

His pale complexion turned red. "I don't understand this. Have we hurt you, Mr. Findley? Have we threatened you in any way? Haven't I served as your personal liaison in a satisfactory manner?"

"You're not my liaison," Turk said. "Allison is."

"There *is* no Allison, and this woman *can't* function as a liaison—she has no connection to the Network . . . she doesn't have a working neural node!"

"She speaks English well enough."

"Like a native," I said.

"There you go."

"But—!"

"So I'm appointing her as my translator," Turk said. "From now on, any interaction I have with Vox goes through her. And we're both finished with doctors for the time being. No knives, no drugs. Can you arrange that?"

Oscar hesitated. Then he addressed me directly, in Voxish: "If you were a whole human being you would recognize your behavior as an act of treason, not just against the administrative class but against the Coryphaeus."

They were weighty words. Treya would have trembled. "Thank you, but I know what I'm doing," I said in the same language. "Oscar."

○ ○ ○

It was during this time that Vox began its lumbering, hopeless journey to Antarctica.

Getting any kind of hard information out of Oscar (who continued to pop up with annoying regularity) was impossible; but the nurses who still hovered around us, bringing meals or inquiring about our health like nosy parents, could occasionally be coaxed to talk. Through them I learned that the Voxish consensus had evolved from jubilation ("We transited to Earth, the prophecies are fulfilled") to dismay ("But the Earth is a ruin and the Hypotheticals continue to ignore us") to a stoic rededication to the ancient cause ("The Hypotheticals won't come to us, we'll have to seek them out").

Seeking them out was the hard part. Fleets of drone aircraft were dispatched to survey the landmasses of what had once been Indonesia and southern India, but all they found was an unrelieved wasteland. There was nothing alive there—or at least, nothing larger than a bacterium.

The oceans were anoxic. Back in Champlain, I had done a lot of reading about ocean toxicity. All the CO_2 we were pumping into the air back then—the fossil carbon reserves of not one but *two* planets— had been the trigger event, though it had taken centuries for the full effect to be felt. Rapid warming had stratified the seas and fed huge blooms of sulfate-reducing bacteria, which in turn spewed clouds of poisonous hydrogen sulfide into the atmosphere. The word for this process was "eutrophication." It had happened before, without human intervention; eutrophication episodes had been blamed for some of the planet's prehistoric mass extinctions.

Vox's administrative class had studied the few surviving records of the Terrestrial Diaspora and concluded that we ought to proceed to the site of the last known human habitation, near the southern pole, on the shore of what used to be called the Ross Sea. In the meantime, robotic craft would extend the aerial survey as far as Eurasia and the Americas.

When I told Turk all this he asked me how long the trip to Antarctica would take. Turk still thought of Vox more as an island chain than a seagoing vessel. But although it was vastly larger than any ship Turk had ever sailed or even imagined, it *was* a ship, with a surprisingly shallow draft and decent maneuverability for its colossal size. A couple of months to reach the Ross Sea, I told him. I promised I'd take him down to see the engine decks sometime soon . . . and it was a promise I meant to keep, for reasons I wasn't yet willing to explain.

There was a whole lot I *couldn't* explain, for the simple reason that we had no privacy. In Vox Core, the walls had ears. Also eyes.

Not necessarily for the purpose of spying. All those nanoscale eyes and ears, embedded in structural surfaces, fed their data to the Network, which sorted it for anomalies and issued alerts whenever an unusual situation arose: a health crisis, a technological failure, a fire, or even a violent argument. I was guessing, however, that an exception had been made in our case. Back when I was Treya I had been taught that when interacting with an Uptaken like Turk Findley, no word or gesture was too trivial to be sifted for

clues about the Hypotheticals or the state of existence the Uptaken had experienced among them. So
we were almost certainly being listened to, and not
just by machines. I couldn't allow myself to say anything I didn't want the administrators to overhear.
Which ruled out much of what I *needed* to say, and
needed to say quickly.

(And even if the administrators weren't listening,
the Coryphaeus surely was. I had been thinking a lot
about the Coryphaeus . . . but I didn't want the Coryphaeus to know that.)

I also wanted Turk to have at least a basic understanding of the geography of Vox Core and how it
operated, because the knowledge might be useful later.
So for the next few days I tried to act like a compliant
and acceptable liaison, doing what Treya had been
trained to do even though I was no longer Treya nor
wanted to be.

I introduced Turk to the book room just down the
corridor. The book room had been prepared years in
advance as a way of educating the Uptaken, and it
was just what the name suggested: a room housing a
substantial shelf of books. *Real* books, as Turk said
admiringly when he saw them. Books printed on paper and bound in boards, freshly minted but startlingly archaic.

They were the only such books in all of Vox, and
they had been created explicitly for the use of the
Uptaken. The books were mostly histories, assembled
by scholars and translated into simple English and
five other ancient languages. They were reasonably
reliable texts, according to my understanding. Turk

was interested but intimidated by the dozens of titles, and I helped him pick out a few volumes:

The Collapse of Mars and the Martian Diaspora
On the Nature and Purpose of the Hypothetical Entities
The Decline of the Terrestrial Ecology
The Principles and Destiny of the Polity of Vox
Cortical and Limbic Democracies of the Middle Worlds

—and a couple more, enough to give him a rough sense of what Vox was and why it had fought its battles back in the Ring of Worlds. The titles, I told him, were more daunting than the texts.

"Really?" he said. "So what are, uh, 'cortical and limbic democracies'?"

Ways of implementing consensus governance, I explained. Neural augmentation and community-wide Networks had made possible many different kinds of decision-making. Most of the communities of the Middle Worlds were "cortical" democracies, so called because the brain areas they interfaced with were clustered in the neocortex. They used noun-based and logically mediated collective reasoning to make policy decisions. (Turk blinked at the words but kindly let me keep talking.) "Limbic" democracies like Vox worked differently: their Networks modulated more primitive areas of the brain in order to create an emotional and intuitive (as opposed to a purely rational) consensus. "To put it crudely, in cortical democracies citizens reason together; in limbic democracies they *feel* together."

"I'm not sure I understand. Why the distinction? Why not a cortical-limbic democracy? Best of both worlds?"

Such arrangements had been attempted. Treya had studied them in school. The few cortico-limbic democracies that had been created had worked well enough for a period of time, and some had seemed idyllically peaceful. But they were ultimately unstable—they almost always decayed into Network-mediated catatonic loops, a kind of mass suicide by blissful indifference.

Not that the limbic democracies had fared much better, though I didn't say so where the walls might hear me. Limbic democracies had their own weaknesses. They were prone to collective insanity.

Except our own, of course. Vox was an exception to all the rules. At least, that was what I had been taught in school.

I kept my troubles to myself, mainly because I didn't want to give Oscar more leverage to use against me. More important, I didn't want to raise any doubt in Turk's mind that I was Allison Pearl, that I preferred to be Allison Pearl, and that I would remain Allison Pearl until the day they strapped me down and forced a Network node into my brain stem.

But the situation wasn't as simple as that.

So, the question I woke up with every day and went to bed with every night: was I *really* Allison Pearl?

In the most obvious sense, no. How could I be? Allison Pearl had lived and (presumably) died on Earth ten thousand years ago, back when Earth was a habitable planet. All that remained of her were a few gigs of diary entries that had somehow survived to the present day. The diary began in Allison Pearl's tenth year of life and ended for no apparent reason in her twenty-third. Treya had absorbed all those diary entries (and thousands of ancillary details about twenty-first-century life) both cortically and limbically, as data and as identity. Certainly Treya had never believed herself to "be" Allison Pearl. But she had carried Allison Pearl like a copybook deep in the meat of her brain. The Network had installed Allison Pearl in Treya's psyche, and the Network had built and maintained rigorous barriers between Allison and Treya.

Rigorous, but not rigorous enough. Because here was a secret I had told no one: even before the Network went down, even before the rebel Farmers destroyed my node, Allison had been bleeding into Treya. And Treya had never objected, nor had she complained to her administrative handlers. Instead Treya had kept the steady drip of Allison Pearl into her daily life a secret—a guilty secret, because there were qualities in Allison that Treya had coveted for herself.

Treya was obedient. Allison was defiant. Treya was willing to submerge her identity in the greater identity of Vox. Allison would sooner have died. Treya believed everything she was told by duly anointed authorities. Allison distrusted all authority, on principle.

But even that distinction falls short of absolute truth. Better to say that, through Allison, Treya had begun to discover the possibilities of skepticism, defiance, rebellion.

So ask again. What *was* I, now that the door between Treya and Allison had been thrown wide open? Was I Allison, or was I Treya *being* Allison?

No! Neither. I was a third thing.

I was what I had made of myself from all these in-
compatible parts, and I was entitled to *all* my memories, real and virtual. Vox had cultivated both Treya
and Allison, but Vox hadn't counted on the consequences of the mixture. And *fuck* Vox, anyway! There
it was, the heresy Treya had always resisted and for
which the voice of Allison had silently begged: *Fuck
Vox*, fuck its quiet tyranny, fuck its frozen dream religion, and fuck its craven obsession with the Hypotheticals.

Fuck *especially* the madness that had brought Vox
to this ruined Earth, and fuck the more profound
madness I believed was about to break loose aboard
her.

Fuck Vox! And bless Allison Pearl for making it
possible to say so.

Though Oscar had agreed to withdraw the surgical
knives, he hadn't abandoned the project of convincing me to submit to surgery. He conducted the cam-
paign secondhand, confronting me with people I
couldn't refuse to speak to, people who were or had
been Treya's friends and family.

They were my friends and family, too, in a real
sense, though I wasn't the person they had known,
much less the person they wanted and expected me to
be. And I was human enough to be hurt by their incomprehension and their grief.

One day Oscar brought my mother (Treya's
mother) to see me. My father (my Vox-father) was an
engineering worker who had been killed in the col-

lapse of an exchange tunnel not long after I was born. As a child I had been cared for by my mother and a crew of aunts, all of whom loved me and whom I had loved. And enough of Treya remained in me that I couldn't help reaching out to the woman whose arms had so often comforted me, couldn't help looking into her terrified eyes while I told her no, her daughter wasn't dead, only transformed, freed from a harsh but invisible bondage. She understood none of it. "Don't you want to be *useful*?" she asked me. "Don't you remember what it means to be part of a family?"

I remembered altogether too well. I ignored the question and told her I still loved her. And truly, I did. But she wasn't consoled. Why should she be? She had lost her daughter. Treya was gone, and I was just some stubborn golem who had taken her place. And in the moment I told her I loved her, I saw from her frozen expression that she hated me in return, actually hated me; that the person she loved wasn't me but a shadow I had ceased to cast.

Well, maybe she was right. I would never be the daughter she had known. I was what I had become. I was the thing I was and the name of the thing I was was *Allison, Allison, Allison Pearl*. I whispered it to myself long after she had left the room.

I didn't mean to take these troubles to Turk. Turk had troubles of his own. He wore his stoic come-what-may attitude proudly, and I guessed he had earned it, but fundamentally, inescapably, he was alone here, a stranger in what must have seemed to him a terrifyingly strange land. Our rooms adjoined, and some nights I woke to hear him pacing or mumbling to himself, confronting fears I couldn't imagine. It seemed to me that he must feel like a man trapped in a dream, aware of the lunacy of it but helpless to break through to a saner reality.

I tried not to pin my own hopes and fears on him. But I couldn't help thinking that for all our differences we were more alike than not. I found myself wondering whether he might have crossed paths with Allison Pearl back in the impossibly distant twenty-first century, some chance encounter in a faceless American crowd. Surely if anyone in Vox Core was equipped to understand Allison Pearl, it was Turk. So maybe it wasn't surprising that on one of those nights when neither of us could sleep I went into his room for comfort. We talked at first, the kind of talk we could have with no one but ourselves, intimacies shared not because of but despite what we knew about each other. "I am the thing most like you in the world," I said, "and you're the thing most like me," at which point it was inevitable that we would go to bed and take some solace there, and in the end I didn't care what the walls might hear or to whom they might whisper their dangerous secrets.

2.

In the morning I toured him through Vox Core, heel to head.

Of course he couldn't see all of it, or even more than a representative fraction. Vox Core above ground was the size of a modest twenty-first-century city. Below ground, in the hollow of the island, it was bigger: unravel all those complex spaces onto a two-dimensional grid and it would have been the size of Connecticut or maybe even California. We avoided the damaged zones that were still being decontaminated and rode vertical transit downward. We paused whenever the tube walls allowed a broad perspective, so Turk could see the plazas and terraces and tiers, the wide agricultural levels bathed in artificial daylight, the dormitory complexes set like alabaster chips in forested wildspaces.

Then I took him to the lowest levels of Vox, the engineering decks. The engines that drove Vox were immense—more a territory than an object—but I showed him reactor units the size of small towns, bathed in an eternal wash of desalinated water; I showed him a shadowy acreage of mu-metal chambers in which magnetic fields directed flows of molten iron; I led him past superconductive field coils around which moisture condensed like snow and was swept away in gales of forced air. Turk was awed, which would play well with the administrators who were no doubt monitoring us. There were ears in the walls even here.

But there were no ears where I took him next. We rode a transit stem up as far as it would go, then transferred to a smaller transport that slid up the spine of Vox's tallest tower. Two more transfers and we arrived at the highest accessible public platform in Vox Core, essentially a roof with a view.

Back when Vox had sailed the oceans of habitable worlds, this platform had not been enclosed. Now an osmotic perimeter had been established—I told Turk it was a "force field," a quaint and inaccurate term but one he more or less understood. "It doesn't seem to be working too well," he said. "Smells a little like a pig farm out here."

I guessed it did. The air was rank and windless, though we could see clouds speeding past aloft, seemingly close enough to touch. I felt sick with vertigo even before we approached the rim. For the first time I almost regretted the loss of my node: missed its calming presence, an invisible anchor. I felt as if a brisk wind would carry me away.

Vox was moving steadily south by southeast, out of the Indian Ocean and into the South Pacific. The sea here was faintly purple to every horizon, the sky a poisonous shade of ocher. I hated the look of it.

Turk peered into the misty distance. "The whole world's like this?"

I nodded. It was the decline and death of these oceans that had spurred the great Terrestrial exodus, which in turn had fed the bitter rivalries and conflicts of the previously settled Middle Worlds. "And the Hypotheticals did nothing to prevent it. Doesn't that seem strange? That they would protect the planet from the expanding sun but do nothing to prevent a catastrophic human die-off? Apparently they're happy with an Earth populated exclusively by bacteria. No one knows why."

"Your people expected to find something different."

They weren't *my people*. But I didn't correct him. "They expected to enter into direct communion with the Hypotheticals as soon as they arrived on Earth. It's a religious idea, really. The people who founded Vox were fanatics by any rational measure. The history books won't tell you so, but it's true. Vox is a cult. Its beliefs were built into its Network and scripted into its limbic democracy. When you're Networked all these doctrines feel reasonable, they feel like common sense. . . ."

"But not to you."

Not anymore. "And not to the Farmers. The Farmers are something less than citizens. They were Networked into compliance but not into communion."

"They were slaves, in other words."

"I suppose you could say that. They were taken as prisoners back in the Middle Worlds, generations ago. They refused to accept full citizenship, so they were modified into cooperation."

"Harnessed and put to work."

"That's why they destroyed their nodes as soon as the Network crashed." Though the survivors—the ones who had stayed in their environmentally sealed farmlands under the out-islands—would have been re-yoked by now. The rebels, of course, were all dead. Including Digger Choi, whose life Turk had attempted to save. Saved him for all of half an hour, maybe. If the warplanes hadn't got him, he would have died choking on the poisonous air.

Turk pressed up against the security railing that followed the edge of the roof, surveying what had become of the exterior land of Vox. The island was unprotected from the atmosphere and looked as if it had entered some grim and final autumn. The forests were dead. Leaves were brown and scattered, fruit rotted. Even the limbs of the trees looked leprous and fragile. The wind of passage was dismantling the woodlands branch by branch.

"Vox," I said, "I mean the collective Vox, limbic Vox, considered itself redeemed when we managed to pass through the Arch. But you're right, what they found isn't what they expected, and disappointment is setting in. That's what we need to talk about, up here where no one can hear us. We need to make a plan."

He stood a moment gazing over the ruined lands. Then he said, "How bad do you expect it to get?"

"Assuming Vox fails to find a door into Paradise down in Antarctica, it could get—well, really bad. The idea of merging Vox with the Hypotheticals is a foundational faith. It's the reason Vox exists. It's the promise we were all given at birth, along with our nodes. No dissent from it has ever been possible, nor would it have been tolerated. But now—"

"You're up against an awkward truth."

"*They* are. I'm not one of them anymore."

"I know. I'm sorry."

"Sailing to Antarctica is an act of desperation, and it's only postponing the inevitable."

"Okay, so reality sets in sooner or later—then what? Chaos, anarchy, blood in the streets?"

I was Voxish enough to feel a trace of shame at the answer to that question. "There have been other limbic cult communities in the past, and when they fail . . . well, it's ugly. Fear and frustration are amplified by the Network to the point of self-destruction. People turn on their neighbors, their families, ultimately themselves." There was no one to hear us, but I lowered my voice. "Social breakdown, maybe communal suicide. Eventually starvation when the food supply fails. And no one can opt out. You can't just reconfigure the prophecies or choose to believe something else—the contradiction is built into the Coryphaeus."

I had seen hints of it even today, as we traveled

through the city—a general sullenness too subtle for Turk to pick up on but plain enough to me, like the sound of thunder on a rising wind.

"And there's no way to protect ourselves?"

"Not if we stay here, no."

"And nowhere to go even if we had a way out. Christ, Allison." He couldn't stop staring at the mottled horizon, the rotting forest. "This was a pretty nice planet, once upon a time."

I stood closer to him, because we had come to the heart of the matter. "Listen. There are aircraft on Vox that can fly from pole to pole without refueling. And because you're Uptaken, the Arch is still open to us. We *can* leave. If we're careful and lucky, we can get ourselves back to Equatoria."

And in Equatoria we could surrender to Vox's ancient enemies, the people who had nuked Vox Core in an attempt to prevent us from provoking the Hypotheticals. The cortical democracies despised and feared Vox, but they wouldn't refuse to accept a pair of earnest refugees—I hoped. They might even help us make our way from Equatoria to one of the pleasanter Middle Worlds, where we could live out our lives in peace.

Turk was giving me a hard look. "You can fly one of these vehicles?"

"No," I said. "But *you* can."

I told him all of it then. I told him the plan I'd worked out in the long nights when I couldn't sleep, nights when Treya's loneliness threatened to shut down Allison's defiance, nights when it was almost impossible to find a space between those two borders of self, impossible even to name myself with any real conviction. The plan was practical, I believed, or might be. But it required a sacrifice Turk might not be willing to make.

When he understood what I was asking, he didn't give me an answer. He said he'd have to think about it. I accepted that. I said we could come up here in a few days and talk about it again.

"In the meantime," he said, "there's something else I need to do."

"What?"

"I want to see the other survivor," he said. "I want to see Isaac Dvali."

CHAPTER NINE

SANDRA AND BOSE

After she left Bose's condo Sandra had to drive to her apartment for fresh clothes, so she was most of an hour late for work. Not that she really cared, under the circumstances. Yesterday, Orrin Mather had been accused of a violent outburst—perhaps, or *probably,* if what Bose had told her was true, because Congreve or someone above him had been paid (in cash or longevity) to keep Orrin locked up. Sandra tried to contain her anger during the drive, but succeeded only in damping it down to a low simmer.

She had disliked Arthur Congreve since the day he was appointed supervisor, but it had never occurred to her that he might be as corrupt as he was unpleasant. But she knew Congreve had connections with municipal government—a cousin who was a sitting councilman—and although the street cops at HPD thought he was too stingy with admissions, the chief of police had made approving visits to State not once but twice since Congreve had been installed.

She parked carelessly and hurried through the metal detector at the building's entrance. As soon as she was badged up, she walked directly to the isolation wing.

It looked like any other part of the State Care building. "Isolation" didn't imply dank, sealed cells, as it might have in a federal prison. The isolation ward was just a little more generously supplied with locks and unbreakable furniture than the open wards, designed to segregate potentially violent patients from less aggressive inmates. Such cases were relatively few: the State system was empowered to deal with chronic homelessness, not outright psychosis. In a sense these were the least troublesome of the patients who passed through the system; they required little debate among the staff and were usually transferred to psychiatric hospitals in short order.

Whatever else Orrin Mather might be, he wasn't a psychopath. Sandra would have bet her degree on it. She wanted him out of isolation as soon as possible, and she meant to begin by getting his side of the story.

It was sheer bad luck that Nurse Wattmore happened to be presiding over the entrance to the locked ward. She should have buzzed Sandra through without comment, but she didn't. "Sorry, Dr. Cole, but I have my instructions," and she proceeded to page Congreve while Sandra stood and helplessly fumed. Congreve appeared promptly. His office was only a few doors down the corridor, and he took Sandra by the arm and steered her there.

He closed the door behind him and folded his arms. His office was at least twenty degrees cooler than the temperature outside—the air-conditioning murmured stoically in its vents—but the air smelled stale and greasy. The empty wrappers of fast-food breakfast items littered his desk. Sandra started to speak, but Congreve held up his hand: "I want you to know, first of all, that I'm really disappointed by the unprofessional behavior you've been displaying lately."

"I don't know what you mean. What unprofessional behavior?"

"Talking to this patient, Orrin Mather, after I assigned the case to Dr. Fein. And I have to assume that's where you were headed again this morning."

"Follow-up with a patient is hardly unprofessional. When I conducted his intake interview, I told him I'd be working his case. I wanted to make sure he was okay with Fein and that he didn't feel he'd been abandoned."

"That ceased to be your concern when I pulled you off the file."

"Pulled me off the file for no good reason."

"I'm not obliged to justify that decision or any other I might happen to make. Not to you, Dr. Cole. When the board appoints you to a managerial position you can question my choices; until then you need to take care of the duties I assign to you. You might be better able to do that, by the way, if you show up on time."

It was the first time she had been late in, what, a year and a half? But she was too angry to slow down. "And this story about Orrin assaulting an orderly—"

"Excuse me, were you a witness to that event? Do you know something you haven't told me?"

"It can't be true. Orrin wouldn't hurt anyone."

The objection was feeble and she knew she had made a mistake as soon as she said it. Congreve rolled his eyes. "You determined this after a twenty-minute interview? That makes you a pretty remarkable diagnostician. I guess we're lucky to have you."

Her cheeks were burning. "I talked to his sister—"

"You did? *When?*"

"I met her outside the facility. But—"

"You're telling me you consulted with the patient's family on your own time? Then I guess you must have written up a formal report . . . or at least a memo to me and Dr. Fein. No?"

"No," Sandra admitted.

"And you fail to see a pattern of unprofessional behavior here?"

"That doesn't explain—"

"Stop! Just *stop,* before you make it worse." Congreve softened his tone. "Look. I admit your work has been satisfactory up to this point. So I'm willing to write off recent events as stress-related. But you really need to step back and think about things. In fact, why don't you take the rest of the week off?"

"That's ridiculous." She hadn't anticipated this.

"I'm reassigning your caseload. All of it. Go home, Dr. Cole, calm down, and deal with whatever it is that's distracting you from your duties. Take a week, minimum—more, if you like. But don't come back until you've recovered some objectivity."

Sandra was one of the most reliable employees at State and Congreve knew it. But he probably also knew she had been seen at lunch with Bose. Congreve simply wanted her out of the way until Orrin was dealt with. To whom had he retailed his conscience, Sandra wondered, and what was the going price these days?

She wanted to ask him these questions and might have done so even at the risk of her job, but she stopped herself. She was only digging herself in deeper, and in the end this wasn't about her or Congreve, it was about Orrin. Fatally offending Congreve wouldn't do Orrin any good at all. So she nodded curtly, trying not to register the triumphant glare he gave her.

"All right," she said. She tried to sound plausibly compliant, if not cowed. A week. If he insisted.

Out the door, down the hallway, thinking furiously: she still had her pass and her credentials, should she need to come back . . . She paused at her own office to gather a few loose notes. Stepping into the corridor again she almost bounced off Jack Geddes, the orderly. "Come to escort you off the premises," he said, obviously relishing the astonishment on her face.

This was beyond insulting. "I told Congreve I was leaving."

"He asked me to make sure."

Sandra was tempted to say something bitter in return, but it would probably be lost on the orderly. She shook his hand off her arm but forced a smile. "I'm not popular with management right now."

"Yeah, well . . . I know that tune, I guess."

"Dr. Congreve says there was some kind of an incident with Orrin Mather yesterday. You know Orrin? Skinny kid, he's in the locked ward now?"

"Hell *yeah* I know him. And it wasn't just an 'incident,' Dr. Cole. He's stronger than he looks. He was making for the exit like his ass was on fire. I was the one who had to wrestle him down and hold him till he could be sedated."

"Orrin was trying to escape?"

"I don't know what else you'd call it. Dodging nurses like he was carrying the ball to the goal line."

"So you, what, you tackled him?"

"Ma'am, no—I didn't have to. I stood in front of him and told him to calm the fuck down. If anything, he tackled me."

"You're saying *he* initiated the violence?"

She must have sounded skeptical. Geddes stopped in midstride and rolled up the loose right-hand sleeve of his uniform. There was a thick bandage on his forearm, midway between wrist and elbow. "All due respect, but what's that look like to you, Dr. Cole? The little shit bit me so hard I needed a dozen stitches and a fucking tetanus shot. Locked ward, yeah. A locked *cage* would be better."

The heat enveloped Sandra like a clenched fist as she crossed the parking lot to her car.

Weather like this made it all too easy to imagine anaerobic bacteria blooming in the deeps of the sea, as in Orrin's doomsday scenario. Out in the Gulf, Sandra had heard, there was already a deepwater anoxic zone that expanded every summer. The shrimping business had dried up and gone elsewhere, years since.

The sky was a sullen shade of blue. As yesterday, as the day before, cauliflower clouds stalked the horizon but brought no relief. When she opened the door of her car it released a gust of broiling air that smelled like molten plastic. She stood a while, letting the feeble breeze cool the interior.

When she climbed in she realized she had nowhere to go. Should she call Bose? But she was still thinking about what he had told her about himself before she left his apartment this morning. *I guess you need to know this about me before we go any farther,* he had said. Above all, she needed some time to think.

So she did what she almost always did whenever she had unscheduled free time and a problem on her mind: she drove out to Live Oaks to see her brother Kyle.

CHAPTER TEN

TURK'S STORY

1.

The conversation with Allison left me with more questions than I could count, but the one that mattered most was: how successfully could I lie?

I had lied to more than a few people over the course of my life, for good and bad reasons. There were truths about myself I didn't like to share, and often enough I altered them in the telling. But I didn't consider myself a natural-born liar, and that was unfortunate, because I would have to become one now. The lie I needed to tell—the lie I would have to enact in every waking moment and ideally in my sleep—was the pivot on which our futures were balanced.

Vox progressed steadily toward Antarctica, making pretty good speed, or so it seemed to me, for a floating island with a population of some few million souls. Twice more I went with Allison up to the high towers of Vox Core to discuss what we couldn't discuss down below, and every time the view was the same, the same ruined wasteland riding in the same discolored sea. The days grew longer—it was summer in these latitudes—but the sun hugged the horizon as if it was afraid of coming untethered from it. To the best of anyone's knowledge Vox was the only remaining human habitation on Earth. I didn't discuss it with Allison, but maybe the awareness of that lonesome truth was part of what drew us closer together.

I set about teaching myself to navigate the city's passageways and gangways. The Voxish people were peculiar in the way they denominated public and private spaces, but I learned to recognize the signs that distinguished homes from dormitories and dormitories from meeting places. I even picked up a few words of the Voxish language, enough to make myself understood in the local markets, though if I wanted to buy anything—an item of food, say, or one of the copper necklaces Voxish men wore for decoration—I needed Oscar to complete the exchange in Networkspace. I arranged to have my hair cut short in the Voxish style, and before long I could pass (or so Allison said) as a native, seen from distance. Up close, of course, I was something no Networked citizen would ever mistake for normal.

The feeling worked both ways. Viewed from a distance, Vox was a community like any other, populated by men and women working at their jobs and raising their kids and doing all the other predictable things human beings do. Get in among those people, however, and you could feel the Network running like a river behind their eyes. Enthusiasms and disappointments swayed them in unison, like wind combing a field of wheat. And as the days passed that invisible wind began to gust and turn uneasily.

I knew what it was Allison wanted from me. And I knew it might be our only hope of survival. But the hardest thing to hide was my fear of it: the fear of what I would have to do and the fear of what it would cost me.

2.

Oscar was never going to trust Allison. He considered her a traitor and wasn't bashful about saying so. But Oscar was the administrator in charge of us, and for our plan to succeed he would have to trust one of us, at least to some extent. So I made it my business to cultivate that trust. I began to ask his advice even when Allison had already rendered an opinion. I went to him with questions about the history books I was reading. I was aloof and a little skeptical, which was what he expected. But he was eager to ingratiate himself, and all it took to raise his hopes was a grateful word now and then. I think he believed he might eventually be able to convert me to the cause of Vox—whatever that cause was or was becoming.

Oscar's advantage in this duel was the Network: its omnipresent eyes and its powers of calculation. My advantage was that I was neither Networked nor a Vox-born native, which made me a little bit inscrutable. So when I first demanded to see Isaac Dvali, Oscar was surprised but willing to cooperate. And when I insisted on bringing Allison along with me, Oscar gnashed his teeth but agreed.

It turned out Isaac wasn't far away from the rooms

I shared with Allison. He was being treated in a hospital unit a couple of corridors aft of us, and Oscar escorted us there, ignoring the sidelong looks of the medical workers as we passed. He warned me, not for the first time, that Isaac's injuries had been grave and that I might be shocked at what I saw.

"I've seen a few things," I told him. "I'm not easy to shock."

Spoke too soon, as it turned out.

Isaac wasn't under guard but he was attended by medical staff at all times, and Oscar had to consult and mollify a few of that flock before we were finally admitted to the room in which he lay surrounded by the machinery that was keeping him alive.

The first time I had seen Isaac Dvali was at his father's compound in the Equatorian desert. There had been something uncanny about him even then—an adolescent boy who had been hybridized with Hypothetical nanotechnology and raised in isolation from the rest of the world. I had never really gotten to know him during the time we had been together in the badlands—I doubted anyone had ever really gotten to know him—but I was friendly toward him, and I believed he welcomed that friendship. It was Isaac, probably more than any of us drawn into the temporal Arch, who deserved a second shot at life.

But not this life, I thought, and not like this.

Much of his body had been destroyed in the attack on Vox Core. What was salvaged had been badly burned. It was a testimony to Voxish medical science, and to the power of the Hypothetical biotech embedded in him, that Isaac had survived at all.

Allison hung back queasily as I approached Isaac's

nest of tubes and wires, while Oscar hovered at my shoulder. "Many parts of him had to be regrown," Oscar was whispering. "His left leg and arm, his lungs . . . most of his internal organs in fact. Only a fraction of his brain tissue was salvageable."

Isaac's head was encased in a gelatinous cowl that filled in the missing portions of his skull. His right eye, jaw, and cheekbones were intact; everything else was a foaming, pinkish mass. Skin, bone, and brain tissue were slowly being reconstructed from within, Oscar said.

I took a step closer, and Isaac's single good eye rolled to follow me. I guessed that meant there really was someone buried inside this living wreckage—an arguably human being.

"Isaac," I said.

"It's unlikely that he can hear you," Oscar whispered.

"Isaac, it's Turk. Maybe you remember me."

The boy made no response. His good eye remained moistly observant. The other socket looked like a cup filled to brimming with scarlet jelly.

"You're hurt pretty bad," I said, "but they're fixing you up. Takes time. I'll come and see you once in a while while you're getting better, all right?"

He opened his toothless mouth and sighed.

I could tell by Allison's expression that the encounter had made her angry, though I wasn't sure why. She waited until we were back in the pedestrian walkway before she turned on Oscar. "You're not just treating him," she said coldly. "I saw the interface. You *Networked* him."

"Isaac is special. You know that. Of all the Uptaken, Isaac is the one who was linked to the Hypotheticals even before he was taken up by the temporal Arch. He's the most effective intermediary between Vox and the Hypotheticals. Did you expect us to rely on *words* to communicate with him? Isaac needs to interact with the collectivity of Vox, not just me or you or Mr. Findley or any other individual."

"You're grafting your own madness into him."

Oscar answered with a few words in his own language.

It was a Voxish proverb, Allison told me later. Loosely translated: *The bee must not pass judgment on the hive.*

3.

As we sailed south, Vox sent out fleets of unmanned aircraft to map the continents of the Earth at increasingly finer scales. The drones flew at the upper limits of the atmosphere, as much spacecraft as aircraft, and their cameras and sensors were sensitive enough to penetrate the near-perpetual shroud of high haze.

They were designed to seek out any evidence of human activity, past or present. At first, all they found were lifeless ruins. I talked Oscar into letting me see some of the images the aircraft had relayed to Vox, but the video was bland and uninformative. Many of the last human cities had been built in the boreal lands of the northern hemisphere (places I still thought of as Russia or Scandinavia or Canada), but they had been abandoned now for more than a thousand years.

All that remained were faint suggestions of roads and foundations, blemishes on the otherwise trackless uniformity of the circumpolar deserts.

I had read in the history books about the Terrestrial exodus. Calling it that made it sound as if the Earth had been systematically evacuated, but the truth was much uglier. Even the vast number of refugees who flooded across the Arch to Equatoria had constituted only a fraction of the planet's population. The rest had simply died, over a grueling few centuries of progressive impoverishment. They died of starvation as crops failed and arable land shrank, died of asphyxia as anaerobic blooms choked the oceans and poisoned the air. Hydrogen sulfide seeping from the seas had sterilized the coastal plains and river deltas; then, inexorably, over decades, the hinterlands had also succumbed. Massive fires swept through ravaged forests, adding tons of liberated carbon to the thickening atmosphere. Decades of lightless cold were followed by decades of rising heat as the climate began to oscillate like a cracked bell.

The trigger had been pulled back in my day, Oscar said. Human beings had burned much of the carbon stored on Earth as oil, coal, and natural gas, and the consequences of that would have been bad enough. But it was the discovery of oil deposits in the Equatorian desert, a bounty of light sweet crude, easily extracted and imported by sea across the Arch of the Hypotheticals, that had signed the planet's death sentence. Maybe we could have burned all our own carbon and survived the consequences, but pumping two worlds' worth of CO_2 into the atmosphere had overwhelmed any conceivable coping mechanism.

I told Oscar that made us sound pretty stupid. No, he said. It was sad but completely understandable. Ten billion human beings without any cortical or limbic augmentation had simply acted to maximize their individual well-being. They hadn't given much thought to long-term consequences, but how could they? They had no reliable mechanism by which they could think or act collectively. Blaming those people for the death of the ecosphere made as much sense as blaming water molecules for a tsunami.

Maybe so. But it was depressing all the same, and I didn't hide my reaction. If I wanted Oscar to trust me I had to let him see my feelings. Some of them.

He said I should try to look at it through the lens of time. All this world's death, all its grief, was finished now. And when the destiny of Vox was fulfilled, a new era would begin: an age in which humanity would consort with its masters on an equitable basis. "Much will be made clear, Mr. Findley. Miracles will become possible. You'll see. You're lucky to be aboard Vox at such a time."

"You really believe that?"

"Of course I do."

"On the basis of a few prophecies?"

"On the basis of the calculations and inferences of the founders of Vox. Those calculations were sound enough to carry us across the oceans of a half dozen worlds. And sound enough to get us to Earth."

"A dead planet."

He smiled. Oscar had held back a nugget of information, like a stage magician waiting for the right moment to pull a paper flower out of his sleeve. "Not *entirely* dead. We have new images from Antarctica. Look."

He showed me another video segment. Like the rest, it had been shot from high in the troposphere; like the rest, it was hard to interpret. At first glance it appeared to show one more stretch of generic desert, from a part of the world that in my day had been buried in ice. I might have been looking at boulders or pebbles: the scale was marked in characters I couldn't read. But at the center of the image was a blip of regularity, and the image stabilized and resolved as the aircraft moved closer. There was something structural there, for sure. Mist-obscured squares and rectangles in dusty pastel colors. Some of these objects, Oscar said, were nearly the size of Vox Core. And they weren't ruined or abandoned buildings, not in the ordinary sense. It was increasingly obvious as the view honed down to a narrow field that some of the structures had left long, linear trails in the Antarctic dust. They were *mobile.*

"We believe these are the work of the Hypotheticals," Oscar said mildly.

I guessed he was right. The structures didn't look like anything human beings would build. But the image abruptly faded to a staticky blank. The drone aircraft's sensors had failed, Oscar explained. More drones had been sent to the same site, but they had failed, too. Oscar chose to interpret the failures optimistically. "Clearly, the Hypotheticals still have a presence on Earth. Just as clearly, they registered the presence of the unmanned vehicles and reacted to them. Which means—I think the conclusion is inescapable—that they're aware of *us.*" His smile was fixed and unworried. "They know we're coming, Mr. Findley. And I believe they're waiting for us to arrive."

CHAPTER ELEVEN

SANDRA AND BOSE

The institution where Sandra's brother, Kyle Cole, lived was called the Live Oaks Polycare Residential Complex. It was located on a broad expanse of land that had once been a ranch. A creek ran nearby, and there was, in fact, a grove of live oaks on the property.

When she first arranged to have Kyle committed to this place Sandra had been curious enough to run a search on the term "live oaks"—why "live"? Live as opposed to *what*? But it turned out the trees were called live oaks because they stayed green in winter, prosaically enough. In Texas, she had read, a grove of live oaks was called a "mott."

She had tried out the term on the receptionist once, back when she was new in the state and still bashful about her New England accent. "I'd like to take Kyle out to that mott of live oaks by the creek."

The receptionist had given her a blank stare. "I mean the grove of trees," Sandra added, blushing. Oh. Well, surely.

Mott or not, it had become a ritual, weather permitting. Most of the day staff recognized her by now; Sandra knew the majority of them by name. "Another hot one today," the attending nurse said, helping Sandra help her brother out of bed and into a wheelchair. "But Kyle likes the warm weather, I think."

"He likes the shade of the trees."

That was, of course, a surmise. Kyle hadn't expressed a preference for the shade of the trees or for anything else. Kyle couldn't walk or control his bowels or speak a coherent sentence. When he was distressed he scrunched up his face and made a hooting sound. When he was happy—or at least not *un*-happy—he grimaced in a way that showed his teeth and gums: an animal's smile. His happy-sounds were soft sighs, formed deep in his throat. *Ah, ah, ah, ah.*

Today he seemed happy to see Sandra. *Ah.* He turned his face toward her as she wheeled him down the stone-paved pathway and across the green lawn to the live oaks. The nurse had put an Astros cap on him, to keep the sun out of his eyes. The baseball cap threatened to fall off as he craned his neck. Sandra straightened it for him.

There was a picnic table in the grove, more for visitors than for the patients, most of whom weren't ambulatory. Today she and Kyle had the grove to themselves. The shade, and a moist coolness that seemed to rise up from the creek, made the heat tolerable and almost pleasant. There was, thank God, a breeze. The oak leaves trembled and seined the light.

Kyle was five years older than Sandra. Before what the doctors called his "accident," Sandra had always been able to share her troubles with him. He had taken his role as big brother seriously, though he joked about it. "I don't have any advice for you, Sandy," he used to say. He was the only person she would allow to call her Sandy. "All my advice is bad advice." But he had always listened, carefully and thoughtfully, and that was the important thing.

She still liked talking to him, though he couldn't understand even a syllable of what she said. His eyes followed her when she spoke, perhaps because he liked the sound of her voice, and she wondered, despite what the neurologists said, whether there was still some fragment of working memory inside him, an ember of awareness that might occasionally flicker with recognition.

"I'm in a little bit of trouble these days," she began.

Ah, Kyle said, a sound as gentle and meaningless as the rustling of the leaves.

It was the Spin that had killed her father and ruined her brother.

Sandra had considered and reconsidered the event over many years, looking for an ultimate cause. She would have liked to pin her hatred on some particular thing or person. But in this case, blame was slippery. It glided over potential targets but refused to stick. And ultimately, behind all the trivial and quotidian facts, behind the million unfathomable contingencies, there was the Spin. The Spin had changed and mutilated many lives, not just her brother's, not just her own.

In a perverse way, the Spin had been good for Sandra's mother. Sandra's mother was an electronics engineer whose career had stalled out, until the Spin rendered satellite communications obsolete and created a booming market for aerostatic signal-relay devices. She had been hired by a company owned by the aerostat tycoon E. D. Lawton, where she designed an airborne antenna stabilization system that became an industry standard. Her work was much in demand and she was often away from home.

The opposite was true of Sandra's father. The initial chaos and confusion that followed the disappearance of the stars from the sky had triggered a global recession in which her father's software business had wilted like a Christmas poinsettia after New Year's Day. That—or the Spin itself, the blunt and simple fact of it—had thrown him into a state of depression that occasionally lifted but never entirely went away. "He just kind of forgot how to smile," Sandra's brother once explained; and Sandra, ten, had accepted this nonexplanation somberly.

Easy for us, Sandra thought, the generation that followed: we're so *accustomed* to these truths, that the Earth was encircled by nameless alien beings capable of manipulating even the passage of time; that to these godlike beings the human race was both trivial and somehow significant. You lived with it because you had always lived with it. Sandra herself had been born at the tag end of the Spin, about the time the stars (scattered and strange though they had become) reappeared in the sky. She may have owed her own existence to a last burst of optimism or desperation on the part of her parents, the affirmative act of creating new life in a world that had seemed to be crumbling into anarchy.

But the return of the stars had made no real difference to her father. It was as if some internal process of decay had taken root within him and could not be halted in its advance. No one ever said anything meaningful about this. Sandra's mother, when she was home, labored to create an impression of normalcy. And because neither Sandra nor Kyle dared to contradict her, the illusion was surprisingly easy to sustain. Her father was often ill. He spent a lot of time upstairs, resting. That wasn't difficult to understand, was it? Of course not. It was sad; it was inconvenient; but life went on. It did, at least, until the day Sandra came home from school and found her father and her brother in the garage.

Sandra was three weeks away from her eleventh birthday when it happened. She had been surprised to find the house empty. Kyle, home from school with a cold, had left his computer unfolded on the kitchen table. It was playing a movie, something noisy with airplanes and explosions, the sort of thing he liked. She switched it off. And that was when she heard the car motor growling. Not the car her mother drove to work but the family's second car, the one parked in the garage, the one her father used to drive before he hid himself in the upstairs dimness.

She understood suicide, or at any rate the idea of it. She even knew that some people committed suicide by locking themselves in a closed space with an idling engine. Carbon monoxide poisoning. She supposed—it was a thought she harbored mainly in the bitter months that followed—that she even understood her father's wish to die. People could get that way. It was like a sickness. No one should be blamed for it. But why had her father taken Kyle into the garage with him, and why had Kyle agreed to go?

She opened the door that connected the garage to the kitchen. The exhaust fumes made her dizzy, so she turned back and went outside and lifted up the big garage door to allow clean air to flow in to flush out the poison. The door slid open easily even though her father had stuffed rags into the gaps to keep the fumes from leaking away. It wasn't even locked. Then she opened the car door on the driver's side and managed to lean across her father's lap and turn the engine off. Her father's head had lolled onto his shoulders and his skin had turned a delicate, uncanny shade of blue. There was a crust of dried spittle on his lips. She tried unsuccessfully to wake him. Kyle was up front beside his father, wearing a seat belt. Had he been expecting to go somewhere? Neither of them stirred when she shook them, when she shouted.

She called 911 and waited in front of the house for the ambulance. Minutes passed like hours. She thought about calling her mother but her mother was at a trade show in Sri Lanka and Sandra didn't know how to reach her. It was a sunny afternoon in May, beginning to feel like summer in the Boston suburb where Sandra lived. There was no one else on the street. It was as if the houses had gone to sleep. As if all the neighbors had been sealed indoors, like dreams the houses were dreaming.

The medics who arrived took Sandra to the hospital with them and found a place for her to sleep. Sandra's mother arrived back from Colombo the following morning. Sandra's father, it turned out, had been dead long before Sandra discovered him. There was nothing she could have done. Kyle's young body had put up a fiercer resistance to the poison he was breathing, a doctor explained. He was alive, but his brain was irreversibly damaged and he would never recover his higher functions.

Sandra's mother had died seven years after her father, of a pancreatic cancer that had been diagnosed too late for meaningful treatment. Her will had stipulated a sum of money to be held in trust for Sandra's education and a far more substantial amount to pay for Kyle's continuing needs. When Sandra moved to Houston she had asked the estate's lawyers to find Kyle a residence nearby, if there was an acceptable one, where she could visit him regularly. The Live Oaks Polycare Residential Complex was what they had chosen. Live Oaks was devoted to caring for severely disabled patients and was rated as one of the best such facilities in the country. It was expensive, but no matter; the estate could afford it.

Kyle had been sedated for the flight west. Sandra had arranged to be present when he woke up. But if waking up in a strange bed in a strange room had caused him any distress or anxiety, Kyle had shown no sign of it.

He sat in the midday warmth as if waiting for her to speak. Today, unusually, Sandra wasn't sure where to begin.

She started by telling him about Jefferson Bose. Who he was and how much she liked him. "I think you'd like him, too. He's a policeman." She paused. "But he's something else, too."

She lowered her voice, though there was no one else in the mott to hear her.

"You always liked stories about Mars from the Spin days. How the human colonies turned into whole civilizations while Earth was wrapped up in the Spin barrier. How they had a fourth stage of life, where people could live longer if they took on certain obligations and duties. Remember that? The stories Wun Ngo Wen told the world, before he was killed?

"Well, Mars doesn't talk to us anymore, and some pretty unscrupulous people have turned those Martian pharmaceuticals into something uglier, something they can sell for profit on the black market. But there were people around Wun Ngo Wen, people like Jason Lawton and his friends, who took Martian ethics seriously. I used to hear rumors, and there were always stories online, about that. About clandestine groups who took the longevity treatment the way the Martians did. Keeping it pure and not selling it, but sharing it, the way it was made to be shared, all strings attached. Using it wisely."

She was nearly whispering now. Kyle's eyes still followed the motion of her lips.

"I didn't used to believe those stories. But now I think they're true."

This morning Bose had told her he wasn't just a cop. He told her he had connections with people who followed the Martian customs. His friends hated the black market trade, he said. The police could be bribed, but Bose's friends couldn't, because they already had taken the longevity treatment—the original version. And what he was doing, he was doing in their interests.

She said this, very quietly, to Kyle.

"Now, the question you probably want to ask," the question, as an older brother, he surely *would* have asked, "is, do I trust him?"

Kyle blinked, meaninglessly.

"I do," she said, and she felt better for confirming it aloud. "It's what I don't know that worries me."

Like the meaning, if any, of Orrin Mather's sci-fi story. Like the bandage on Jack Geddes's arm, and what it might imply about Orrin's capacity for violence. Like the scar Bose had tried to conceal from her, and which he had still not explained.

Time passed. Eventually a nurse came down the pathway to the grove of live oaks, moving slowly in the heat. "Time to get this fella back to bed," she announced. Kyle's hat had fallen off, though that didn't matter so much in the shade of the trees. His hair was thinning prematurely. Sandra could see his scalp, pink as a baby's skin, through wisps of pale blond hair. She picked up the Astros cap and put it on him, gently.

Ah.

"Okay," she said. "Rest easy, Kyle. See you soon," she told him.

Sandra had studied psychiatry in order to understand the nature of despair, but all she had really learned was the pharmacology of it. The human mind was easier to medicate than to comprehend. There were more and better antidepressant medications now than when her father had endured his long decline, and that was a good thing, but despair itself remained mysterious, clinically and personally, as much a visitation as a disease.

The long drive back to Houston took her past a State Care internment facility, one of the places her patients went after they were assigned custodial status. Passing the State camp inevitably tweaked her conscience. Usually Sandra avoided looking at it—it was comfortingly easy to overlook. The entrance was marked only with a small and dignified sign; the facility itself was hidden beyond a grassy ridge (yellow and sere); very little of it showed from the highway, though she glimpsed the tops of the guard towers. But she had been up that road a couple of times and knew what lay beyond it: a huge two-story cinderblock residence surrounded by makeshift expansion housing, mostly sheet-metal trailers donated by FEMA from surplus stock, encircled by wire fencing. It was a community of men (mostly men) and women (a few), carefully segregated from one another and endlessly waiting. Because that was what you did in such a place: you waited. Waited for your turn in an occupational rehab program, waited for the slim possibility of transfer to a State Care halfway house, waited for letters from distant and indifferent relatives. Waited with slowly hemorrhaging optimism for the miraculous advent of a new life.

It was a town made of wire and corrugated aluminum and chronic despair. *Medicated* despair—she herself had probably written some of the prescriptions that were perennially renewed at the camp dispensary. And sometimes even that wasn't enough—Sandra had heard that the biggest security problem at the compound was the flow of intoxicants (liquor, pot, opiates, meth) smuggled in from outside.

There was a bill before the Texas legislature to privatize the residential camps. Attached to the bill was a proviso that "work therapy" could be construed as permission to hire out healthy inmates for roadwork or seasonal farm labor, to defray the public expense of their internment. If it passed, Sandra thought, the legislation would mean the end of any tattered idealism still attached to the State Care project. What had been intended as a way of providing comfort and protection to the chronically indigent would have become a cosmetically acceptable source of indentured labor—slavery with a haircut and a clean shirt.

The watchtowers disappeared in her rearview mirror, hidden among the baking yellow hills. She thought about how angry she had been at Congreve, who had taken her off Orrin Mather's case to prevent her from rendering an inconvenient diagnosis. But how clean were her own hands? How many souls had she committed to internment just because they matched a profile in the Diagnostic and Statistical Manual? Saving them from the cruelty and violence of the streets, yes, saving them from exploitation and HIV and malnutrition and addiction, and there was enough truth in that to salve her conscience; but in the end, saving them for what?

It was almost dark when she got home. September now, the days getting shorter, though it was still hotter than high August. She checked for any fresh message from Bose. There was one, but it was only another installment of Orrin's notebook.

Her phone buzzed while she was microwaving dinner. She picked up without looking at the display, expecting Bose, but the voice on the other end was unfamiliar. "Dr. Cole? Sandra Cole?"

"Yes?" Feeling wary, though she couldn't say why.

"I hope you had a rewarding visit with your brother today."

"Who is this?"

"Someone with your best interests at heart."

She was conscious of the fear that began in her belly and traveled up her spine and seemed to lodge, somehow, in her heart. *This is not good,* she thought. But she didn't put down the phone. She waited, listening.

CHAPTER TWELVE

TURK'S STORY

1.

What is majestic about them," Oscar was saying, "almost *incomprehensibly* majestic, is their physical structure—trillions upon trillions of diverse components, from the microscopic to the very large, distributed over an entire galaxy! A human body is trivial, less than microscopic by comparison. And yet we matter to them! In some way, we're a significant part of their existence." He wore the abstracted smile of a man contemplating a sacred vision. "And they know we're here, and they're coming to meet us."

He was talking about the Hypotheticals.

For the first time, Oscar had invited me to his home. Before today I hadn't really envisioned Oscar having either a home or a family. But he had both, and he wanted me to see them. His home was a low, pleasant wood and stone structure deep in one of the starboard tiers of Vox Core, set around with delicate thin-leafed trees. The members of his family present when I visited were three women and two children. The children, his daughters, were eight and ten years of age. One of the women was his permanent partner; the other two were more distant members of the family—the Voxish language had a word for the relationship but Oscar said it wasn't easy to translate into English; we settled on "cousins." The family shared a meal of braised fish and vegetables, during which I answered polite questions about the twenty-first century; then the cousins escorted the noisy daughters away. Oscar's partner, a mild-eyed woman named Brion (with the customary string of titles and honorifics), lingered after dinner but eventually excused herself. Which left Oscar talking to me about the Hypotheticals as the artificial daylight faded to dusk.

It wasn't just casual conversation. I began to understand that Oscar had invited me here to pose a difficult question or make some onerous demand.

"Even if they know about us," I said, "what's that mean?"

He touched a control surface in the table, calling up a two-dimensional image that floated in the air between us. It showed a recent aerial view of the Hypothetical machines as they inched their way across the Antarctic desert: three featureless boxes accompanied by a half dozen smaller rectangles, objects as bluntly simple as drawings in a high school geometry text. "Over the course of the last week," he said, "they changed direction. The path they're now following intersects precisely with our current location."

The pride he took in this apparent confirmation of

Voxish prophecy wasn't just his own. I had seen the
same knowing smile on other faces today.

"These machines, or devices similar to them, have
crossed and recrossed all the continents of Earth.
Now that we know what to look for we can recognize and analyze their tracks. Evidence suggests they
may even have traveled across the ocean floors—
that's not impossible. Our scholars believe they're
mapping the topography of the Earth to a very close
approximation."

"Why would they want to do that?"

"Any answer would be speculative. But think of it,
Mr. Findley. These machines are the local incarnation
of a system of intelligence that literally spans the
galaxy, and they're coming *for us!*"

If so, they weren't in any hurry. The Hypothetical
machines were traveling at two or three kilometers
per hour over flat land. And they were still more
than a thousand kilometers away, out in the wind-
swept Wilkes Basin, with the Transarctic Mountains between us and them. "For that reason," Oscar
said, "we've decided to send an expedition to meet
them."

He seemed to expect me to share his delight at this
news, as if his enthusiasm was contagious—as it
would have been, I guessed, had I been wired into the
Network. When I didn't respond he continued: "Our
unmanned aircraft consistently fail to function if they
come within a certain distance of the machines. The
same may be true of manned vehicles. Therefore we
propose to travel to a point outside that radius and
proceed on foot."

"Why, Oscar? What do you expect to happen?"

"If nothing else, we can conduct a passive reconnaissance. Or some sort of interaction with the machines might take place."

One of the cousins brought us glasses of juice and left us alone again. The evening breeze moved through the open architecture of the house. A window looked aft, and I could see rain falling over distant regions of the tier, gossamer banners of it, far away.

"In any case," Oscar said cautiously, "we think it would be desirable to have one of the Uptaken on the expedition."

There were only two Uptaken in Vox Core, and I was one of them. The other, of course, was Isaac Dvali. I had been following his progress. Isaac's skull had been successfully reconstructed, and lately he had learned to walk a few paces and pronounce a few tentative words. But he was far too fragile to risk on an expedition to the Antarctic hinterland.

"Do I have a choice in this?"

"Of course you do. At this point, I'm simply asking you to consider it."

In fact I knew I would have to accept. Doing this for Oscar would buttress his belief in my possible conversion to Voxish principles. And it was necessary for Oscar to believe in that possibility, if Allison's plan was to have any chance of succeeding.

If there still *was* a plan. If we hadn't already surrendered to our own lies.

The truth was that I had no home in the world but Vox. And Vox, as Oscar insisted, was eager to adopt me, if I was in a mood to accept it.

I tried to behave like a man for whom that offer held some attraction.

Maybe, on some level, it did. Now that I knew it better, Vox had ceased to be a frightening abstraction. I had learned how to dress so that I wouldn't stand out in a crowd, and I understood at least the most basic social customs. I continued to study the books I had been given, trying to pry comprehensible stories out of the legalistic prose. I knew that Vox had originated as a planned polity in the global ocean of a planet called Ester, a Middle World in the chain of habitable planets. I had learned to name the founders of Vox's limbic democracy and to enumerate its five hundred years of wars and alliances, victories and defeats. I could recite a little of the vast collage of theory and speculation that constituted the Voxish Prophecies. (Some of us who had disappeared into Equatoria's temporal Arch ten thousand years ago were named in those prophecies, eerily enough. Our second coming had been calculated to the day and hour.)

In other words I had begun to create a Voxish identity for myself in every way I could, short of having a node installed at the base of my neck.

Meanwhile Allison was moving in the opposite direction, away from her past and deeper into her *impersona*. The price she paid was social isolation and a chronic, brittle loneliness. And that served a purpose, too. She wanted her overseers to believe she was losing touch with reality.

After I left Oscar I made my way back to the quarters I shared with her. I found her sitting at a table, shoulders hunched, doing what she had been doing daily and obsessively for weeks now: writing. She wrote on sheets of paper with a pencil. Paper hadn't been hard to come by, since Vox manufactured small amounts of it for various purposes. Vox didn't use conventional pens or pencils, however, but once I explained the concept to Oscar he had agreed to have a machine shop produce a few samples—rods of graphite in carbon-fiber tubes, more like what we used to call "mechanical" pencils.

The original Allison Pearl had been an obsessive writer, which was one reason her diaries had been so useful to the Voxish scholars who re-created her. I put my hand on Allison's shoulder to let her know I was home. Leaning over her I caught a glimpse of her cursive script. (Big letters, shakily produced: she had been given Allison Pearl's urge to write but not the physical skill itself.) Vox was anchored relatively close to the mainland of Antarctica, in a deep basin where the Ross Ice Shelf had once been; Allison had visited one of the high towers today, and she was writing about what she'd seen.

> ... the mountains are the Queen Maud Range in the ancient atlases, gray bleak teeth under an ugly sky dead as everything else on this ruined planet, green clouds dropping yellow rain on the windward slopes. It's like a judgment on humanity and tho I know humans have moved on from this place it still looks like a monument to our mistakes, how we lived lives with consequences we could never truly predict or understand ...

She cupped her hand over the paper and looked up at me.

"Oscar wants me to go inland," I said.

Her eyes flared, but she kept silent.

I told her about the proposed expedition. We talked about that a while, the way we talked about everything these days, calculating the effect our words might have on an unseen audience. She didn't like the idea, but she didn't argue about it.

Eventually she went back to her writing. I picked up one of my books (*The Collapse of Mars and the Martian Diaspora*) and took it to bed with me, remembering what Oscar had said about the "incomprehensible majesty" of the Hypotheticals. The Hypotheticals had created a string of worlds linked by Arches, one end anchored on Earth and the other on Mars, the ten vastly distant habitable planets between them comprising a continuous extended landscape, something the book called a "distributed interstellar topology." Mars had never been an easy place for human beings to live, despite our engineering of it, and a doorway to greener, kinder worlds had been a gift too great for the Martians to refuse. But without their careful husbandry Mars had reverted to its essential nature as a cold, dry planet— one more hostile desert in a universe that seemed full of them. The Martians, like the Earthlings, had lost a habitable homeworld.

I remembered stories about the Martian ambassador Wun Ngo Wen, who had arrived on Earth during the Spin. His Mars had sounded like a saner place than Earth. The Martians had already tapped Hypothetical technology in a modest way, using it to create their famous longevity treatment. But according to the book they had eventually repudiated that and every other form of Hypothetical technology. Most of the early bionormative philosophers had been Martians, the book said. Not that they opposed biotechnology in itself—the first cortical democracies had been Martian inventions—but they insisted on restricting themselves to *human* biotech, which could be fully understood and controlled.

That was a shortsighted and oppressive doctrine, the book suggested.

I had put down the book by the time Allison came to bed. We still slept together, though we hadn't made love for weeks. It was our unguarded moments that put us most at risk: there was no telling what dangerous inferences the Network might draw from our sighs and gasps. The script we had written for ourselves would play out more plausibly without passionate interludes.

But I missed her, and not just physically. I woke that night and found her mumbling a slurry of English and Voxish words, asleep but not at rest, her eyelids trembling and her face wet with tears, and when I touched her cheek she moaned and turned away.

2.

The day before the expedition was scheduled to leave I visited Isaac Dvali in the medical suite. Oscar insisted on coming with me: he took a professional interest in my interactions with Isaac. "Your presence always has a measurable effect on him," he told me. "His pulse rate increases when you're with him. The electrical activity in his brain becomes more intense and more coherent."

"Maybe he just likes company."

"No one else has this effect on him."

"Could be he recognizes me."

"I'm sure he does," Oscar said. "In one way or another."

Isaac's condition had improved considerably and most of the life-support machines that had been attached to him had been taken away. A crowd of physicians and nurses still hovered out of earshot, but he ignored them and looked directly at me.

He could do that now. The reconstruction of his ruined head and body was almost complete. The flesh on the left side of his skull was still translucent, and when he opened his mouth I could see the hinge of his jaw moving like a crab in a milky tide pool. But his new left eye had lost its bloodshot opacity and it focused in tandem with the other. I took a step toward the chair where he was reclining. "Hey, Isaac," I said.

His jaw did its crab-dance under a veil of capillaries. "Tuh," he managed to say. "Tuh-tuh—"

"It's me, it's Turk."

"Turk!" He nearly shouted it.

One of the Voxish physicians whispered to Oscar, who translated: "Isaac's voluntary motor functions are much better now but his impulse control is still very poor—"

"SHUT UP!" Isaac screeched.

Isaac had been touched hard by the Hypotheticals, which made him the next best thing to a living god. I tried to imagine how Oscar felt, being chastised by a deity with poor impulse control.

"Hey, I'm here," I said. "Right here, Isaac."

But the effort at speech had already wearied him. His eyelids went to half-mast. His arms trembled against the restraints that bound him to his chair. I looked over my shoulder and said, "Does he really need to be tied down?"

More consultation with the Voxish physicians; then Oscar said in a barely audible whisper, "Yes, I'm afraid so, for his own safety. At this stage of his recovery he could easily hurt himself."

"You mind if I stay a while longer?"

I had addressed the question to Isaac, but it was Oscar who fetched me a chair. When I sat down Isaac's eyes veered nervously until they found me again. An expression that might have been anxiety or relief played over his pale face.

"You don't have to say anything," I told him. He trembled against his restraints.

"He responds positively to the sound of your voice," one of the physicians suggested.

So I talked. I talked to Isaac for most of an hour, registering his occasional grunts as encouragement. Since I wasn't sure how much he understood about Vox or how he'd got here, that was what I talked about. I told him how we had been taken up by the temporal Arch in the Equatorian desert and how we had come to Vox after a passage of ten thousand years. We were back on Earth now, I said—Vox had some business to attend to here—but Earth had suffered considerably in all the centuries we'd been gone.

I got the feeling Oscar didn't like me saying any of this. Probably he had hoped to introduce Isaac to Vox in his own way and in his own words. But the doctors seemed pleased with Isaac's physical reaction, and Oscar wasn't willing to provoke another outburst.

It was Isaac himself who ultimately shut the session down. His eyes wandered and he began to look sleepy. I took that as a cue. "I don't want to tire you out," I said. "I'll be away for a little while, but I'll come and see you again soon, promise."

I stood up. That was when Isaac began to shake—not a gentle tremor but a full-blown convulsion. His head whipped from side to side and his eyes bulged against their paper-thin lids. The team of doctors hurried toward him as I backed away. "Turk!" he shouted, spittle frothing on his lips.

Then he stiffened. His eyes rolled up until only the whites showed. But his lips and tongue and jaw began to move, forming precise English words: *"Majestic!"* he whispered. *"Billions of diverse components distributed over an entire galaxy! They know we're here! They're coming to meet us!"*

The same words Oscar had used.

I glanced at Oscar. His face was nearly as pale as Isaac's.

"Turk!" Isaac shouted again.

One of the physicians pressed a silvery tube against Isaac's neck. His body slumped back into the chair, his eyes closed, and the chief medic gave me a look that needed no interpretation: *Leave. Now.*

3.

Allison came with me to the aircraft docks the day the survey expedition was due to leave. The docks were situated on a high platform above the city, protected from the toxic air by a transparent osmotic filter. A crowd of soldiers milled around us, their gear stacked on the deck waiting to be loaded. Ocher-colored clouds swept past, somber in the raking light of the sun.

Allison hugged me and said good-bye. "Come back," she said, and then, recklessly, she whispered into my ear: "*Soon.*"

Uttering even that single word was a risk. She must have hoped the Network wouldn't hear her; or, if it did, that the word would sound like a lover's appeal to a man who was beginning to edge out of her grasp.

But that wasn't what she meant. What she meant was, *We have to act soon or we'll lose our best shot at escape.*

She meant, *We could be exposed at any time.*

"I will," I whispered back.

Meaning: *I know.*

CHAPTER THIRTEEN

SANDRA AND BOSE

It was past ten by the time Sandra finally managed to get hold of Bose. When she explained what had happened he told her to sit tight, he'd be there as soon as he could. Less than half an hour passed before he buzzed her from the security gate in the lobby. She let him in and listened until she heard the sound of the elevator opening in the hall. She waited for his knock before she unhooked the latch and opened the door.

He was in his off-duty gear, jeans and a white T-shirt. He apologized for not returning her calls sooner. She asked if he wanted coffee: she had put on a fresh pot. He shook his head. "Just tell me what the guy said. Best you can remember it."

The voice had been gruff and a little nasal, an older man's voice. It was the insinuating familiarity of it that had first made her afraid. *Someone with your best interests at heart,* the caller had said. No, not likely.

"Is this about Kyle? Is he okay?"

"No more or less okay than ever," the caller said. "Brain damage, right? Which is why he's stored in that vegetable locker for the rest of his life."

"Tell me who you are or I'm going to hang up."

"That's your prerogative, Dr. Cole, but again, I'm trying to help you, so don't be in a hurry about it. I know you were visiting your brother today, and I know a couple of other things about you. I know you work at State Care. I know you took an interest in a patient there, Orrin Mather. And I know about Jefferson Bose. You took an interest in Officer Bose, too."

She gripped the phone but didn't answer.

"Not that I'm saying you're *fucking* him, necessarily. But you've been spending a lot of time with the guy, considering you only met him a couple of days ago. How well do you really know him? You might want to ask yourself that."

Just hang up, she thought. Or maybe she ought to listen—it might be important to be able to tell Bose what the caller wanted. She felt invaded, but she tried to muster her thoughts. "If you're trying to threaten me—"

"Pay attention! I want to *help* you. And you *need* a little help. You have no idea what you wandered into here. How much did Bose tell you about himself, Dr. Cole? Did he tell you he's the only honest cop on the Houston payroll? Tell you he's interested in busting a life-drug ring? Well, let me paint you another picture of Jefferson Bose. Something maybe a little less flattering. A man with a failing police career and shitty prospects for promotion. A man who's been trying unsuccessfully to interest the Federal Bureau of Investigation in his theory about controlled chemicals coming into the country through a local importer. A man who has fuck-all evidence to *support* that theory, and is reduced to trying to depose a mentally retarded night watchman. Let me add, a man who's not above seducing a female State Care worker in order to *get* that deposition. You've been taken advantage of here, and you have to start facing up to the truth."

"Go to hell."

"Okay, you don't believe me. Fair enough. Why should you? We could argue all night. But I said I wanted to help you. Or to help you help your brother, Kyle, if you prefer. Now, I have to give Officer Bose his due—he's not completely full of shit. There are folks in Houston who are involved with the life-drug trade, that's a fact. And yes, the trade is illegal. But ask yourself—maybe you *have* asked yourself—is it such a bad thing, what they're doing? A treatment that can add thirty or forty years to a person's life, what's so sinful about that? What gives the government the right to keep it from us? Because it's bad for their, what, *social planning*?"

"If you're trying to make a point—"

"I'm asking you to think outside the box, Dr. Cole. You're young, you're healthy, you don't need the Martian treatment—that's fine. You might feel different when that pretty skin starts to sag, when you come to the time of life when there's nothing to look forward to but a hospital bed or a grave. Okay, not yet and probably not for a long time. But things happen. Suppose you get a bad diagnosis—not years from now but next week—stage four cancer, nothing they can do for you with ordinary medicine. Well, the life drug isn't just for what they call longevity. You live longer because it's inside you, patrolling your body for bad cells, tumors, all that filth. It'll *cure* your cancer. You still want to keep that drug locked up? Condemn yourself to death for the sake of what they call *genomic security*? Pardon me if I call that bullshit."

"I don't see what this has to do with anything."

"I'm saying, okay, you're not in a position right now where you need this treatment for yourself. And maybe you're such a staunch advocate of whatever-the-fuck principle is involved you never *will* want it, at least for yourself. But I want to remind you again, it's a *cure*. It's a cure for things there's no other cure for. Diseases of the body. Also of the brain."

She managed to say, a little breathlessly, "This is absurd."

"On the contrary. I've seen it happen."

"You're talking about a criminal act."

"I'm talking about a bottle the size of your index finger with a colorless liquid inside. Consider what it could do for Kyle. You take your brother out of Live Oaks and you administer this drug. He'll run a fever for a while but after a couple of weeks he's good as new, all that damaged brain tissue completely restored . . . or close enough that you can help him get his life back. Think about your responsibility as a doctor and as a sister. Even with the best therapy money can buy, Kyle's wasting away—he's half dead already, he's dying by inches, you *know* that. So what do you do? Do you let him go? Or do you do this one thing, this simple thing, this thing other people are doing every day for far more selfish reasons? Ask yourself. It's a practical proposition. The bottle I'm talking about, I'm holding it in my hand right now. I can get it to you anonymously and safely. No one will know anything about it but you and me. All that has to happen is, you stop interfering with Dr. Congreve's business. Tomorrow morning you get up, you drive to State, you apologize to Congreve, and you sign a document recusing yourself from Orrin's case for conflict of interest."

Despite the heat, despite the sweat trickling down her cheek, Sandra felt cold. The window curtains rose and fell in a fitful breeze. At the other end of the room the video screen flickered in mute hysteria.

"I won't sacrifice Orrin Mather."

"Who said anything about *sacrifice*? So Orrin goes into State Care. Is that so awful? A clean place to live and some daily supervision, no more sleeping on the street—it sounds like a decent outcome to me, taking the long view. Or don't you have any faith in the system you work for? If State's such a bad deal, maybe you should reconsider your choice of career."

Maybe she should. Maybe she had. Maybe she shouldn't even be listening to this. "How do I know I can believe you?"

"The reason you can believe me is that I took the trouble to make this call. Please understand, I'm not threatening you in any way. I'm simply attempting to do business with you. Admittedly there are no guarantees. But isn't it worth gambling, when your brother's future is at stake?"

"You're just some voice on the phone."

"All right, I'm going to hang up now. I don't need you to say yes or no, Dr. Cole. I just want you to think about the situation. If you contribute to a satis-factory outcome in this matter you'll be rewarded. Leave it at that."

"But I—" she began.

Uselessly. The caller was gone.

She explained it all to Bose, surprisingly calmly—or maybe not so surprisingly, given the two glasses of wine she'd poured and gulped while she was waiting for him to arrive. Her mother, who used to take a drink or two in stressful moments, had called the ef-fect "Dutch courage." Sandra glanced at the label on the wine bottle. Napa Valley courage.

"Bastard," Bose said.

"Yes."

"He must have had you followed. And he's well connected enough that he was able to find out who you were visiting at—what's it called?"

"Live Oaks Polycare Residential Complex."

"Where your brother lives."

"Kyle, yes."

"You didn't tell me you had a brother."

"Well, it didn't—I wasn't *hiding* it from you."

He gave her a speculative look. "I didn't think you were. Did you notice anything while you were out there? An unfamiliar face, maybe a car on the road?"

"No. Nothing."

"And nothing distinctive about the voice?"

"He sounded like he might be an older guy. A little phlegmy. Otherwise, no." She had checked to see if her phone had recorded the caller's number, but of course it hadn't. "I'm not even sure why this person thinks I'm worth threatening or bribing. Congreve already bumped me from Orrin's case. Any medical decision is out of my hands."

"Unless they can compromise you, you're still a dangerous loose end. You could testify about Congreve's behavior if the matter came up in court. You could go to authorities with what you already know."

"But without Orrin's testimony—"

"At this point I don't think these folks are worried about what he might say in court. I think they're worried about what he saw in the warehouse and where that knowledge might lead a federal investigation, if he's allowed to talk freely about it. Getting Orrin declared incompetent is just the first step. I expect they want him drugged and permanently out of sight. Or worse, dead."

Sandra whispered, "They can't do that."

"Once he's in internment," Bose said gently, "things can happen."

Well, yes. She had seen the statistics. In the past year there had been half a dozen violent assaults at the local internment camp, not to mention deaths from drug overdoses or deliberate suicide. On a per-capita basis the State camps were relatively safe—far safer, statistically, than living on the street. But, yes, things could happen. Maybe things could even be arranged to happen.

"So how do we stop them?"

Bose smiled. "Slow down."

"I mean, tell me what I can do."

"Let me give it some thought."

"We don't have a lot of time, Bose." Orrin's final review was scheduled for Friday, and Congreve could call it sooner if he felt pressured.

"I know. But it's past midnight and we both need to get some sleep. I'll stay here tonight—if that's okay with you?"

"Of course it is."

"I can sleep on the couch if you like."

"Don't you *dare*."

In the morning, over breakfast, sitting at her kitchen table and watching Bose plow through the eggs she had scrambled for him, Sandra thought about what the anonymous caller had said about Kyle.

"The longevity drug," she said, "would it really help someone like my brother?"

Last night, in the dark of her bedroom, she had told Bose about Kyle and her father. Bose had put his arms around her while she told the story. When she finished he hadn't said anything falsely consoling— hadn't said anything at all; he had just kissed her forehead, gently, and that was enough.

"It might repair the physical damage. But it wouldn't restore him to what he was before. It wouldn't bring back his memories or his skills or even his original personality."

She remembered scans of Kyle's brain the neurologist at Live Oaks had shown her, huge patches of necrotic tissue like the wings of a deadly black moth. Even if those areas were magically repaired they would still be blank and empty. After the treatment Kyle might be trainable, he might even learn to speak . . .

but he would never recover completely. (Or, if he did, he wouldn't be *Kyle*. Did that matter?)

"And," Bose said, "the treatment would change him in another way. Once the biotech infiltrates your cells, it's there for good. Some people find that idea abhorrent."

"Because it's derived from Hypothetical technology?"

"Presumably."

"According to Orrin's notebook," Sandra said, "the Martians eventually abolished the procedure."

"Yeah, well—on that subject Orrin's guess is as good as anybody's."

"We still don't know where he came up with all that stuff."

"No," Bose said.

"But I guess we don't have to, right? All we have to do is keep him safe."

Bose was silent for a while. Sandra had come to respect these silences, the cadences of his thoughts. She opened the kitchen window, wanting fresh air, but the breeze that blew through was hot and faintly metallic.

Bose said, "I'm worried about how dangerous this has become for you."

"Thank you. So am I. But I still want to help Orrin."

"I'm sorry about all this. Getting you involved in it. Short of doing what the caller suggested, I think you're pretty much out of a job at this point."

"I expect so."

"And you're not the only one. I was called into the precinct captain's office yesterday. He said I have a choice. I can keep my distance from whatever's going on at State Care or I can turn in my gun and badge."

"I take it you're not planning to keep your distance?"

"I'll worry about my career tomorrow. We need to get Orrin out of that building. Then he and his sister can lay low until all this is resolved, one way or another."

"Okay, great. How do we do that?"

Another evaluative silence. "You absolutely sure you want to get deeper into this?"

"Just tell me what to do, Bose."

"Well, it depends." He scrutinized her. "Are you willing to go back there and apologize, make it look like you're cooperating?"

"That's your plan?"

"Part of it."

"All right, suppose I do go back . . . what then?"

"You give me a call as soon as Congreve leaves for the night. I'll come by when I hear from you. Then we'll see if we can pry Orrin out of the locked ward."

CHAPTER FOURTEEN
TURK'S STORY

1.

The "vanguard expedition," as Oscar insisted on calling it, consisted of fifty people, mostly soldiers but including a half dozen manager-class civilians and twice that many scientific and technical personnel, plus all their gear and an aircraft big enough to accommodate us.

Allison had told me one of these vehicles could be flown by a single pilot with a nodal link. The link made it possible to gain access to the control interfaces—the real pilot was the ship itself, quasi-autonomous subsystems that enacted the operator's intentions. Touch menus and visual displays popped up on any available surface. Exterior views were distributed throughout the cabin on virtual windows, one of them on a wall opposite the bench where Oscar and I were seated.

The view was uniformly drab until we crossed onto the mainland and approached the Queen Maud Range. There was still a trace of glaciation on the highest peaks of these mountains. The ice was clean, distilled by evaporation from the cesspool of the sea, and in the shadowed slopes it gave back a crisp blue radiance.

Coming down the windward slope into the interior desert we ran into heavy cloud and intermittent snow. I asked Oscar whether it was safe to fly under these conditions. He looked at me as if I'd asked a child's question. "Yes, of course."

He was visibly anxious for a different reason. Generations had lived and died in the expectation that Vox would one day meet and merge with the Hypotheticals, but it was Oscar's generation that was confronting the fulfillment of that prophecy. By joining this expedition he had put himself at the cutting edge of the encounter. That was a spectacular piece of luck, from Oscar's point of view—whether good or bad remained to be seen.

Wind and squalls persisted all the way to our landing point.

Maps from my day would have been a poor guide to Antarctica as it existed now. The great ice sheets had disappeared centuries ago, and the Ross Sea and the Weddel Sea had joined to separate East Antarctica from the huge islands off its western coast. Oscar said the place where we landed was in what geological surveys had once called the Wilkes Basin, roughly seventy degrees south latitude. It was a flat, pebbly wasteland.

We suited up as soon as the aircraft touched ground. We wore thick, insulated outer garments to keep us warm and tight-fitting masks that fed us canned air. The ship's airlock opened onto a landscape that was bleak but not actually ugly. All of Antarctica was a desert, but deserts are often beautiful: I thought of the Equatorian outback, or the deserts of Utah and Arizona, or the old pictures of Mars before it was terra-formed, pre-Spin. The terrain here was nearly Martian in its stony lifelessness. The climate was cold, Oscar said, but not cold enough to sustain a permanent icecap, and relatively dry. A late-summer snow-fall like this would likely melt off before the day passed. The snow came down in intermittent flurries, drifting into hollows and blurring the outlines of the low, parallel ridges that stretched into the distance.

The sun was a dim incandescence behind the clouds, close to the horizon. We could expect another few hours of daylight but we were fully equipped to operate in darkness. The soldiers loaded portable high-intensity lights and a host of other gear onto self-powered carts with big, articulated wheels. Then they fell into formation and advanced, the civilians following behind.

We navigated by compass. The Hypothetical machines were still invisibly distant. We had landed well outside the perimeter that had been defined by the loss of the drone vehicles. How the attempt to cross that perimeter would affect us and our gear was an open question. "Of course we trust the Hypotheticals," Oscar said. "But they have autonomic functions just like any other living thing. Events can happen without conscious volition, especially given the hugely different scales of time and space on which they operate." But none of that seemed as real or substantial as the tug of the wind, the monotonous crunch of gravel under our feet, or the faint stink of hydrogen sulfide that infiltrated our masks.

We had marched for most of an hour when one of the technical crew, consulting an instrument, called a halt.

"This is the perimeter," Oscar whispered: the point of proximity beyond which all pilotless drones had mysteriously failed.

Three of the soldiers marched ahead while the rest of us waited nervously. The snow had thinned and there were open patches of sky above us, but daylight was fading fast. The science crew aimed a couple of their lights into the gloom.

The point men halted at a fixed distance, then waved us on. We followed from a prudent distance, announced by sweeping beams of light—we would be hard to miss, I thought, if the Hypotheticals happened to be looking.

But we were well inside the perimeter now, and nothing had happened.

The temperature dropped with the fall of night. We cinched the hoods of our survival gear tight around our face masks. The wind remained brisk but the squalling snow stopped suddenly, and in the clear air we could make out the shapes of the Hypothetical machines ahead of us, startlingly close. The technicians hurried to aim their mobile lamps.

We had been calling these structures "the Hypothetical machines," but from the ground they looked less like machines than huge geometric solids. The nearest of them was a perfectly rectangular cube, half a mile on a side and moving at a slow but (barely) perceptible speed. Now that we were close to it I believed I could feel that ponderous motion under my feet, a gentle seismic tremor.

We approached the cube in silence. The soldiers on point were dwarfed by it. The technicians began to angle up their lamps, playing the beams against the nearest vertical face, a featureless surface the texture of sandstone. Because of its regularity it was hard not to think of this thing as an absurdly large *building,* but it was a building without windows or doors, as enigmatic as a sealed pyramid.

For a while we did nothing but stare at it. Oscar said it must already have detected our presence; but if it did, it failed to react in any obvious way. Then the technical crew got down to business. They erected tripods and secured their lamps on them; they unpacked sensors and recording devices and anchored them in the pebbly, cold soil. A steadily increasing number of fiercely bright beams divided the desert into a quilt of light and dark.

On the plain beyond the cube, scattered over a couple of kilometers, were a half dozen objects of similar size and different but equally simple shapes— huge cylinders, octagons, truncated spheres, conical sections. Some were sandstone-colored, like the cube; others were black, cobalt blue, obsidian black, cadmium yellow. Any one of them could have enclosed a small city, and all of them were creeping at the same patient speed toward the distant mountains and the sea. "So immense," Oscar said breathlessly, "these objects, but such an insignificant fraction of the whole body of the Hypotheticals." The stark light cut shadows into his mask and made him look like a timid animal peering out of a hole. "It would be easy to commit the impertinence of fear."

Way too easy, out here on the polar desert of the planet that had given birth to the first human beings and had become an unmarked grave for billions more. While the scientific crew activated sensors and surveying devices, I walked without Oscar's permission (but he scurried after me) to within a few hundred yards of the base of the cube.

It was old. It wasn't weathered or cracked, and for all I knew it might have been manufactured a day or an hour ago, but it *felt* old—age seemed to radiate from it like cold air from an icefield. Inches ahead of it the thin layer of new-fallen snow was disappearing from the desert floor, sublimating into the night air.

"The Hypotheticals are endlessly patient, Mr. Findley. They're older than most of the stars in the sky. To be so close to their work . . . this is a sacred moment."

We all wore earpieces to facilitate communication. I had turned down the volume on mine—the few simple Voxish words I had learned weren't much use here—but we both heard a burst of excited chatter erupt from the technical crew. Two beams of high-intensity light swept upward.

The beams diffused into what appeared to be a pale cloud at the top of the cube. Snow or mist, I thought; but no—elsewhere, the sky was clear. The cloud appeared to be boiling off the top of the cube itself—and the other, more distant objects were generating similar clouds, pale mists that sifted down gently despite a wind that should have dispersed them.

I took an instinctive step backward. Then: "*Look*," Oscar said in a hushed voice.

Something had landed on the arm of his protective suit. Oscar regarded it with a kind of terrified reverence. A snowflake, I thought at first. But on closer inspection it was more like a tiny crystalline butterfly—two pale and perfectly translucent wings beating over a body the size of a grain of rice.

Oscar lifted his arm so we could get a better look. The winged crystal had no eyes or segments or any other division in its body. It was just a curl of something like quartz, with legs (if you could call them that) as fine as eyelashes, which it used to cling to the fabric of Oscar's suit. Its wings beat against the pressure of the wind. It looked as harmless as a piece of costume jewelry. The cloud descending the walls of the cube was composed of countless numbers of these things—millions, maybe billions of them.

Then, out along the periphery of the lights, a soldier began to scream.

2.

The soldiers reacted quickly and professionally: they grabbed the portable lights and began waving the civilians back the way we had come. They did this despite the fact that hundreds or thousands of these tiny crystalline butterflies were swarming them, obscuring their vision and covering their clothing.

The butterflies were settling on me and Oscar, too, but not as aggressively. When I flicked my arm they fell away and dropped to the ground, inert. And when I brushed them away from Oscar they scattered from my hand.

Nevertheless we ran. Everyone was running now. The lamps the soldiers carried cast wheeling, hectic beams ahead of us. Through my earpiece I could hear barked commands and more screams, while the cloud of crystalline devices swirled around us like silent snow.

Other members of the expedition began to fall away behind us. I saw this in serial glances, looking back over my shoulder. Anyone who dropped to the ground was instantly swarmed, covered in a glassy drift, becoming a pale mound that heaved at first but quickly *settled*—I don't have a better word for it. I began to understand that these men and women were dying.

The technicians died first. The soldiers wore heavier protective clothing, but even they were slowly being overwhelmed. The lamps, when they dropped them, raked light at static angles across the plain.

Twice I had to stop and brush Oscar free of the butterflies. I was too terrified to wonder why I was apparently immune to them. Oscar clearly wasn't: his protective clothing was ragged now, torn in places by their small but razor-sharp legs, and some of those ragged patches were speckled with blood. I worried about his mask and oxygen supply and I tried to make sure I cleared the most vulnerable parts first.

For a while we ran arm-in-arm, which seemed to keep the swarms at bay. All the panicked chatter and terrified screaming that had filled my earpiece slowly began to fade, and the final silence, when it came, was even more terrifying than the screams. I couldn't say how long or how far we ran. We ran until we couldn't run any more, until there was no sound but the roar of my own labored breath. Then I felt a sudden resistance, Oscar's arm tugging me backward, and I thought, *They got him, he's dead weight—*

But he wasn't. When I turned to face him I found his suit was clean: there were no butterflies on him. His face through the moist blur of his mask was shocked but relatively calm. "Stop," he gasped. "We're out of range. We're beyond the perimeter now. Please, *stop.*"

I took a long look back.

We had come a fair distance. The abandoned lamps were still working, the Hypothetical machines plainly visible in a skewed crosshatching of artificial light. Nothing human was moving.

The wind blew grains of snow around our feet and the stars glittered overhead. We stood shivering, waiting for whatever might come out of the darkness after us—another attack, a straggling survivor. But there was no one, nothing.

Then, in quick succession, the distant lamps began to blink off.

We reached the aircraft guided by signal-finders built into our suits. It was a long walk but we were too shaken to talk much. Oscar eventually managed to establish voice contact with Vox Core, and he exchanged curt messages with managers and military personnel. Remote telemetry had broadcast most of what happened, and Vox was already attempting to analyze the data. "Probably," he said at one point, "our presence triggered a defensive reflex of some kind." Maybe so. But I wasn't Voxish and I didn't have to believe in the benevolence of the Hypotheticals—I didn't have to make excuses for a senseless slaughter.

Our aircraft rested on the Antarctic plain like some incongruous deposition from a vanished glacier. I asked Oscar whether he would be able to pilot it back to Vox.

"Yes. Really, I just need to tell it to carry us home."

"You sure? You're bleeding, Oscar."

He glanced down at his ravaged clothing. "Not badly," he said.

Once we passed the airlock he stripped off his gear. His upper body had sustained a number of small cuts, none of them deep or life-threatening. He told me where to find a medical kit, and I smeared his wounds with something that stopped the bleeding.

A few of the tiny crystalline butterflies—dead or dormant—were still clinging to his discarded survival gear. Oscar emptied a ration box, tweezed one of the dead butterflies between his thumb and forefinger and dropped it inside. A sample for analysis, he said. Then we dumped the rest of our tattered clothes out the airlock.

"They didn't touch you," Oscar said, once we were aloft and the aircraft was following a programmed route to Vox.

What had been a crowded crew cabin on the flight out now seemed grimly and cavernously empty. The air, our bodies, even the fresh clothing we put on all reeked of hydrogen sulfide.

"No . . ."

"Because they *recognized* you." His voice had been reduced to a shocked querulousness.

"I don't know what that means, Oscar."

"Obviously, they recognized you because you were Uptaken."

"I don't understand what happened any more than you do. But I'm not Isaac—I don't have any Hypothetical biotech inside me."

"Mr. Findley," he said, "are you still denying it, even now? A human body doesn't pass through a temporal Arch the way it might pass through one of the spatial Arches. We know this from many years of study. You weren't *preserved*, like a frozen vegetable. In all likelihood you were re-created from stored information. The reconstruction may seem flawless to human eyes and human instruments. But *they* know you for one of their own."

I was too exhausted to argue. Oscar was clinging to one of the few expectations this encounter had actually borne out: that the Hypotheticals had recognized me and singled me out for salvation. He believed he had survived because I was beside him, helping him. He imagined he had been saved, in other words, by a truculent and stupid demigod.

CHAPTER FIFTEEN

SANDRA AND BOSE

Sandra arrived at the State Care intake facility at noon. The parking lot was silvered with heat mirages and the air was thick and oppressive, worse, if that was possible, than yesterday. The guard manning the desk at the entrance—his name was Teddy—sat basking in the breeze from a small rotary fan, but he stood up hastily when he recognized Sandra. "Dr. Cole! Hi! Hey, listen, I'm sorry, but I have instructions not to let you pass—"

"That's okay, Teddy. Give Dr. Congreve a call and tell him I'm here and that I'd like to speak to him."

"I guess I can do that—yes, ma'am." Teddy murmured into a handset, waited, murmured again; then he turned to Sandra and smiled. "All right. Again, sorry about that! Dr. Congreve says you can go to his office. He wants me to tell you you should go there directly."

"Do not pass Go. Do not collect two hundred dollars."

"Pardon me?"

"Nothing. Thanks, Teddy."

"You're welcome! Have a nice day, Dr. Cole."

Congreve was wearing a triumphant look when Sandra stepped into his office. She reminded herself that she was here to play a role, the same way she had played Desdemona in her high school production of *Othello. My noble father, I do perceive here a divided duty.* Not that she was much of an actress. "Sorry to bother you, Dr. Congreve."

"I'm surprised to see you, Dr. Cole. I thought you understood you were to take the rest of the week off."

"I do understand. But I wanted to apologize for my behavior, and I thought I should do it in person."

"Really? That's a sudden change of heart."

"I know it seems that way. But I've had time to think it over. Time to do a little soul-searching, you could say. Because I do value my career here at State. And looking back, I believe I acted improperly."

"In what way?"

"Well, by overstepping my authority, to begin with. I took a proprietary interest in Orrin Mather, and I guess I resented it when you gave the case to another physician."

"I explained to you why I thought that was a good idea."

"Yes, sir, and I understand now."

"Well—I appreciate you saying so. It can't be easy for you. What's so special about this particular patient, can you tell me that?" Steepling his hands, regarding her thoughtfully, assuming a grave judiciousness.

"I don't suppose he *is* special. He just seemed particularly . . . I don't know. Fragile? Vulnerable?"

"All our patients are vulnerable. That's why they're here. That's why we're in the business of helping them."

"I know."

"And it's why we can't afford the luxury of identifying too closely with them. The best gift we can give the men and women under our care is absolute objectivity. That's what I meant when I called your behavior unprofessional. Do you see what I'm driving at?"

"Yes sir, I do."

"And do you understand why I suggested you take some time off? Usually, when a physician begins to project his own anxieties onto his patients, it's because he's tired or distraught."

"Really, I'm fine now, Dr. Congreve."

"I'd like to believe that. Is there anything happening in your personal life that might be interfering with your work?"

"Nothing I can't handle."

"Are you sure of that? Because if you want or need to talk about it, I'm willing to listen."

God forbid. "Thank you. No, it's just . . ." She sighed. "Honestly, it's the weather as much as anything. My air-conditioning's broken and I haven't had a decent night's sleep for days. And yes, the work is sometimes a little overwhelming."

"All the staff are feeling it. Well, I'm pleased you decided to come to me with this. Do you honestly feel fit enough to go back to work?"

"Yes, sir. Absolutely."

"I won't say we can't use you. How about we ease up on the caseload for the next couple of weeks? Maybe you can tutor Dr. Fein—I'm sure he could benefit from your experience."

"I'd like that."

"Not on the Mather case, of course."

She nodded.

"In fact we've run into some complications in that regard. I'll need a formal letter from you acknowledging that you voluntarily turned over the Mather file to Dr. Fein. Are you willing to do that?"

She pretended to be surprised. "Is that really necessary?"

"It's a formality, but yes."

"If you think it would be helpful, then of course I'll submit a letter."

"Well, then. All right, Dr. Cole. Take the rest of the day off and come in tomorrow." He smiled. "On time."

"Yes, sir."

"And we'll forget about this unpleasantness."

Not likely. "Thank you. Actually, if it's all right, I was hoping I could spend the rest of today in my office. I don't want to do consults, but there are four or five case reports I need to write up."

Congreve gave her a careful look. "I guess that would be all right."

"Thank you."

"You're welcome. And I have to say I appreciate your attitude. As long as that doesn't change, we should get along fine."

"I hope so," she said.

o   o   o

Sandra went to her office, feeling slightly unclean, and opened up her desktop interface. How long until Congreve went home? He was usually out of the building by six, but a consultation or a board meeting could keep him later. In the meantime she systematically went through her files, pulling and deleting anything personal. It was funny how *separate* she already felt from State, as if her years here had faded into a single blurred image, a picture on an antique postcard.

When that was done—and it didn't take long—she took a printed copy of Orrin's document out of her bag and began to read. As usual, the document raised more questions than it answered.

At half past three she stood up, stretched, and headed to the staff washroom. She was surprised to find Jack Geddes sitting in a chair in the hallway opposite her door, humming to himself. "Hey, Jack," she said. "Are you guarding the medical staff now?"

"Just keeping an eye on things." His grin was lopsided and insincere.

"Dr. Congreve's orders?"

The grin lapsed. "Yeah, but—"

"I see. Don't worry. I'll be right back."

"None of my business what you do, Dr. Cole." But his eyes followed her to the washroom door and watched her when she returned.

Back in her office she took out a pad of paper and a pen and wrote the word **QUESTIONS** at the top.

Then she paused, nibbled the pen top, collected her thoughts.

Re: Orrin Mather document
1. Did Orrin write this or is it someone else's work?

If someone else, who?

It occurred to her that she might be able to find out whether the document was a blatant act of plagiarism. She called up a search function on her desktop and entered a couple of text strings from the document. No meaningful matches. Which proved only that the text, if it existed outside of Orrin's notebooks, hadn't been posted to the Web—a positive result would have been significant; a negative result proved nothing.

2. *Is this a work of fiction or a delusional construct?*

She couldn't answer that without access to Orrin. Bose had said there was something about the Findley warehouse later on in the document, which suggested that Orrin had contributed at least a few words of his own to the story. Which led to the next question:

3. *Is there a real "Turk Findley," and, if so, is he connected to the Findley who operates the warehouse?*

She searched a Houston-area phone directory and found a whole raft of Findleys, but nothing between Tomas and Tyrell. No T. Findleys, either.

4. *Is there a real Allison Pearl?*

According to Orrin's document, Allison Pearl had lived in Champlain, New York. Feeling more than a little foolish, Sandra accessed a Champlain directory and searched it. It listed five Pearls. The majority were singletons, none of them A. or Allison. Two were couples, listed under the male partner's name. Mr. and Mrs. Harvey Pearl and Mr. and Mrs. Franklin W. Pearl.

She opened her phone and closed it again twice before she worked up the courage to tap in one of the numbers. *Idiotic,* she thought. She might as well try to place a call to Huck Finn or Harry Potter.

Harvey Pearl answered on the fourth ring. He was friendly but bemused. Nope, no Allison here. Sandra apologized hastily and hung up. She could feel herself blushing.

One more call, she told herself; then she could give up and forget about it.

Mrs. Franklin Pearl answered this time, a younger and friendlier-sounding voice. Sandra asked meekly whether she could speak to Allison.

"Um—may I ask who's calling?"

Sandra's pulse quickened. "Well, I don't even know if I have the right number . . . I'm trying to find an old friend, Allison Pearl, and last I heard she was in Champlain, so . . ."

Mrs. Pearl laughed. "Well, this is Champlain, and you got the name right. But I doubt Allison's your old friend. Not unless you met her in grade school."

"Excuse me?"

"Allison's ten years old, hon. She doesn't *have* any grown-up friends."

"Oh. I see. I'm sorry . . ."

"She must be a popular woman, though, the Allison you're looking for. We had another call for her a while back. A man who said he was with the Houston police."

Oh! "Did he give his name?"

"Yes, but I don't recall it. I told him the same as I'm telling you—sorry, but it's not our Allison. Good luck finding the one you're hunting for, though."

"Thank you," Sandra said.

A staff conference—Sandra wasn't invited—kept Congreve in the building well past his usual departure time. He knocked at her office on his way out, a few minutes after seven. "Still here, Dr. Cole?"

"I'm just finishing up."

"Did you prepare the letter I asked for?"

"It'll be on your desk in the morning."

"Fine."

She glanced out the door as he left. Jack Geddes was still sitting in the hallway, chair tipped back, humming to himself. She listened until Congreve's footsteps had faded down the corridor. The State facility had begun to take on its after-hours aspect. Most of the day staff had already left; the open-ward patients were back from the commissary, some of them watching TV in the common room. She heard a couple of orderlies laughing together down by the main entrance.

She closed the door and went back to her desk. Then she opened her phone and tapped in Bose's number.

CHAPTER SIXTEEN

TURK'S STORY

1.

The medics kept Oscar and me in a weeklong quarantine, scanning us for any sign of contamination. They failed to find anything unusual in our bodies or our psyches, though that wasn't conclusive—Hypothetical devices were perfectly capable of eluding detection. But we measured consistently clean, and the sample we had brought back with us, the crystalline butterfly in its sealed container, remained dead or dormant.

News of what happened out in the Wilkes Basin quickly spread through Vox. Collective grief for the lost soldiers and scientists was written in the faces of the medics who examined us and in Oscar's face, too. I asked him what it was like to feel an emotion amplified by the entire population of a city.

"It's painful," he admitted. "But it's better than be-

ing alone. What was unbearable was what we felt after the attack that shut down the Coryphaeus—so
many dead, and no way to *share* that grief. It was
agonizing, horrible beyond belief."

"Coryphaeus" was the word scholars had chosen
to translate a concept for which there was no English
equivalent. In the ancient dictionaries it was defined
as a noun from classical Greek: the leader of a chorus, a choirmaster. In Vox it referred to the nest of
feedback loops and functional algorithms that regulated the input and output of the community's neural
nodes. It was the emotional heart of the Network—
Allison had called it "the parliament of love and conscience."

Solitary grief (like guilt, like love) was an inescapable part of the human condition, or at least it once
had been. We had endured it for most of our tenure as
a species. I guessed it wasn't a bad thing to be able to
share that burden in a way that lessened the pain, and
maybe there was something admirable in the willing-
ness of the people of Vox to shoulder their country-
men's burden of tears. But the price of that anodyne
was reckoned in personal autonomy; it was reckoned
in privacy.

I tried to give Oscar the impression that I was sympathetic and even curious. That, too, was part of the
plan.

As soon as we were released from quarantine I hurried back to the quarters I shared with Allison. She
ran to me as the door slid open and came shivering
into my arms.

We couldn't say any of the things we wanted and needed to say. We settled for a few self-conscious endearments. After a while we fixed a meal in the kitchen dispensary and Allison accessed (clumsily, with a manual interface) a video stream that was the local equivalent of a newscast. The final images from the vanguard expedition were playing on a loop, slowed down so that events happened as if in an underwater ballet. The glassy butterflies dropped out of the darkness and settled like lethal snowflakes on the soldiers and technicians; the human figures froze in astonishment, then jerked and danced like unstrung marionettes as they were systematically swarmed and killed.

The loop ran for two cycles before I asked Allison to turn it off.

After the disaster a drone aircraft had been sent to survey the site from a safe distance. But by daybreak there was no sign that anything unusual had happened—no human bodies, no trace of the analytical gear or of the crystalline insects that had destroyed it. Nothing but the immense and indifferent Hypothetical machines, patiently grinding across the Antarctic wasteland.

2.

Soon, Allison had whispered to me at the aircraft docks, which meant I had to cultivate Oscar's confidence despite what had happened in the Wilkes Basin. I arranged to meet him on a platform overlooking the nuked sector of Vox Core—I wanted to see how the reconstruction work was going. I left early for the appointment and took a roundabout route.

The better I had come to know Vox Core, the less

monolithic it seemed. The five elements of Voxish urban design (Oscar had explained this) were terraces, zones, enclosures, plains, and tiers, each of these terms having a precise technical definition—as I walked and rode that morning I passed through three terraces and an enclosure and caught a glimpse of a plain from a bridge that spanned two tiers. Vox Core ran on a seasonless diurnal cycle, sixteen hours of artificial daylight and eight hours of night, but every sector had its own unique and shifting *quality* of light. I crossed a terrace in which the light was as diffuse as rainy daylight and I walked through an enclosure illuminated by a point-source as bright as the noonday sun. Come nightfall the busy slopes would glitter like separate cities, while the wooded or grassy plains slipped into silent darkness.

The last time I had come to the ruined sector of the city it had been an ugly and impenetrable mass of debris. Now most of that debris had been collected and recycled or dumped into the sea. Lingering radiation had been "chelated" (Oscar's word) by some technology I didn't understand, and the reconstruction was proceeding briskly. The main crater had been retained as a memorial, but it was already scalloped with new slopes and elegantly landscaped terraces.

I met Oscar at a workers' commissary overlooking the site. The food we were given was good but the portions were small: supplies were low due to the loss of farming manpower after the transit to Earth. We talked a while about Allison. I told him I was worried about her, that her bouts of depression were becoming more frequent and more severe. I mentioned her crying jags, her intermittent crippling anxiety.

"This isn't unexpected," Oscar said. He gazed from our table across a low wall and into the crater. Below and aft of us, robotic construction machines were cutting foamed-granite pillars for a new terrace. "The fact is, she simply can't become what she wants to be—what some part of her mind insists she *is*. And the conflict is compromising her health and her sanity."

"All she wants to be is Allison Pearl."

"Allison Pearl is nothing but an illusion, all inference, synthesis, and ancillary data. Treya's belief that she *is* Allison is a symptom of the separation trauma that happened when her link to the Network was broken. I know you're sympathetic to her, and I understand the source of that sympathy. She's a connection to your past. That's what she was meant to be. That's why we engineered the Allison Pearl impersona in the first place. But she's not a time traveler from the twenty-first century, Mr. Findley."

"I know that, but . . ."

"But?"

"Her hostility to Vox seems pretty authentic."

He shrugged. "She's entitled to her grievances. Grafting the impersona into her neocortex was a controversial act from the beginning, though of course no one expected a prolonged Network failure to compound the effect. But she can't solve the problem by hiding from it. 'Allison Pearl' simply isn't a stable configuration. What Treya needs more than anything is to have her limbic node restored."

I nodded as if I conceded the point. In the crater, machines shaped like segmented snakes dismantled the spars of a damaged enclosure. I asked Oscar whether it made sense to reconstruct the city when the Hypothetical machines were headed for us, presumably for the purpose of rapturing us all into heavenly communion.

"No one knows what union with the Hypotheticals might mean in practical terms. Undoubtedly we'll all be changed—spiritually, intellectually, physically. But we might still need a city to live in."

"You don't find that frightening?"

"As an individual I might be frightened. Collectively, we're braver than that."

"I'm sorry, but it's hard for me to imagine what that's like—the node, the Network, the Coryphaeus."

"I've described how they function."

"Subjectively, I mean. What it feels like."

"If you're talking about the implant, the surgery is entirely painless . . ."

"Oscar, not the *surgery*! What does it feel like, living with wires inside your head?"

"Ah. Well, they're not wires. They're spindles of artificial nervous tissue and opsin proteins—no," holding up his hand to cut off my objection, "I *do* understand what you're asking. All I can tell you is that it feels like nothing at all. Of course, my own node was installed at birth. But I can describe what it was like when the Network failed, if you think that would be helpful."

I nodded. The terrace trembled with the distant construction work. The air smelled faintly of granite dust.

"Losing the Network was like losing a sense. Like a subtle blindness. One of the node's functions is to facilitate communication. Even in a simple conversation, the limbic interface helps us perceive and interpret nuances we might otherwise miss. At least when both parties are so equipped. Excuse me if this sounds insulting, but to us a nodeless person can appear insensitive almost to the point of imbecility."

"Uh-huh . . . is that how I seem to you?"

He smiled. "I've learned to make allowances." That was Oscar's sense of humor—about as deep as it went.

"At some point, though, a kind of emotional consensus emerges, right? And that's what I can't quite picture."

"Maybe the word 'emotion' is misleading. It's subtler than that. Conscious judgment is beyond the reach of the Coryphaeus. But consider how much of human cognition is *un*conscious. For instance, Mr. Findley, both you and I often make decisions on the basis of moral intuition. We call that intuition 'conscience.' Conscience doesn't arise out of deliberate, systematic reasoning. Which is not to say it's unreasonable or illogical! Suppose you see a man drowning in a river and you swim out to save him—do you think about it first? Do you calculate the risks against the benefits? Obviously not; you act out of an instinctive identification with the drowning man; you feel his distress as if it were your own and you act to relieve that distress despite your fears. Or, if you fail to act, you might feel guilt or remorse. This isn't a trivial phenomenon. Acts of conscience have overturned governments and toppled empires—even in your time."

"And we didn't need nodes or Networks to do it."

"No. But at the same time, individual conscience is notoriously unreliable. An individual might talk himself out of doing the right thing. Or he might be genuinely uncertain about what the right thing *is*."

"You're no more infallible than I am, Oscar."

"But when I sum my conscience with a thousand or a million others, errors become less likely and self-deception almost impossible. That's what the Coryphaeus does for us!"

He had given me a textbook argument for limbic democracy, and he was utterly sincere about it. But he hadn't really answered my question. "I don't want to know what it's good for. I want to know how it feels."

He thought for a moment. "Take the recent food rationing. Historically, rationing has always produced black markets, hoarding, even violent resistance—yes? But you won't find any of that in Vox. Not because we're saints, but because our collective conscience is muscular enough to prevent it. The sum of our better instincts—which is just another name for the Coryphaeus—knows the rationing is necessary and fair. And so, as individuals, we *feel* it as necessary and fair."

"It still sounds like coercion."

"Does it? Tell me, did you ever break into a neighbor's house and steal his property?"

"No—"

"And is that because you were *coerced,* or because you knew it would be wrong? Only you can answer that question, but I have to assume it's because you felt it would be a shameful act, that you would make yourself abhorrent in your own eyes and in the eyes of others by committing it. Well, that's how I feel about cheating on my rations. And I'm secure in the knowledge that my neighbors feel exactly the same way."

I had been abhorrent in my own eyes more often

than he could have guessed, but I raised a slightly different question: "What if the consensus is wrong? Conscience isn't infallible even if you count hands."

"Perhaps not infallible, certainly less *likely* to be wrong."

"I'm new here, Oscar, and it's not my place to criticize, but I saw a lot of Farmers killed in the rebellion. You folks didn't bother taking prisoners, either. You left the survivors out to die. Is your collective conscience okay with that?"

"That decision was taken when the Network had ceased to function. Had the Coryphaeus been active we might have behaved differently."

"What about keeping Farmers as bonded serfs? You've been doing that for centuries, according to the history books."

"I won't debate the historical reasons for doing what was done. I'll grant you it's an uneasy compromise. And you're right, of course, we're *not* morally infallible. We don't claim to be. But compare our history with that of any other nation or culture, death for death, injustice for injustice—compare."

"I'm not sure that's a claim you want to make, given that we're sitting next to a bomb crater."

"That was the result of a cortical republic enacting its own radical bionormative ideology. Reason breeds more monsters than conscience, Mr. Findley."

Maybe so. I let a few moments pass.

"About Allison," I said. "That is, Treya. If she replaced her node, would the suffering stop?"

"It might take time for her to adjust," Oscar said, giving me an evaluative stare. "But the conflicts that are troubling her would quickly be resolved."

White plumes of dust lofted up from the crater, drawn toward filters in the artificial sky. There was the sound of distant hammering. It occurred to me that I was constructing a deception as systematically as those machines were constructing new tiers and terraces. And I had come to the central pillar of that deception.

"I want to help her," I said.

Oscar nodded encouragingly.

I said, "This isn't easy for me. But I've come to a couple of conclusions since what happened out in the wasteland."

"Yes?"

"I didn't choose to come to Vox. And to be honest? Knowing what I know now, I might have preferred to travel up the Ring, maybe see what those Middle Worlds are like."

"I understand," Oscar said cautiously.

"But I can't do that. I can't undo what's been done and I can't change the future. This is where I'm going to live and die."

His eyes narrowed.

"And if I'm going to live here, I want to live with Allison. But I don't want to watch her suffer."

"There's only one way to relieve her suffering."

"She has to accept the implant."

"Yes. Can you convince her to do that?"

"I don't know. But I'm willing to try."

His expression was cautious, opaque, calculating, the look of a gambler contemplating a bet. He said, "We gave her the Allison impersona so she could bond with you. You're the reason she's clinging to it. You could be the reason she abandons it."

Down in the crater a chorus line of machines began welding iron beams, sparks showering from their fingers like falling stars.

"Maybe if I went first," I said. "I mean, if I volunteered for the surgery."

Oscar's eyes widened. Then, slowly, he began to smile.

CHAPTER SEVENTEEN

SANDRA AND BOSE

Bose phoned as he was pulling into the State Care parking lot. Sandra tucked everything she wanted to keep from her office—a few gigs of files, a photo of Kyle from before he was hurt—into her bag, then went to Reception to meet him.

Jack Geddes was still keeping vigil in the hallway. He stood up from his chair and said, "You leaving now, Dr. Cole?"

"Good night, Jack," she said, which was not an answer. But he watched her head for the main lobby and waved as she turned the corner, no doubt happy to be released from surveillance duty.

Bose's uniform and badge got him past the guard who was posted at Reception. The next hurdle was the night nurse in charge of the locked ward. Sandra led the way.

She knew the night nurse by reputation only. Her

name was Meredith something—Sandra couldn't re-member, and the woman's nametag just said MERE-DITH. She appeared to be in her mid-fifties, with a don't-mess-with-me expression that sat so naturally on her face Sandra suspected it might be congenital. Meredith stepped out from behind her desk when she saw Bose and Sandra approaching, effectively blocking the door to the ward. Before she could say anything Bose handed her a standard release-to-next-of-kin form, which he must have filled out himself. Meredith gave the document a frowning study.

"Just unlock the door, please, ma'am," Bose said. "It's late and I'd like to get this prisoner back to his family."

"Prisoner he may be but he's not *your* prisoner, not right now anyhow. And yes it's late—what brings you around this hour of the night?"

Sandra took the initiative: "I don't believe we've met. I'm Dr. Cole. You're right, it's an unusual time to transfer up a patient, but just bear with us, please. I'll sign the patient out."

Meredith appeared to hesitate. According to staff gossip, the night nurses ran their wards like private fiefdoms. Clearly Meredith didn't appreciate this in-trusion into her kingdom. "Okay, Dr. Cole, but this Orrin Mather's on a special protocol and I don't see anything on his chart about you being his physician of record. What I *do* see is a notation from Dr. Congreve that you were pulled off the case a couple days ago."

"Do you see anything on that chart about prevent-ing a staff physician or a police officer from entering this ward? Because I'm starting to get impatient, Meredith."

Meredith glared but reached for the switch that would unlock the ward door. Then she drew her hand back. "A patient transfer needs authorization from the *attending* physician."

"I'm just asking you to open the door, Meredith."

"Dr. Congreve might not like it."

"If you keep us waiting any longer, *I* won't like it. And I may not be Dr. Congreve, but I can sure as hell let him know you thought it was a good idea to stand here and give us attitude."

Meredith made a lemon-sucking face but threw the switch. "I'm gonna have to talk to Dr. Congreve about this."

"Your choice," Sandra said.

The door ratcheted open. Sandra followed Bose along the corridor toward Orrin's room. The lights had been dimmed, making the green-tiled hallway seem long and subterranean. "Nice work," Bose said, glancing back. "But she's already on the phone."

The next problem was obvious as soon as Sandra used her pass card to open the door to Orrin's room. Orrin lay on the bed as if he'd been dropped on it. Sandra shook him gently. "Orrin," she said. "Hey! *Orrin!*"

His eyes drifted open but the lids stayed at half-mast. "What?" he said softly. "What now, what now?"

He was heavily medicated. "Orrin, it's me. It's Dr. Cole."

He gave her a groggy look. Fucking night staff, Sandra thought. Were they double-dosing everybody on the ward, to keep them quiet? Or just Orrin? "It's dark outside, Dr. Cole . . ."

"I know it is, but you have to get up. Get up and come with us, okay?"

"Officer Bose," Orrin said, still lying there inertly, his hospital gown rucked up over his skinny butt. "Hi."

"Hi there, Orrin. Listen to me. Dr. Cole's right. We have to get you out of here. Take you to see your sister, Ariel. Is that okay with you?"

It took a few seconds for the question to register. Then Orrin offered a loopy grin. "That's just exactly what I want, Officer Bose. Thank you . . . I'm pretty tired, though."

"I know." Bose bent down and put his arm around Orrin's shoulders and helped him to his feet. Orrin wobbled but managed to remain standing.

"Easier with a wheelchair," Sandra said. She ducked out of the room—the corridor was still empty, Nurse Meredith still at her station but talking vigorously into her phone—and grabbed one of the folding wheelchairs from the supply cubby. STATE CARE OF TEXAS / HOUSTON AREA UNIT was stenciled across the leather backpiece. The chair rattled as she wheeled it into Orrin's room, startlingly loud in the stillness of the ward.

Bose helped Orrin into the chair. As soon as he was seated Orrin's chin nodded toward his chest and his eyelids slid shut again. Maybe it was better that way, Sandra thought. She took the handles of the chair while Bose led the way to the exit.

But Meredith was blocking the ward door again, and now she had company—Jack Geddes.

"Hold on right there," Meredith said. "I got Dr. Congreve on the phone, and he says you have no right to remove this patient. So you just wheel Mr. Mather back to his room and you can take up the matter with management in the morning."

Bose ignored Meredith and directed his remarks to Geddes, who had bulled up to him with his chest thrust forward. "This is a police matter. I'm removing Mr. Mather on my authority."

"You don't *have* any authority," Meredith said.

"You can get out of my way," Bose told Geddes, "or I can arrest you for interference, but make up your mind, sir. I wouldn't be here at this hour if this wasn't urgent business."

Sandra imagined Congreve taking the call in his car, turning around, heading back to State. How long ago had he left? Half an hour, forty-five minutes? Had he gone straight home or stopped on the way? She tried not to betray her anxiety by looking at her watch.

Geddes had locked eyes with Bose, a classic stare-down, Sandra thought, but then the orderly sighed and turned to Nurse Meredith. "This man showed you his badge? His papers?"

"Yes, but—"

"Then I can't do nothing about it, ma'am."

Geddes stepped aside. Bose, preternaturally calm, asked Meredith, "Do you need my signature?"

"If you insist on taking him you better *had* sign." Nurse Meredith thrust a clipboard at him. "At the bottom. You, too, Dr. Cole. Be hell to pay when Dr. Congreve gets here. It's on you, that's all I can say."

Bose signed; Sandra added her own slightly shaky signature. Then she wheeled Orrin down the hallway at a brisk clip, following Bose's long stride. Orrin had gone back to sleep, miraculously. She could hear his soft, rasping snores over the rattle of the wheels.

As soon as they were past the main door into the

parking lot Sandra's face began to prickle with sweat. A reef of clouds had hidden all the stars.

"The paperwork you gave them," Sandra said, "was that legitimate?"

"Hardly. It's a standard form. I just scribbled in a few of the boxes."

"That's not entirely legal, is it?"

He smiled. "Another bridge burned."

"They're going down fast."

She took a last look back at State. She would never be allowed inside this building again. She was unemployed, she was free, and she was so frightened she felt like laughing out loud.

They headed toward the motel where Ariel Mather was staying. Orrin slept in the backseat, his body lax against the seat belt, his hospital gown spindled around his thighs. "We'll need to get him some fresh clothes," Sandra said.

"I believe Ariel brought him some clothes from Raleigh, just in case."

A car passed by, speeding in the opposite direction—Sandra thought it might be Congreve's car, though she couldn't be sure. She spent a few moments relishing the thought of Congreve getting the news from Jack Geddes or Nurse Meredith.

"I brought his notebooks, too," Bose said. "Orrin'll be glad to have them back."

"I read what you sent me. But there's more, right?"

"A little more."

"You still want my opinion of it?"

He gave her a curious look. "Anything you have to say, I'm interested."

"At one point you thought the document constituted some kind of evidence."

"Yeah. You may not have read the relevant parts yet."

"But that's not the real question, is it? The real question is, how much of it is true?"

He laughed, but she saw his grip tighten on the steering wheel. "Come on, Sandra. *True?*"

"You know what I mean."

"You really think Orrin's channeling spirits from the year twelve thousand?"

"I willing to bet you've given it some thought. There are corroborative details in there, stuff you could have tracked down. Stuff even *I* could track down. Allison Pearl, for instance. Born and grew up in Champlain, New York. A truly incurious man might not wonder whether such a person really exists. But you're not an incurious man."

"I'll take that as a compliment."

"As it happens, there's no Allison Pearl in the Champlain directory."

He wasn't smiling anymore. "You checked?"

"Only a handful of Pearls altogether. No Allison, but there's a couple with a daughter by that name."

"You called them?"

"Yes."

"Did they tell you I called them too?"

"Yes, but thank you for mentioning it."

"Because Orrin, or whoever wrote that document, might not have picked those names out of the air—

Turk Findley, Allison Pearl. I asked Mrs. Pearl whether she knows Orrin or Ariel Mather or anyone fitting their description."

A question that hadn't occurred to Sandra. "Does she?"

"No. She never heard of them. But that doesn't rule out a connection. Orrin could have come across the name Allison Pearl somewhere, maybe from a neighbor who happens to be a distant relative—I don't know. Or it could just be a coincidence."

"Does that seem likely?"

"Compared to what? The idea that Orrin can travel in time? As far as I can tell the only trip he ever took was Raleigh to Houston on a Greyhound bus."

"So we'll never know?"

He shrugged.

CHAPTER EIGHTEEN

ALLISON'S STORY

1.

Often in the weeks after the first encounter between Vox and the Hypothetical machines I caught myself quietly repeating my own name—*Allison Pearl, Allison Pearl*—anchoring myself to the syllables, the sound of them, the feeling of them in my throat and on my tongue.

As Allison, I had once read a book about the human brain. From that book I had learned the term "neural plasticity," which means the ability of the brain to modify itself in response to changes in its environment. Neural plasticity was what made it possible for me to be Allison Pearl. It was also what made it possible for a living brain to be wired to a limbic implant. The brain adapts: that's what brains do.

When Turk told me he had volunteered for surgery I pretended to be surprised. The implant had been an essential part of our plan from the beginning. But for the benefit of the Network's hidden sensors I was obliged to feel betrayed, I was obliged to argue with him. So I argued. So I wept. It was a convincing performance. It was convincing because it was nine-tenths sincere. I didn't doubt his courage, but no plan is foolproof. I was terrified of what he might become.

Shit happens, as the original Allison once wrote in her diary. No truer words, etc. For instance: the day Turk had his node installed—probably about the time he was being wheeled into surgery—Isaac Dvali came to see me, and he laid my secrets bare.

I knew from the newsfeeds that Isaac's recovery had proceeded at an astonishing rate. Everyone in Vox Core was paying breathless attention to him now. Far more than Turk, Isaac had become what the city's founders had hoped and believed one of the Uptaken ought to be: a living connection to the Hypotheticals—which meant the city's promised transcendence remained at least plausible. Without Isaac, Vox was nothing but a congregation of fanatics whose faith had stranded them on a dead and deadly planet. With Isaac, it was still possible to believe Vox was a community of like-minded pioneers poised at the vanguard of human destiny.

Only days after the disaster in the Wilkes Basin, Isaac had mastered the ability to speak fluent Voxish. His motor skills improved to the point where he could walk unassisted, his body went from frail to remarkably robust, and the reconstructed portions of his skull began to look almost normal. The croaking,

screaming creature Turk had known was gone. The
newly and unsettlingly articulate Isaac had been released from medical care, though he still lived and
slept in the rooms where he had been treated. Lately
he had conducted vague but ingratiating interviews
with scholars and managers, the contents of which
were publicly broadcast. He praised Vox for its dedi-
cation and endurance; he expressed his admiration
for the wisdom of the founding prophecies. For days
now he had been traveling around the city like a
tourist, sometimes mobbed by curious children whose
equally curious parents hung back shyly and didn't
dare speak.

I had followed all this on the newsfeeds. Vox was
listing toward insanity, and the abject worship of
Isaac Dvali was just the latest symptom. I told myself
to expect more of the same. "Expect the unexpected,"
Allison had written in her diary. Not an original sen-
timent but always apt.

And I believed I was well braced for surprises . . .
but I was shocked beyond words when Isaac showed
up at my door, pale as a mushroom and bright-eyed
as an infant, smiling and calling me by name: not
Treya but, amazingly, *Allison*.

I was afraid of him, of course.

I didn't know what he wanted and I was instantly
terrified of the attention he would attract—must already have attracted—just by being here. Somewhere
in the nearby corridors and walks his minders were
surely hovering. The hidden ears and eyes of the Network were pricked and focused.

But all he said was, "May I come in?" And I nodded, mutely, and let the door slide shut behind him.

Somehow I found the courage to ask him to sit down.

He remained standing. "I won't stay long." He spoke in English. It was the language he had been born to, I reminded myself. Under all the layers of synthesis and reconstruction there was still at least some fragment of the Isaac Dvali he once had been, a boy raised in the Equatorian desert by people whose urge to make contact with the Hypotheticals had been almost Voxish in its intensity. He was, like me, like Turk, a divided and incomplete soul. He was also, at least potentially, a very dangerous one.

Apart from his pale skin, his eyes were his most striking feature. When he looked at me my first instinct was to wince. He told me not to be frightened and I said, "That's not so easy."

"You came to my suite when I was sick," he said.

"You remember that?"

He nodded, smiling. "I've learned a lot about you since then."

"About me?"

"From the Network. I know who and what you are. And I think it would be useful if we can talk to each other. I won't hurt you. And I won't tell anyone about your plan to escape."

For months I had been training myself in the art of inscrutability, as a way of keeping that one simple secret. Now the charade had collapsed, and I was too shocked to move.

"No one can hear us," Isaac said.

"You're wrong," I managed to say.

His smile was insistent, maddening. "The Network sensors in this room are disabled. They'll stay that way as long as I'm here."

"You can do that?"

"Because of what I am, because of what the surgeons put inside me, I can influence the Network and even the Coryphaeus."

Was that possible?

The Coryphaeus was the sum and master of the Voxish collectivity, a nested hierarchy of quantum processors distributed throughout Vox Core. Even a nuclear attack had only temporarily silenced it. It had never occurred to me that the Coryphaeus could be *influenced*. But there had never been anyone like Isaac before, either. He had been deeply infused with Hypothetical biotechnology since birth, and his neural implant hadn't simply been added to his brain; his brain had been regrown around it.

"It's true," he said. "At least for now, you can speak as freely as you like."

My heart was pounding. But since Isaac apparently knew about our plan—and since he had announced it out loud—I could only hope he was telling the truth. "You can really shut down the sensors?"

"Yes, or make sure anything they observe is left unanalyzed."

"But if you already know about . . ."

"Your escape," he said. I flinched again. "You were extremely clever about hiding it. Pulse, respiration, cortisol traces in your sweat and urine, all those markers have been at elevated levels for weeks; but the effect was indistinguishable from emotional stress. Stochastic and heuretic indicators—the things you did or didn't say or do—took the Coryphaeus much longer to analyze. But you would have been found out eventually." That Buddha smile again. "If I hadn't intervened."

I took a breath and said, "Then . . . how did *you* know?"

"The Coryphaeus was already beginning to draw inferences. I extrapolated from that. The details aren't clear to me, but I guess you intend to steal an aircraft and take it through the Arch to Equatoria."

"Close enough," I whispered.

"And I hope you succeed."

"Does that mean—what are you saying? Do you want to come with us?"

His smile faded. "That's not possible. When I was reconstructed, important neurological functions were delegated to remote processors inside the Network. Only part of me lives in this body. You understand that, don't you? That a person can have more than one nature?"

". . . Yes . . ."

"I can't come with you, but I may be able to help."

"Help how?"

"Turk can't pilot an aircraft until his node is functional enough for him to gain access to the vehicle's controls. But once the node is *fully* functional, he won't be willing to leave. I assume you understand how narrow that window of opportunity is."

"Obviously, but—"

"Right now Turk sees himself as facing a choice between escape and bondage. Once the node begins to influence his brain, it may seem more like a choice between escape and forgiveness."

Forgiveness for what? I wondered but didn't ask.

"The point is, I can warn you when he's close to that line. And I can help by diverting the attention of the Coryphaeus at the critical time. We can talk about it in more detail later on, but I want you to know you have a friend and an ally. I hope you'll think of me that way."

He sounded so much like a precocious child who wanted to be liked that I almost forgot to be afraid of him. But when he stood up and moved toward the door I nearly panicked. "Wait! The Network surveillance in this room, is it turned off permanently?"

"No, I'm sorry. There are limits to what I can do. Unless I'm physically present, you should assume the Network is listening."

I forced myself to stand close to him. The skin on the right side of his face was seashell-pink and almost poreless, imperfect because it was *too* perfect. His eyes were softly radiant. "One more question."

"What is it?"

"Are you—you know, what they say you are?"

"I'm not sure what you mean."

"What the prophecies say you are. Can you really talk to the Hypotheticals?"

"No," he said. "Not yet."

Less than an hour later Oscar showed up at the door, obviously distraught. He knew Isaac had been here, and he was maddeningly curious about what Isaac might have said, but he couldn't access a Network record of it. He demanded an explanation.

I had known Oscar reasonably well back when I

was Treya, training for liaison duties. Oscar had always had a serene confidence in the purity and purpose of his work. There was a Voxish saying: "He rises and falls with the tide," describing someone who tracks the needs of Vox Core and caters to them uncomplainingly. That was Oscar. But lately his serenity had begun to fray at the edges. The fact that Isaac had chosen to meet privately with a nodeless apostate—and to enforce that privacy even against the Network's routine surveillance—had sabotaged his finely honed sense of order.

I told him Isaac had wanted to reminisce about the twenty-first century.

"Anything you might know about the past he can easily access for himself."

"Maybe he was curious about me. I don't know. Maybe he felt like speaking English for a little while."

"What could you possibly have to say that would interest a being like *him*—even in English?"

That was insulting, so I used an expression Oscar might not have encountered in his formal training: "Fuck you," I said, and closed the door.

2.

No word came from Turk—he had warned me they might keep him overnight after the surgery—and I decided I couldn't sit alone any longer, partly because I was afraid my elevated heartbeat or hormonal chemistry might give the Network another clue to my state of mind, especially if Isaac wasn't paying attention and blocking the sensors. I needed distraction. So I left the suite and rode transit to the nearest large public space, a terrace overlooking a market zone, to watch the parade of lights that marked the Festival of Ido.

Vox Core was a city of rituals and festivals. As Treya, I had always loved them. The part of me that was Allison was surprised that a polity as tight-laced as Vox should be so fond of celebrations. But Vox was a limbic democracy; sharing public emotion was what we did best.

Vox had been founded on a planet called Ester, five worlds away from Old Earth. We still kept the Esterish year of 723 days and the Esterish division of a day into twenty-four hours (a custom as ancient as Earth itself, though Ester's days and hours were slightly longer). Vox had journeyed through all five of those worlds, sailing the isotropic sea that linked every Ring world with the exception of Mars. We marked many of our days with celebrations: celebrations of the Founding, of the Prophecies, of the anniversaries of historical battles and so on. The Festival of Ido commemorated our victory over bionormative forces at the Arch of Terivine—the battle in which we had taken the prisoners who eventually formed the nucleus of the Farmer caste.

It was a martial holiday, with fireworks and drums and torch parades. Most years the celebration was joyous, bountiful. This year the feasts were rationed and there was a note of hysteria in the festivities. Everyone knew it might be the last Ido before the remaking of the world.

Obviously, I couldn't participate. Even if I had wanted to, everyone in Vox Core knew me from the newsfeeds. I was a traitor to my own past, a dissonant note in the story of the Uptaken, and because I was nodeless my behavior would seem opaque and untrustworthy. I wasn't in any danger from the crowds—at least, not yet—but I would be ostracized and ignored if I tried to join them. So I found a place where I could be alone, a wooded patch overlooking the market zone. A half mile or so downslope, as ambient light dimmed toward night, the market square filled with celebrants. They carried luminous rods of various sizes and colors, and they gathered behind a leader who conducted them through the maze of market stalls in a sinuous moving line. The effect was spectacular in the dark and from a distance, a glowing multicolored snake twining around and through itself, swaying to the beat of the drums.

I felt sad, I felt perversely nostalgic. I wasn't Treya anymore and I didn't want to be Treya, but I missed the pleasure Treya had once taken in events like this. That is, *my* pleasure. *She, me, mine, hers.* Deceptively simple words, not as easy to parse as they had once seemed.

Even nodeless, I could tell when a fresh rush of excitement swept through the crowd. I had to look across a gap of treetops to one of the festival's huge video displays to see what had happened. The display showed a group of snakedancers unfurling a banner; on the banner was a portrait of Isaac Dvali, literally glowing in the dark. Cheering and applause echoed up the terrace like the sound of a hard rain falling.

But it wasn't really Isaac they were cheering for. They were cheering for what Isaac represented: the fulfillment of prophecy, the imminent end of days. It was the voice of the doomed Coryphaeus, worshipping itself through the body of Vox.

How do you measure a universal madness? I took as signs the contagious irrationalities, the bland indifference to real problems (shortages of grain and animal protein, for instance), the public obsession with the Hypotheticals that followed the massacre in the Antarctic desert. Images of the Hypothetical machines were everywhere now, and a belief had begun to emerge that the soldiers and scientists killed in the vanguard expedition weren't really dead but had been Uptaken.

Presumably, when the machines eventually arrived at Vox, the rest of us would be similarly raptured into communion with the Hypotheticals . . . or killed; the terms were commutable. Prophecy had always been a little vague on that point. Vox's founders had believed the end of Vox would take the form of what they called *ajientei,* for which the nearest English equivalent might be "enlargement"—the diffusion of human consciousness over galactic space and geologic time, the scale on which the Hypotheticals were presumed to operate.

In any case, our scholars had estimated that at their current rate of progress the Hypothetical machines wouldn't reach Vox for months or even years. In fact certain pious elderly citizens were petitioning to be flown to the machines so they could be Uptaken before they died.

They needn't have worried. Only hours after the Festival of Ido, our unmanned aircraft delivered unsettling news from the Wilkes Basin. The Hypothetical machines had begun to move more quickly than before. In fact they were accelerating—doubling their speed every few hours. That didn't amount to much at the moment, but if the acceleration continued they would arrive sooner than expected. *Much* sooner, the scholars said: a matter of weeks. Possibly days.

Vox rang like a bell with the news.

CHAPTER NINETEEN

SANDRA AND BOSE

We're not safe yet," Bose said when they pulled into a parking space outside Ariel Mather's motel room.

Sandra had no trouble believing him. She had seen how vigilantly he watched his mirrors as he drove away from State. The plan, he said, was to check Ariel Mather out of her room and put her and Orrin in a different motel for the night. In the morning, Bose's "friends" would drive them to a safe place out of town.

Sandra stayed in the car with Orrin while Bose knocked at the door of Ariel's room. Moments later he was back, followed by Ariel with her single scuffed plastic suitcase. Ariel wore denim jeans frayed at the cuffs and a black T-shirt with UNIVERSITY OF NORTH CAROLINA printed on it. Sandra doubted Ariel had been any closer to the University of North Carolina than the thrift shop where she bought her clothes.

"There are people out there who might still think

of Orrin as a threat," Bose explained to her as she crouched into the backseat. "So we're taking you to another motel, just overnight. Tomorrow you can get out of Houston and away from all this. That all right with you, Ms. Mather?"

"Yeah," Ariel said abstractedly. "I don't have any better idea. What's the matter with Orrin? Orrin, you all right? Wake up!"

"He was sedated," Sandra said. "He'll be fine in a few hours. In the meantime it might be better just to let him sleep it off, if that's what he wants to do."

"They *drugged* him?"

"Just a sleeping pill."

"Huh! Honestly, I don't know how you can stand to work in a place that drugs up innocent people for no reason."

"I guess I can't stand it," Sandra said. "I don't work there anymore."

Bose drove side streets until he was sure they weren't being followed, then stopped at an anonymous two-story motel near the airport. By this time Orrin was functional enough to climb out of the car and stagger to his room on the arm of his sister. Sandra waited in the motel's small lobby while Bose carried Ariel's suitcase.

Getting late now, and she'd had almost no sleep herself, but she was alert and slightly buzzed, still processing the adrenaline she had generated back at State Care. Ariel's rough tenderness toward Orrin made her think of her own brother, passing the night in an institution far kinder than State and vastly more expensive. She thought about the man on the phone who had tried to bribe her by offering the longevity drug.

To which Bose's anonymous friends also had access— the original Martian drug, not the hacked commercial version. Would such people also be willing to help Kyle? If so, what would they ask in return?

"It isn't some kind of elaborate secret society," Bose had said—was it really only yesterday? "The original group consisted of people Jason Lawton happened to know." Jason Lawton, the scientist to whom Wun Ngo Wen had entrusted his inventory of pharmaceuticals. "Not people who *took* the treatment, necessarily, though some did, but people who were willing to make themselves custodians of it. To distribute it ethically and, until the laws are changed, secretly. The circle expanded over the years. It's not foolproof and it's not airtight, but we try to take care of each other."

We, she had noticed.

Bose came back to the lobby alone. He said, "It's not a good idea for you to be home by yourself. I figured I'd take a room here for the night." He smiled. "I'll make it a double, if you want to save money."

"So that's what, an *economic* proposition?"

"No," he said, "not quite."

The air-conditioning was anemic, but some things were worth sweating for.

After they made love, lying in the dim and intermittent light cast by passing headlights on the blinds of their room, Sandra ran her finger along the line of Bose's scar, belly to shoulder. When he realized what she was doing he flinched, but then—maybe by sheer force of will—relaxed. She said, "What happened? If you don't mind me asking."

He was silent long enough that she guessed he *did* mind. Then he sat up, bracing himself against the backboard of the bed.

"I was seventeen," he said. "I was in Madras visiting my father. This was after my parents split up. My father was an engineering consultant for a company that installed shallow-water wind generators. The company rented him a bungalow with a sea view but it was in a dicey neighborhood, the security was bad. Thieves broke in one night. They killed my father. Me, I was stupid enough to try to defend him." He covered her hand with his. "They were carrying knives."

If the scar was a knife wound they must nearly have gutted him. "That's terrible . . . I'm so sorry."

"A neighbor heard the scuffle and called the police. I lost a lot of blood—it was kind of touch and go for a while. My mom flew over and took charge, pulled some strings, made sure I got the right kind of medical care."

Sandra wondered if that was why he ended up at HPD: outrage at the crime, a sense of the police as belated saviors. Southern India after the Spin: "I heard it was pretty bad over there for a few years."

"Not much worse than Houston," Bose said. But he was uncomfortable talking about it, and she dropped the subject and let herself drift toward sleep.

It was strange to wake up next to him in an unfamiliar bed, the morning already gone, diesel-scented air seeping in through the poorly sealed motel windows. She sat up and yawned. Bose was still asleep, lying on his back and breathing in a rhythm as regular as waves breaking on a beach. The salty, delicate odor of their lovemaking still clung to the sheets.

She would have liked to lie here indefinitely—and she guessed she could; she was functionally if not officially unemployed; she had nowhere to go—but some Calvinist impulse caused her to pick up her watch from the bedside table. Noon, a little past. The day half wasted. Shocking.

She left the bed without disturbing Bose and used the shower. Her only clothes were the jeans and shirt she'd worn yesterday, and they weren't especially fresh, but they would have to do.

When she came out of the bathroom he was awake and grinning at her. "Breakfast," he said.

"It's a little late for breakfast."

"Lunch, then. I called Ariel's room. Orrin's still groggy but he's feeling better. They're going to the motel coffee shop. Maybe you and I can sneak away for something a little nicer? Then come back here. We're booked for another night, but I can arrange a ride for Orrin and Ariel before dark."

Yes, Sandra thought. And then? Once the Mather sibs were safely out of town . . . what then?

The heat wave still hadn't broken, but the news was predicting storms tonight. Sandra hoped that was true. The sky was dusty and hot, and on the southern horizon the clouds were beginning to build their afternoon cathedrals into higher, cooler air.

Bose's idea of "somewhere a little nicer" to eat lunch turned out to be a chain restaurant off the highway. Sandra ordered a sandwich and ignored the cowboy-motif decor and the aggressively cheerful waitstaff. By the time they were served the noon crowd had come and gone and the warehouse-sized dining room was comfortably quiet. Bose polished off a huge plate of steak and eggs in what Sandra imagined was a kind of postcoital protein binge. Over coffee she said, "I guess we'll never know. About Orrin's notebooks, I mean. Where all that stuff came from and what it means to him."

"There are a lot of things we'll never know."

"He'll go into hiding and we'll do . . . whatever it is we do next. Did you check your phone today?"

"'Turn in your badge and go home.' Voice and text. They probably would have sent a candygram if they knew how to reach me."

"You have any plans?"

"Long- or short-term?"

"Long, I guess."

"I've been thinking about Seattle. It's chilly and it rains a lot."

"Just pick up and go? Just like that?"

"I don't know any other way." He put down his coffee cup. "Come with me."

She stared at him. "Christ, Bose! You just open up your mouth and *say* these things . . ."

"Obviously, I don't know much about your line of work. But my friends are your friends. Come to Seattle and maybe we can help you find something."

"That's just—I can't—"

"You have any reason to stay in Houston?"

"Of course I do." But really, did she? No real friends, no prospect of employment. "There's Kyle, for one."

"Your brother. Okay, but is it possible he could be transferred to a facility in Washington State?"

"That would involve a lot of paperwork."

"Oh. *Paperwork.*"

"I mean, I guess it could be done, but . . ."

He waved a hand apologetically: "I'm sorry—it was a selfish question. It just seems like we're in the same boat here. No fault of your own. You were doing all right before I walked into your life."

No, but he didn't know that. "Well . . . I appreciate the thought." She added almost in spite of herself, "I'll think about it." Because now she *could* think about it. She was unemployed and falling freely. She could risk everything without risking much at all. "Why is this so easy for you? I'm jealous."

"Maybe I've been thinking about it longer than you have."

But no, it wasn't that. It was something more profoundly a part of Bose's nature, a degree of inner calm that was almost eerie. She said, "You're not like other people."

"What's that mean?"

"You know what it means. You just don't want to talk about it."

"Well," he said, fishing his wallet out of his pocket, "we can talk about it after we get Orrin out of town."

Sandra needed a change of clothes, so she persuaded Bose to swing by her apartment long enough for her to run inside and throw a few things into a suitcase.

She packed items from her wardrobe, of course, but she also took her passport, her gig drives, her personal papers. She didn't know when she would be back. Maybe soon. Maybe never. She took a last look around before she left. The apartment seemed already untenanted, as if it had sensed her intentions and dismissed her.

Downstairs she found Bose waiting patiently, playing some kind of tinny shitkicker music on the car's audio system. She tossed her bag into the backseat and climbed in beside him. "I didn't know you liked country music."

"It's not country music."

"It sounds like an alley cat fucking a fiddle."

"Show some respect. This is classic western swing. Bob Wills and the Texas Playboys."

Recorded with a tin can and a string, by the sound of it. "This is what's keeping you in Texas?"

"No, but it's just about the only thing that makes me sorry to leave."

He was tapping the steering wheel in merry rhythm when his phone buzzed. A hands-free app displayed the caller's number in the lower-left corner of the car's windshield. "Answer," Bose said, which prompted the car to cut the music and open the phone connection. "Bose here."

"It's me," a shrill voice said, "it's Ariel Mather—is that you, Officer Bose?"

"Yeah, Ariel. What's wrong?"

"It's Orrin!"

"Is he all right?"

"I don't *know* if he's all right—I don't where he *is*! He went out to the Coke machine and now he's gone!"

"Okay," Bose said. "Wait for us right where you are. We're on our way."

Sandra saw the change that came over him, the way his lips went taut and his eyes narrowed. *You're not like other people,* she had said, and it still seemed true, as if Bose had a deep reservoir of calm inside him— but it wasn't calm now, Sandra thought. Now it was filled with a fierce resolve.

CHAPTER TWENTY

TURK'S STORY

1.

What I saw after the surgery, as I was coming up from anesthesia, not quite awake and not entirely asleep, was a vision of a man on fire—a burning man dancing in a pool of flame, staring at me through ripples of superheated air.

The vision had all the qualities of a nightmare. But it wasn't a dream. It was a memory.

The medical team had shown me the limbic implant before they installed it. I believe they interpreted my horror as preoperative anxiety.

The node was a flexible black disk a few centimeters wide and less than a centimeter thick. It was covered with nubs the size of pinheads from which fibers of artificial nervous tissue would grow, once the node established a suitable blood supply from the surrounding capillaries. Almost as soon as it was installed the implant would power up its link to the Network; within days its artificial nerves would have bonded to the spinal medulla and begun to infiltrate the targeted areas of my brain.

The medics asked me if I understood all this. I told them I did.

Then: the prick of an anesthetic injection, a cold swab at the back of my neck, oblivion while the surgeon wielded his knife.

The burning man had been a night watchman at my father's warehouse in Houston.

He was a stranger to me. The killing was unpremeditated, and in a court of law the charge might have been reduced from murder to manslaughter. But I never went before a court.

Twice in my life I had told some version of that story to another person—once when I was drunk, once when I was sober; once to a stranger, once to a woman with whom I had fallen in love. In both cases the story I told was incomplete and partially fabricated. Even my best attempts at confession inevitably foundered on lies.

The people I had confessed to were all ten thousand years gone, but the dead man was locked in my conscience, where he had never stopped burning. And now I had given the keys to my conscience to the Coryphaeus, and I didn't know what that might mean.

2.

The first change I noticed after the surgery wasn't in myself but in other people, especially their faces.

I felt some of the side effects I had been warned about—transient dizziness, loss of appetite—but the symptoms weren't severe and they passed quickly. What scared me wasn't what I felt but what I might *not* be feeling . . . what I might have lost without knowing I had lost it. I questioned every unguarded impulse and I kept to myself for days, hardly speaking even to Allison (who in any case had begun treating me with a kind of mournful disdain, which I hoped was only theatrical). Both of us knew what had to be done; both of us knew I wasn't yet ready to attempt it.

The medics had prescribed exercises in what they called "interactive volitional skills," meaning the ability to manipulate node-enabled control surfaces—things as simple as turning on a graphic display by a combination of touch and will. These were the same skills I would need to pilot us away from Vox, so I pushed myself up a fairly steep learning curve. Oscar stopped in from time to time to monitor my progress, and on one of these visits he brought me a selection of tutelary devices intended for Voxish children: Network toys that changed color or made music when I told them to. Except mostly they didn't. The node was still infiltrating key parts of my brain, still learning to enhance or suppress activity at selected sites; not all the necessary feedback loops had formed or stabilized. Oscar counseled patience.

It wasn't until I stopped focusing on control surfaces and ventured out into the public spaces of Vox

Core that I *saw* the difference the node had made. I had walked these corridors and passed through these tiers and terraces dozens of times, but suddenly it was as if I had never really seen them. The faces of the people I passed were almost luminous in their expressiveness and complexity. I found I could read the moods of strangers as accurately as if I had known them all my life. The doctors had told me this would happen, but since their explanations had been couched in phrases like "amygdalic linkage" and "mirror neuron profusion" and "chiasmic induction"—Oscar's translations—I had never really grasped the significance of it. Now the effect was almost overwhelming.

I decided to travel up to one of the city's high places, away from the crowds. Taking vertical transit in Vox was like riding an elevator the size of a subway car: it put me eye-to-eye with other passengers. I sat opposite a woman holding a young child in her lap. She noticed me and smiled. It was the smile you might give any amiable stranger, except that in some sense we *weren't* strangers—we were bound by the Network, and wordless intimacies scrolled between us. Her restless eyes and the alternating ease and tension of her body told me she was anxious about the future—it had recently been announced that the Hypothetical machines were accelerating toward us—but she was humbly willing to submit to whatever fate the prophets had mandated for her. It was when she looked at her infant son that her uneasiness grew more focused and concentrated. The boy was five or six months old and his own limbic implant was still a prominent pink bump at the base of his skull. He radiated simple needs and absolute dependency. And she was reluctant to entrust him to the care of the Hypotheticals, no matter how benevolent she believed them to be. Whenever she held her son in her arms, she was tempted by the sin of fear.

I felt the soothing euphoria of the Coryphaeus running through both of them, counterpoint to the text of their bodies and gestures. That was unnerving. And of course they sensed my reaction as keenly as I sensed theirs. The mother frowned and averted her eyes, as if she had seen something distasteful. The child squirmed and arched against her body.

I hurried away at the next stop.

The next time I felt restless I went out at night, when the corridors were dimly lit and mostly empty. I had been working with Network interfaces all day and although I was tired I knew I wouldn't be able to sleep.

News had come from our fleet of drone aircraft that the Hypothetical machines were crossing the Transarctic Mountains faster than expected. Out in the Wilkes Basin the machines had looked like cumbersomely solid objects, but when they encountered rough ground they deformed in order to negotiate large obstacles. In extreme terrain they actually seemed to flow like a viscous liquid, moving edgelessly up narrow passes and steep, chaotic inclines. Estimates of the time it would take the machines to reach Vox were revised downward yet again.

The few people I encountered that night were bristling with conflicting emotions—their faces glowed like torches, to my eyes—and I hurried past them. I had begun to understand what Allison meant about collective insanity. It wasn't just euphoria the Coryphaeus was sharing. Fear smoldered in the Voxish collective like a fire in a coal seam, too strong to be entirely suppressed. I passed a maintenance worker whose anxiety literally radiated from his face, a spiky halo of awe and dread. I felt it myself, a pressure as faint and persistent as the beating of my heart: the longing for a better and larger existence, set against the suspicion that what was approaching from the Antarctic desert might be nothing but a quick and nasty death.

Allison was awake when I got back, and she wasn't alone. Isaac Dvali was with her.

I knew about Isaac's miraculous recovery and the endorsement of the Voxish prophecies that had made him a public hero. His image was everywhere in Vox Core. But he was here without his minders, he was smiling at Allison and she was smiling at me: "We can talk!" she said.

Which made no sense. I stared at Isaac. To my eyes he looked gilded, like a painting of a medieval saint. More subtly, I could see hints of the trauma that had shaped him, sparks in an aura—he was a mosaic of colored glass, coruscating with unexpected energies. I asked him what he wanted.

"Let me explain," he said.

CHAPTER TWENTY-ONE

SANDRA AND BOSE

Ariel Mather paced the floor of her motel room, shaking with anxiety. At first she had insisted on going out to look for Orrin ("right *now!*"), but Bose had convinced her to stay in the room at least long enough to explain what had happened. Sandra sat on the unmade bed, listening carefully and not saying much, letting the crisis unspool around her.

"You went to lunch," Bose prompted.

"Yeah, over to the coffee shop. We had hamburgers. Does that information help you in some way?"

"How was Orrin feeling this morning?"

"Pretty good, I spose, considering he was drugged last night."

"Okay, he was in a good mood. What did you talk about?"

"Mostly about what happened since he left Raleigh. How he came to Houston and got hired by that man Findley. I asked him why he wanted to leave home in the first place—was it something I did wrong, was he unhappy there? He said no and he was sorry I worried so much about him. He said he just felt like there was business in Houston he had to take care of."

"What business?"

"I asked him that but he was cagey. And I didn't push, because I figured it was all over with now. We were going home—so I *thought*."

"What else did you talk about?"

"The weather. This damn heat. It gets hot in Raleigh, but Texas! I don't know why anybody lives here, honestly. Nothing much else than that. While we ate Orrin kept his notebooks in his lap, you know, those ratty notebooks of his, the ones you gave him back yesterday."

"Did he say anything about them?"

"He showed me a couple of pages this morning, but he was real shy about it. There are words in there I didn't think he knew . . . words *I* don't know. I asked him, did he write this? Sort of, he says. I asked him how you can 'sort of' write something—was he holding the pen that made these words or was he not? He was, he says. Somebody with him at the time? No, he says. Then you wrote them, I said. Whatever they mean. He said it was just a story. But I don't know about that, the way he clings to those pages. Why? Does that have something to do with him running off?"

"I don't know," Bose said. "What happened after lunch?"

"He asked me for some walking-around money."

"Walking around?"

"That's what we called it back in Raleigh. He worked

odd jobs to help with the rent but he didn't usually have any money of his own, so I used to give him a little cash on Saturdays so he could walk down to the store and buy something, or maybe go to the municipal pool or get himself lunch at McDonald's. He didn't like to be away from home without money in his pocket." Ariel stopped pacing and shook her head. "I gave him forty dollars to keep him happy. I didn't think he'd take it and run. What's forty dollars in a city like this? After lunch we went back to the room to wait for you two. Then he says, Ariel, I'm going to the lobby and get change for the Coke machine. I said I would give him coins. He said no, I already gave him money, he wanted to change a bill. Twenty minutes and he's not back, so I went to look for him. He wasn't down at the soda machine and when I went to the lobby he wasn't there, either. The clerk told me he saw Orrin waiting for a city bus at the highway stop."

"Going which direction?" Bose asked.

"You'll have to ask the clerk."

"Was Orrin alone or was he with somebody?"

"Clerk didn't say anything about anybody else."

Sandra waited until Bose had wrung out of Ariel all the information she was capable of giving. Then she said, "I have a couple of questions, if it's all right."

Bose seemed surprised. Ariel sighed impatiently but nodded.

"Last time we talked you said Orrin was gentle, that he would never hurt anyone. Do you remember that?"

Ariel's lips went taut. "Of course I remember."

"But when he tried to leave State he fought with the orderly who tried to restrain him."

"That's a lie."

"It may be, but the orderly was wearing a bandage the next day. He claims Orrin bit him."

"I wouldn't take anything those people say seriously. I thought you mentioned you quit that job?"

"I did. I don't work there anymore. I just want to get clear on this."

Ariel paced a few moments more. Then she said, "Nobody's perfect, Dr. Cole. I told you Orrin's gentle, and that's the truth. Maybe I exaggerated last time we talked, but you were working for the people who locked him up—I didn't want to say anything to make it worse."

"Exaggerated how?"

"Orrin had a few encounters when he was growing up. He's slow to anger, Dr. Cole, and he hates fights, but that doesn't mean he never got in one. The neighbor children used to bother him. Called him names and all that. Mostly Orrin would run away, but every once in a while he'd lose his patience."

Sandra and Bose exchanged glances. Bose said, "How often did this happen, Ariel?"

"Oh, I don't know. Maybe once or twice a year when he was younger."

"Was it ever serious? Did he get hurt, did he hurt anyone else?"

"No . . ."

"Whatever you can tell us might help us find him."

"I don't see how." Pause. "Well. Once he hit the Lewisson boy hard enough he had to get stitches over his eye. Other times it was just scuffles. Maybe a black eye or two. Sometimes Orrin got the worst of it. Sometimes not." She added, "He always felt bad about it afterward."

"Okay, thank you," Bose said. "Anything else Orrin

talked about this morning that you can recall? Anything at all, even if it seems unimportant."

"No. Just the weather, like I said. He was interested in the weather report coming over the radio in the coffee shop. They're calling for heavy rain tonight. That excited him. 'I guess it's tonight,' he said. 'Tonight's the night.'"

"Any idea what he meant by that?"

"Well, he always did like storms. You know. The thunder and all."

Bose convinced Ariel to stay in her room, "otherwise I'll end up looking for the both of you." And Ariel had calmed down enough to see the sense in it.

"You'll call me, though, right? Soon as you know anything?"

"I'll call you whether we know anything or not."

Back in the motel lobby, Bose talked to the desk clerk for a few minutes. Orrin had been waiting for the downtown bus, the clerk said. No, he hadn't actually seen Orrin get on. Just noticed him waiting out there. Skinny guy in torn jeans and a yellow T-shirt standing in the sun by the side of the road. "Begging for heat stroke in this weather, if you ask me. Those buses only come along every forty-five minutes."

"So what do we do?" Sandra asked when Bose had finished.

"Depends. Maybe you want to stay here with Ariel?"

"Or maybe I don't."

"I can think of a couple of places we might look."

"You're saying you know where he went?"

"I have an idea or two," Bose said.

CHAPTER TWENTY-TWO

ALLISON'S STORY

Isaac Dvali explained how he'd turned off the Network surveillance. Turk sat warily still, watching Isaac, watching me.

"It's true," I said when Isaac finished, and I told him the rest of it: that I'd talked to Isaac days ago, that Isaac knew about our plan, and that (at least for the moment) the Network couldn't hear a word we said.

I wasn't sure he believed me until he stood up and came across the room and we looked at each other, our first honest look since we had begun planning our escape. Then we were in each other's arms, trying to say all the things we wanted to say and managing only a happy-sad incoherency. But words didn't matter. It was enough to be able to hold him without making a lie of it. Then my hand touched the node at the back of his neck: a patch of papery skin, a fleshy bump. He flinched, and we drew apart.

He turned to Isaac. "Thank you for doing this—"

"You're welcome."

"—but it's a little confusing. I knew Isaac Dvali back in the Equatorian desert. You look like him, allowing for what happened, and I know they rebuilt you from Isaac's body. But a lot of you must be pure Vox. And to be honest, you don't sound much like the Isaac I knew."

"I'm *not* the Isaac you knew. There isn't a word for what I am."

Turk was looking at him with Networked attention, reading the invisible signs. "What I'm saying is, I don't understand why you're here. I don't know what you want."

Isaac's smile disappeared and a cold light came into his eyes, a light even I could see. "It doesn't matter what I *want*. It never did! I didn't ask to be injected with Hypothetical biotechnology when I was in my mother's womb. I didn't ask to be cycled through the temporal Arch, I didn't ask to be brought back to life when I was decently dead. What I *wanted* was never germane. It isn't now. My neural functions are shared with processors embedded in the Network. I'm chained to Vox, I can't exist without it, and Vox is about to be consumed by something . . . incomprehensible." He made a visible effort to control himself. "The Hypotheticals don't care about anything as trivially brief as a human life. It's the Coryphaeus that interests them. When the Hypothetical machines reach Vox, they'll absorb the Coryphaeus and dismantle Vox Core. Nothing human will survive."

I said, "How do you know that?"

"I can't talk to the Hypotheticals—I'm not what Oscar thinks I am—but I can hear them ticking out in the dark. Not their thoughts—their *appetites*." His face went slack and he closed his eyes—listening, maybe. Then he shook his head and looked at Turk. "You were there when I was in pain. Not because you thought I was a god. Not because you could use me. Not like the doctors, hovering over me like crows over carrion."

"That's little enough," Turk said.

"If you can save yourselves, I want to help. That's also *little enough*."

"What about you?" I asked.

A trace of a smile returned to his face, but it was bitter. "If I can't leave, I might be able to hide. I've been trying to create a protected space inside the Network. Not for my body but for my *self*. I mean to try. But the Hypotheticals are very powerful. And the Coryphaeus . . . the Coryphaeus is insane."

The Coryphaeus is insane.

As Treya I hadn't given the Coryphaeus much thought. Few of us did. The Coryphaeus was an abstraction, a name for the processors that quietly and invisibly mediated between Network and node. Our teachers had shown us a diagram to explain it:

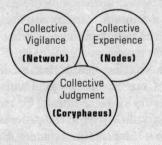

—and that was as much as we had ever wanted or needed to know. The system was stable, self-protecting, self-perpetuating, and it had worked flawlessly for five centuries. What could it mean, then, to say that the Coryphaeus had gone mad?

The problem was the Voxish prophecies. Our founders had written them into the Coryphaeus as unalterable axioms—embedded truths, permanently exempt from debate or revision. That hadn't mattered when the rapture of the Hypotheticals was a distant goal toward which we moved in gradual increments. But now we had come to the blunt end of the question. Prophecy had collided with reality, and the obvious inference—that the prophecies might have been mistaken—was a possibility the Coryphaeus was forbidden to consider.

That conflict was being played out in the surveillance and infrastructure systems that bound together our lives and our technology; it was being played out in the limbic interfaces and private emotions of everyone who wore a node. "What makes it especially dangerous," Isaac said, "is that we can't predict the result. The most likely outcome is an asymptotic trend toward self-destructive behavior in both the organic and inanimate aspects of the system." He added, "It's already happening . . . more quickly than I anticipated."

I asked him what he meant, then wished I hadn't.

"The end of Vox is days away. That means there's no need for a surplus food supply. Or surplus people, if they're not a willing part of the process." He looked away, as if he couldn't bear to meet our eyes. "The Coryphaeus is killing the last of the Farmers."

° ° °

I refused to believe it until I had seen evidence. As soon as Isaac left I rode vertical transit to one of the high towers and found a panoramic window. It was night, but the sky was unusually clear and the moon was bright on the northern horizon.

The Farmers had lived in the hollow spaces under the outlying islands of the Vox archipelago. They had numbered about thirty thousand souls before the rebellion—fewer, but at least half that many, after.

Now: none.

The out-islands were sinking. The Coryphaeus had cut them loose from the central island and opened their ancient accessways to the sea.

Any Farmers who survived the initial flooding, perhaps by climbing to the highest tiers of their enclosures, were dying as I watched. The Ross Sea drew the islands down in great upwellings of violet-colored froth. Geysers of water erupted from severed transit tunnels and ports. Cliffs of salt-encrusted granite heaved up dripping from the poisonous sea, then turned and settled beneath it forever, leaving oily residue and the tangled branches of dead forests.

I stood there for most of an hour, too shocked even to weep.

CHAPTER TWENTY-THREE

SANDRA AND BOSE

Bose took her past the place where Orrin had once rented a room. It was a five-story walk-up in a part of town you drove through with your doors locked: windows like eyes shut against the sullen indifference of the heat-stricken street, a doorway littered with broken syringes. Up in one of those rooms, Sandra thought, in the long afternoons before the night shift began, Orrin must have patiently filled his notebooks, page by page, day after day. "You think he came back here?"

"No," Bose said. "But I don't know how well Orrin knows the rest of the city. He has forty dollars in his pocket and I doubt he ever hailed a cab in his life. He's taking transit and he might have decided to stick to the route he knows."

"Route to where?"

"To the Findley warehouse," Bose said.

o   o   o

So they followed the bus routes Orrin once would have taken to work, hot streets clotted with traffic under a sky dark with thunderheads. The afternoon light was fading by the time Bose turned off into a neighborhood of single-story industrial buildings set back in lifeless yellow lawns. The buildings housed small manufacturers and regional distributors, none of which seemed especially prosperous.

Bose parked in the lot of a corner gas station with a coffee-and-doughnut shop attached to it. Sandra said, "Are we close to the warehouse?"

"Close enough."

Bose suggested coffee. The restaurant, if she could dignify it with that name, held a dozen small tables, all vacant. The windowsills were dusty and the green linoleum was peeling where the floor met the walls, but at least the place was air-conditioned. "Better get something to eat," Bose said. "We might be here a while." She ended up carrying a muffin and coffee to a corner table. From this angle she could see the street, the long row of anonymous buildings on the far side, the threatening sky. Was one of these buildings the Findley warehouse?

Bose shook his head: "The Findley warehouse is around the corner and a couple of long blocks down, but the nearest bus stop is just across the street—see it?"

A rusty transit sign bolted to a light standard, a concrete bench tagged with ancient graffiti. "Yes."

"If Orrin comes by bus, that's where he'll get off."

"So we're just going to sit here and wait for him?"

"You're going to sit here. I'm going to scout around

the neighborhood in case he got here ahead of us, though I doubt that. I don't really expect him until after dark."

"You're basing this on what, intuition?"

"Did you finish reading Orrin's document?"

"Not all of it. Not yet."

"You have it with you?"

"A printout. In my bag."

"Why don't you read the rest of it, and we'll talk about it when I get back."

She read it while Bose did his drive-around, and she was within a few pages of the end when he pulled back into the lot. He parked behind the restaurant's Dumpster where the car would be hard to see from the street—an act of prudence or paranoia, she thought. "Find anything?" she asked when he came through the door.

"Nope." He ordered another coffee and a sandwich and she heard him ask the woman behind the counter, "You mind if we sit here a while more?"

"Sit as long as you like," she said. "We do most of our business at lunch. It's mainly drive-through after three. Make yourselves comfortable. Long as you buy a little something now and then."

"There's a tip in it for you if you keep a fresh pot brewing."

"We're not allowed to accept tips for counter service."

"I'll never tell," Bose said.

The woman smiled. "Looks like the rain's starting. Good time to be indoors."

Sandra saw the first fat drops strike the restaurant window. Moments later, water was washing down the glass in quavery sheets. Rain bounced from the steaming asphalt of the parking lot, and the scent of moist, tepid air seeped under the door.

Bose peeled a layer of plastic wrap off his sandwich. "You finished Orrin's story?"

"Just about."

"You understand why I think he's headed here?"

She nodded tentatively. "Orrin—or whoever wrote this—obviously knows a few things about the Findley family. Whether they're *true* or not is a different question."

"I'm more concerned with what's going on in Orrin's head than what's true. Remember what he told Ariel? 'Tonight's the night.'"

"He has unfinished business. Or at least he thinks he does."

"Right. What he doesn't know is that Findley and his people are on high alert. There are private security cars parked all around the perimeter of the warehouse."

"Private security? What, like Brinks?"

"No, not like Brinks. These guys aren't bonded and they don't advertise."

Sandra shivered and told herself it was because of the sudden damp in the air.

Outside, in the flooding rain, a city bus pulled up. A puddle had formed around a blocked storm drain and the bus's wheels splashed the three indifferent blue-collar guys who were waiting for it. They got on. Nobody got off. The bus pulled away.

"Orrin could get hurt," she said.

"We see him, we take him back to Ariel and make

sure they both get out of town. That's the plan. If he gets past us there's really nothing we can do."

The wind picked up. There was one tree on the entire street—a spindly sapling on the lawn that hedged the sidewalk—and it bent before the storm like an arthritic pensioner. The restaurant's plate-glass windows rattled.

Sandra found her thoughts returning to the scar on Bose's body and the story of his father's death in India. "Those thieves who broke into your father's place in Madras," she said.

He gave her a startled look. "What about them?"

"What were they after?"

"Why do you want to know?"

"I'm curious." I'm entitled to be, Sandra thought.

Silence. Then: "Maybe you guessed. They were after the drugs."

"What kind of drugs?"

"The kind of drugs you seem to think they were after. Martian drugs."

"Because your father wasn't just an engineer, he was involved with Fourths."

"He despised the people who were only interested in longevity. He hated the word. He used to say it wasn't longevity that mattered, it was maturity."

"Your mother knew about this?"

"My mother was the one who recruited him."

"I see. So the scar . . ."

"What about it?"

"I didn't get out of med school without a course in anatomy. Unless the knife that cut you had a blade under an inch long, it would have damaged major organs. Not usually a survivable wound, especially if you had to wait for help."

She was so accustomed to Bose's perpetual calm that she was startled when he wouldn't meet her eyes. After a time he said, "It was my mother's decision."

Sandra had come to this surmise last night, but it was still slightly shocking to hear him admit it. "To give you the Martian treatment, you mean."

"As a last resort. For the purpose of saving my life. It was a hugely controversial decision, among the people who knew about it. But I didn't have a choice—I was comatose when it happened."

Cellular technology engineered by the Martians from samples of Hypothetical debris, grown in bioreactors and injected into his damaged body, repairing it, working in him even now . . . She recalled something he'd said just a couple of mornings ago: *Once the biotech infiltrates your cells, it's there for good. Some people find that idea abhorrent.*

This body she had touched: not wholly human.

"That's why you care so much about Findley's import business."

"Findley and the people he works for are corrupting and debasing something that might be vital to the future of all of us. They're more than ordinary criminals. They're the kind of people who'll commit murder—not for the sake of a few extra years of life, which might be understandable, but for the privilege of retailing it."

"Like the people who killed your father."

"Exactly like."

A fresh pulse of rain rattled the window. The streetlights had come on, serial halos of yellow light. Bose reached over the table to touch her hand, but she drew it away without thinking.

CHAPTER TWENTY-FOUR

TURK'S STORY

1.

Isaac Dvali visited us once more before our planned escape. As before, he screened us from the Network's embedded sensors, but I wondered whether there wasn't one surveillance device still operational—namely, my own node. If the Coryphaeus wanted to know what was happening, couldn't it just look through my eyes?

"Don't make the mistake of thinking of the Coryphaeus as a personality," Isaac said. "It isn't. And it can't do what you're suggesting."

"Still . . . it's in my head."

"Not to spy on you. Vigilance is a Network function. The Coryphaeus will try to influence your emotions and your unconscious beliefs, but it hasn't established full connectivity yet. For now it can't act except through the agency of other people. If it wants to speak to you, it will have to use someone else's voice."

"You think it might do that? Speak to me?"

"I think it will do anything in its power to keep you from leaving."

We finalized our plans, simple as they were. Allison and I would travel separately to the high tier that housed the military aircraft. We would need one of the larger vehicles to get to the Indian Ocean and past the Arch without refueling. There wouldn't be a posted guard at the aircraft bays—there was little need for guard details in a tightly Networked community—but civilians or technicians who happened to be present might try to interfere with us, especially if the Coryphaeus figured out what we were up to. Once we were aboard I would attempt to pilot our ship out of the docking bays. If we got that far, it should be possible to isolate the vehicle (and my node) from any signals originating from Vox Core.

During this time Isaac would be shielding us from the attention of the Coryphaeus. Whether he had enough influence to leverage our escape was an open question, but it might at least improve the odds.

Isaac stood up to leave. He hesitated at the door of the suite, fragile child and luminous monster in equal parts, and asked almost wistfully whether we had any more questions. I said no. Allison shook her head.

"Please be careful," he said, giving me a studying look. "The deeper the node embeds itself, the better the Coryphaeus knows you. On some level, it's already negotiating with you. Sooner or later it will offer you something you want. And you might find it hard to say no."

In the remaining hours I practiced operating Oscar's Network toys, reassuring myself that I could get the appropriate response from them at least nine times out of ten. I could already interact fairly confidently with the ordinary Networked control surfaces (video feeds, temperature controls, etc.) in the suite. A military aircraft was a vastly more complicated device, but it didn't need more from its pilot than a reliable communication of intent. I figured I was just about good enough to give it that.

I slept a few hours while Allison kept an eye on the video feeds. The murder of the Farmers had made her somber and deeply wary. Newsfeeds reported minor outbreaks of violence throughout Vox Core: A woman had committed suicide by leaping from the high wall of a housing tier. A man had stabbed his infant daughter with a kitchen knife. Waves of conflicting emotions were propagating almost too quickly for the Coryphaeus to identify and extinguish them. And there was worse news. Allison shook me awake: "You have to look at this," she said.

I followed her out of the bedroom. What she wanted to show me was fresh video from an overflight of the Hypothetical machines. As the sequence began, the Hypothetical machines were crawling through a dry glacial valley toward the shore of the Ross Sea. No doubt they were closer to us than they had been the day before, but otherwise there seemed to be nothing unusual about the image. The angle of vision altered subtly as the drone continued to circle beyond the safe limit. I wondered what I ought to be looking for—and then it was obvious. Suddenly, simultaneously, all the Hypothetical structures began to deform and dissolve.

Almost at once, there was nothing on the ground where the machines had been but a dense gray fog. The camera zoomed in until fog filled the entire screen, not fog anymore but a granular swarm of small objects. I used my Network skills to overlay a scale gauge in metric units. It told me the objects were all uniformly sized, each one a little more than a centimeter on its longest axis.

Which only confirmed what I already knew: these were the same crystalline butterflies that had swarmed the vanguard expedition in the Wilkes Basin—now in vastly greater numbers. The Hypothetical machines must have converted their entire mass into this form.

The swarm moved like a nebulous arrowhead toward the sea.

"That's how they'll come for us," Allison said. She gave me a look that meant, *We need to leave NOW.*

2.

We had decided to travel separately to the aircraft docks. Allison had worked out a route that avoided heavily populated neighborhoods, and she left the suite before corridor illumination had ramped up to full daylight. The plan was that I would wait a few minutes before I followed, keeping some physical distance between us and lulling any suspicions the Coryphaeus might have begun to harbor.

But soon after Allison left there was an alert from

the door. I opened it to find Oscar outside, smiling nervously. He said, "May I come in?" And I had to say yes.

Back on Earth—Earth the way it had been when I was growing up—I had heard about species of fish that lit up under the sea: bioluminescence, it was called. There was something like that in the way I saw Oscar's face through my Network-enhanced perception: a soft glow of euphoria, tempered by flashes of fatigue and suppressed doubt and, under all that, an indigo pulse of suspicion, regular as a heartbeat.

I was, of course, just as transparent to him. It was mood-reading, not mind-reading, but he could still catch me in a lie. I hoped any emotional turmoil I couldn't hide would look like a natural reaction to the crisis.

Oscar said, "Is Treya here?"

"No. I don't know when she'll be back."

"I'm sorry. I want to issue an invitation—to both of you. Please, come to my home, Mr. Findley. Come and bring Treya. My family is there." He was radiating a bright but shallow sincerity, the way a wood-stove radiates heat. "Five hundred years of history is reaching a climax. You shouldn't be alone when it happens."

"Thank you, Oscar, but no."

He gave me a penetrating stare. "It's too bad you didn't make the decision to join the Network sooner. You're very close, but I think you still fail to understand how lucky you are, how lucky we all are, to be alive at this moment of history."

"I do understand," I said. "And I appreciate the offer. But I'd rather face it alone."

That was a lie. Worse, it was a mistake. He *knew* it
was a lie. His suspicion flared. He said, "May I talk to
you, just for a little while?"

So I had to ask him to come in, to sit down. While
he gathered his thoughts I reminded myself that I
couldn't fool him (or the Coryphaeus) with an outright falsehood—it had been stupid to try. The best I
could do was to tell the truth, selectively.

"Some of us in the managerial class have raised
questions about you," he said at last. "When you sub-
mitted to surgery, those voices were largely silenced.
And now that we're only hours away from—*final
events,* the question is moot. But over time I've come
to think of myself as your friend." (He believed what
he was saying.) "And as your friend it's been a pleasure to watch you moving toward a real alignment
with Vox. You're almost there. It's perfectly obvious.
But you persist in hesitating, almost as if you were
frightened of us." He cocked his head. "*Are* you
frightened of us?"

The truth. "Yes," I said.

"Vox isn't just a polity. It's a state of being. You feel
that, don't you?"

He was drawing a distinction between *understanding* and *feeling,* between the fact and my experience
of it. "I do feel it," I said. Also true. I felt it because of
what was happening inside my head. The medics had
explained this to me. There was a part of the brain
called the medial prefrontal cortex, not strictly part
of the limbic system. It modulated moral judgment,

and it was the last area the node would infiltrate and manipulate. I said, "It feels like . . . well, like standing on the porch of a house on a winter night. There are people inside, and in a way they're family . . ."

Oscar liked that: he beamed and smiled.

"But I can't shake the thought that if I cross that door I won't be welcome. Because they'll know me for what I am."

"What are you?"

"Different. Foreign. Ugly. Hateful."

"Different in your history, but not in any way that matters."

"You're wrong about that, Oscar."

"Am I? You can't be sure until you let us know you."

"I don't want to be known."

"Whatever it is you're hiding from us, I promise it won't make a difference to Vox."

"What I'm saying, Oscar, is that I'm not an innocent man."

"None of us is innocent."

"I'm a murderer," I said.

All true.

The burning man in his aura of blue fire:

I killed him because I was angry, because I was humiliated, or maybe just because a storm had blown through Houston on the heels of a record heat wave. Maybe there's no point asking why.

In the dark, as oily rain sheeted off rooftops and plunged down gutters, I walked along an empty back street carrying a jug of methyl hydrate in a plastic bag. In my right pocket I had a box of matches, also wrapped in plastic, and, for insurance, a butane lighter the store clerk had told me was waterproof.

I was eighteen years old. I had taken public transit from the suburb where I lived with my parents, changing buses three times. There had been nobody on the last bus but a few sullen night-shift workers, and I hoped I looked like one more sodden and unlucky minimum-wager. The bus wound through an industrial park as grim as a prison compound. I got off and stood a moment under a bus stop sign, alone. The bus lumbered around a corner, belching diesel fumes; then the street was empty. The warehouse where my father ran his criminal enterprise was a couple of blocks away.

I didn't know much about the business except that it had been the subject of arguments between my mother and my father, as far back as I could remember. I had spent some of my childhood in Istanbul, where we lived for six years—that was why my friends called me Turk. In Istanbul, as in Houston, we had lived in a comfortable part of town while my father worked in much less desirable neighborhoods. My mother was a Louisiana Baptist by heritage and she had never gotten accustomed to the mosques, the burqas—even though Istanbul was a cosmopolitan city and we lived in a Westernized district. For a while I thought that was why they argued so often. But the arguments continued after we moved back to the States. And although they tried to keep it from me, I eventually understood that it wasn't the long hours or the foreign interludes of my father's work that upset my mother, it was the nature of the work itself.

Her shame and discomfort were expressed in small ways. She wouldn't answer the phone unless the call came from a known number. We seldom visited relatives on either side of the family, nor were we visited by them. As the years passed, my mother grew quiet, sullen, withdrawn. Once I hit adolescence I began to spend more time out of the house—as much as possible. Better the street than these drawn curtains and whispered conversations.

Maybe that makes it sound worse than it was. We were at least superficially comfortable. We had money; I went to a decent school. Furtive though my father's business might be, he was successful at it. I overheard argumentative phone calls in which he inevitably prevailed. Sometimes men in neatly pressed suits came to see him, and they spoke to him softly and deferentially. I had occasionally wondered whether my father might be a criminal, but the idea seemed ludicrous on the face of it. I guessed he might be operating on the far side of some trivial law, maybe dodging taxes or import duties, but I had learned from television and the Internet that such behavior could be lovable and even, looked at in the right light, heroic. The Spin years had taught us that when the rules break down it's root hog or die; and in those days you did what you had to do to keep a family together and food on the table.

I loved my father. I told myself so, and I believed it. It was only later that I collided with his disdain for conventional ethics, his pathological need to be obeyed.

The sluicing rain was useful cover. My father's business was housed in a building older than the Spin, a twentieth-century building with brick walls and small high windows of green leaded glass. It fronted on this dreary street, but the real work was conducted from the rear, where the loading bays were. My father had taken me here twice before, against my mother's objections, to give me a sanitized tour of the warehouse—he may have hoped to bring me into the business at some point in the future. And I had scouted the area myself just two days ago, working out a plan. I cut down a narrow passage between two adjoining buildings to the laneway at the back. Long ago, a railway spur had serviced these warehouses. The spur line had been paved over but the asphalt had scabbed away in places to reveal the old steel rails, glittering in the smoky orange light of the street lamps. The rain was coming down pretty hard but I could hear the slosh of flammable liquid in the jug I was carrying.

Last year I had fallen in love with a girl named Latisha Philips—fallen in love the way a seventeen-year-old falls in love, stupidly, wholeheartedly. Latisha was an inch taller than I was and so sweetly good-looking that I woke up most mornings afraid she'd figure out she could do better than Turk Findley. She was smart, too. If scholarship programs hadn't been cut to the bone during the post-Spin austerity drives, she might have qualified for an Ivy League college. She wanted to be a marine biologist. She wanted to save the oceans from acidification. She attended local protests against the sulfur-aerosol launches.

Her family was neither rich nor poor. They lived in a neighborhood adjoining the gated community where my father owned a house. I believe they rented. I didn't mention Latisha to my parents because I

knew my father would disapprove of her. There had
been hardscrabble Findleys in Texas and Louisiana
since before those states joined the Union, and part of
my father's legacy was a racism so offensive he had
long since learned to conceal it in polite company. Istanbul had been a particular strain for him, but he
found plenty to complain about in Houston. When
he was at home he dropped his veneer of tolerance
like a pair of tight shoes. The world was being mon-
grelized, he said, and he knew exactly who was to
blame. I didn't know whether my mother shared
these views. If so, she never spoke about them; like
me, she had learned to ignore my father's rants even
as she pretended to listen to them.

His racism was almost antiquarian, poisonous
but—so I thought—toothless. Nevertheless I wasn't
eager to introduce him to Latisha, who happened to
be black. I had already met her family. Her father was
a pharmacist; her mother had moved to Houston
from the Dominican Republic twenty years before and
currently worked at Walmart. They had always treated
me with a cautious but sincere cordiality.

I followed the old railbed until I was opposite the
loading bays at my father's warehouse. I found a dark
space between two concrete abutments and hunkered
down where I couldn't be seen, not that there was
much chance of anyone coming by. The warehouse
was closed, and although my father occasionally
stayed late to take care of unscheduled business, this
wasn't one of those nights: he had come home for
dinner and settled into the sofa with a drink in his
hand and a twenty-four-hour news channel to glower
at. The rain fell continuously and I was drenched and

shivering, although it had been a stiflingly hot day—
the rain fell from some colder, higher place than these
cloistered back alleys. I watched the warehouse at-
tentively for half an hour. From my earlier scouting
trips I had concluded that there would be no one here
after midnight but the night watchman, a skinny
drifter my father had hired from the bus depot downtown. By watching the windows I had even established his regular routine: an hourly fifteen-minute
walk-through of the upper and lower floors, the rest
of his time spent in a small room with a single frosted
and wire-reinforced window. I guessed he had a video
monitor in there, by the way the light flickered.

I had known my father would be a problem, but I
was serious about Latisha. We had even talked about
marriage. Or "elopement." Some arrangement that
would leave my father out of the loop until it was too
late for him to interfere. No fixed date because Latisha, at least, deserved a shot at whatever higher education she could afford to get. But our plans were
real. Or at least I had thought so.

Real enough that I had confided in my mother over
the kitchen table. She had listened carefully and
wordlessly. Then she sat back in her chair and said, "I
don't know what's good and what's bad anymore, if I
ever did. But if you do this, it's probably best you get
out of the house." She added, plaintively, "I would
like to meet Latisha one day. When that becomes possible. Until then I won't say anything to your father."

I'm sure she meant not to. But over the summer
something must have aroused his suspicion, I didn't
know what: an undeleted text message, a phone conversation overheard. He hadn't questioned me but he

had questioned my mother, and she caved in and told him what she knew.

My father believed in direct action. I didn't know he had done anything at all until my calls and texts to Latisha started bouncing. I went to her house but her parents wouldn't let me talk to her; they said she had decided to break off the relationship. Maybe so, but I refused to believe it until I had spoken to her myself. I kept an eye on the house but there was little sign of Latisha apart from a couple of trips out in the company of her mother.

I got a note to her through a girl she knew, enclosing a more secure IP address—I had changed it without telling my parents. That night I waited for a return message, but when it came it was abrupt and unapologetic.

> *Sorry Turk yr father talked to my father made an offer: my college tuition paid provided we break up, shitty deal but now my folks insist on it, only chance for a good school & so forth, not too proud to milk a bigot for his money etc. I would tell them go to hell but really what kind of life could we have broke and young + even tho I love you how long til we start to hate each other for what love cost us? Don't blame anyone but me I know I have a choice & Im probably making the wrong one but its my life & I have to think of the future. Crying now, pls don't write anymore.*

It was from this low brick building that my father had extracted the cash that paid for our house, our backyard pool, the clothes on my back, and the sedition and betrayal of my best hopes. Out of this warehouse and whatever business he conducted here had come my mother's chronic unhappiness and my own wholesale humiliation. That was why it had occurred to me with the force of revelation that the building ought to be burned down. For the purpose of revenge, yes, but also as a purification by fire. I had read that on the battlefield wounds were sometimes cauterized to stop uncontrollable bleeding. And I was bleeding, and this building was my wound.

Rainwater gurgled down a storm drain by my feet, stranding scraps of paper, cigarette butts, a discarded condom as pale and flaccid as a jellyfish. The night watchman worked his rounds. I could see the sway of his flashlight on the high windows as he moved from room to room. When he was (as I calculated) at the far end of the building I crossed to the loading bays and mounted a few steps to the steel door, painted military green, that was the building's back entrance. Mounted beside the door was a two-step lock: you used a physical key to uncover a numerical touchpad. I had taken the key from the top drawer of the desk in my father's home office, and I remembered the entry code from the last time he had brought me here (because it had struck me as ludicrously obvious: the year of his birth).

Whatever part of Latisha's tuition my father had arranged to pay, he probably considered it a bargain. My father was never ostentatious about his wealth but I had lived in his house long enough to overhear the occasional veiled reference to offshore holdings and IRS audits aborted by expensive lawyers. He could have sent me to Yale twice over if I had shown any aptitude for schoolwork. None of this money had been applied to the premises of the warehouse, however. The corridor inside had been overpainted with cheap yellow enamel, the floor was ocher linoleum, the ceiling lights were flyspecked fluorescent tubes. A door to the right opened into the storage and forwarding area, stairs to the left led to second-floor offices.

My plan was to douse the hallway, start the fire, pull the alarm by the exit (to give the watchman some warning), and run. Whether the fire would be quickly controlled or whether it would spread, whether the damage would be significant or just another financial nuisance for my father, whether I would be caught and punished for it or whether I would buy a ticket out of town and change my name—I didn't know, it didn't matter. My rage mattered, my humiliation mattered. So I took the jug of methyl hydrate out of the plastic bag I'd wrapped it in. I put it on the floor. I unscrewed the cap and tipped it over.

The floor had sagged over the years. The liquid puddled and spread toward the interior of the building. The reek of it was eye-wateringly sharp. It filled the crevices in the linoleum and crept steadily down the hallway, pooling here and there. There seemed to be much more of it than a two-gallon jug could possibly have contained.

I took the matchbook out of my pocket and peeled off the wrapping that had protected it from the rain. The matchbook was dry but my hand was wet and I ruined two matches before I managed to strike one into a steady flame. I wondered if the fumes in the corridor might themselves be flammable, whether I was about to be immolated by my own act of revenge. I decided I didn't care.

I was in the act of tossing the match when the door to the right opened and the night watchman stepped through.

Maybe there was a surveillance camera in the hallway, though I hadn't seen one, or maybe I had tripped a warning light in the watchman's cubby just by coming through the door. Or maybe he had left his post for the purpose of taking a piss. All I knew was that he was suddenly standing in the hallway a couple of yards away, staring at me. He was a skinny guy in jeans and a sweat-stained open-collar shirt. He had a big angular head and his hair was shaved close. He couldn't have been much older than I was. His eyes bugged out in surprise. A small river of flammable liquid forked around his old brown shoes.

He opened his mouth to say something. But I had already tossed the match. It tumbled through the air, leaving a coiled trail of smoke. I had time to take a single startled step backward. The night watchman just gawked. I don't think he understood what was about to happen.

The flames were blue and they ran along the surface of the liquid and around the rims of the watchman's shoes. Then some critical boundary between vapor and air ignited. There was a vast exhalation of hot air, and I was pushed off my feet. I turned and scuttled out the door into the gouting rain. Now the doorway was a curtain of flame and smoke, but through it I could see the watchman burning. He tried to run, and that might have saved his life, but his feet went out from under him. He did a kind of dance before he toppled into the flaming liquid. The dry flooring burned like tinder. He looked like he was screaming, but I couldn't hear anything over the rush and bite of the flames.

I thought of Allison making her way to the aircraft docks. Maybe she was there already, waiting. Waiting for me, while the rest of Vox waited for a ticket to heaven.

"You don't have to carry that weight alone," Oscar said. He sounded as indulgent and unshockable as the pastor at First Baptist, where my mother used to take me when I was a child. "We'll share it with you, Mr. Findley. The Coryphaeus will share it with you, once your interface is complete."

The limbic implant was doing its work. I was sorely tempted to accept his offer of salvation, same as I had been at First Baptist, back when my sins were trivial things. Lay your burden down, young man. Lay it at your savior's feet. Even as a child, I had understood why so many weeping souls made the journey to the altar. The Coryphaeus knew me, word and deed, inside and out. My sins were its sins.

Oscar watched me closely. "But you're still not ready to take that last step. Unconditional forgiveness from a polity of your peers . . . you want it, but you won't accept it."

A forgiveness that would last as long as it took the Hypotheticals to show up. Or had I been wrong about that, too? Maybe Vox really would be redeemed, maybe Vox would live forever. There was a presence in my head that insisted it would. I said, "I'm not sure every sin deserves to be forgiven."

"The man you killed has been dead ten thousand years. Clinging to a single tragic misjudgment is a vain and wasteful act."

"Not talking about *my* sin, necessarily."

"Oh? Whose, then?"

"It was more than murder, Oscar. The death of all those Farmers. It was an act of genocide."

Whatever Oscar saw in my face, it made him flinch. He glittered with sudden uncertainty. "The Farmers would never have been taken up by the Hypotheticals . . . their death was always inevitable."

"They were only here because Vox enslaved them and brought them here."

"*Necessity* brought them here."

"Someone made the decision."

"We all made the decision!"

"And you all forgave yourselves for it."

"The *Coryphaeus* forgave us. The Coryphaeus is our conscience."

"I don't mean to offend you, Oscar, but doesn't it seem to you that a conscience that can rationalize genocide might be defective?"

He stared at me, radiating violet spikes of anger and resentment. Then he shrugged. "You haven't lived with your node long enough. Before long you'll understand."

That's what frightens me, I thought.

"None of this matters now," he said. "Come with me."

I wanted to. All the years of my adult life I had lived in the harsh light of the burning man. I longed to let the Coryphaeus shoulder my sins. And if the price I paid was oblivion or death, maybe that was nothing but belated justice. At least I would die clean.

Did I deserve to die clean?

"I'd rather be with Allison," I said. "When the time comes."

"Then why isn't she here? I know you feel responsible for her, but she's an aberration, an empty vessel. Even her affection for you is artificial. You're Networked now—you must have seen that in her."

I didn't want to tell him what I had seen in her.

"Go on, Oscar," I said. "Go be with your family."

He started to object, then closed his mouth and nodded in resignation. Maybe he saw how deeply I envied him, and maybe he was too kind to mention it.

He stood up. "All right. Good-bye, Mr. Findley," he said.

The door closed behind him. I waited until I was sure he had cleared the corridor. I told myself it was time to go. But it would be so much easier to rest, I thought. To let what would happen, happen. It was a foolishness, a terrible vanity, this idea of escape. An insult to the millions who had already lived and died in Vox Core and to the millions more whose bright hopes were burning behind my eyes.

I took a last look around. I thought about Allison, waiting for me. Then I headed for the aircraft docks.

CHAPTER TWENTY-FIVE

SANDRA AND BOSE

Before Bose could say anything else—before Sandra could even begin to consider what he had told her—another bus pulled up at the stop across the street. She turned her head to watch.

Under the orange glare of a streetlight, the shiny-wet bus looked like a floating hallucination. Nobody got on. Two men got off. Just a couple of shift workers carrying dinner pails. The bus pulled away, and the men hurried off wherever they were going—not in the direction of the Findley warehouse.

"It's getting late," Sandra said. She wasn't ready to think about what Bose had admitted about himself, and Bose seemed willing to back away from the subject. "What if he doesn't show up?"

"I think he will," Bose said.

"Because of what he wrote?"

"Whatever else they might be, I think Orrin believes

his notebooks are prophetic. The passage about Turk Findley setting fire to the warehouse—in Orrin's mind that's not something that *did* happen, it's something that *might* happen. He wants to change the outcome."

"Obviously he knows a few things about the Findley family—if any of it's true."

"The basics weren't hard to confirm. Findley spent a few years in Istanbul. He has an eighteen-year-old son. The high school his son graduated from also has a Latisha Philips registered the same year."

"Did you talk to her?"

"No. What would I say? She's not implicated in any of this."

"Or the son?" Whose nickname, Sandra presumed, was Turk.

"Hard to do that without tipping off Findley."

"So maybe we can assume Orrin talked to the boy, or overheard something and drew his own conclusions, and he incorporated that into his story."

"Logically, yeah. He's not psychic."

"Well, he predicted the storm," Sandra said. The rain eased off every once in a while but it always came roaring back, as if half the Gulf of Mexico had levitated over the city and yielded to gravity.

"But he was wrong about other details. Orrin's document says the warehouse was empty except for the night watchman. It's not, not tonight. Also, one of the reasons Orrin was so upset when he was fired is that he thought *he* was supposed to be the watchman on duty when Turk set fire to the place."

"He was predicting his own death?"

"In a sense. But not because he wants to die. Orrin

doesn't strike me as remotely suicidal. I think he came here to prevent the thing he was predicting, whether he's the victim of it or not."

Bose sketched out the scenario for her. Orrin, working at the Findley warehouse, somehow uncovers a plan on the part of the boss's son to commit an act of arson, and he incorporates that knowledge into his ongoing notebook fantasies. The notebooks are the work of a troubled young man who happens to be smarter than anyone including his sister imagines he is, but whose grip on reality is tentative at best. Unexpectedly fired from his job, and then locked up at State, Orrin panics: he believes the time of the planned arson is close and he thinks he can stop it if he can get free. (Which was why he bit Jack Geddes during his clumsy attempt to break out, Sandra thought.) Once Bose and Sandra cut him loose, he borrows car fare from Ariel and sets out to prevent Turk Findley from committing an unforgiveable act.

Sandra thought about it. "Seems like your timeline is a little off. Orrin was fired before he could have known anything about Turk's romantic problems."

"We don't know who his source is. Maybe it was secondhand. Maybe he stayed in touch with someone at the warehouse. The pertinent passages in the document are the most recent ones, and we don't know for sure when they were written."

"Why would he even care whether Turk Findley sets fire to his father's business? Orrin already lost his job there—work that paid less than minimum wage and barely covered the rent on a flophouse room."

"I don't know," Bose admitted. "A few days ago I was hoping you could tell me."

She didn't have an answer for him, then or now. "What if the explanation is even stranger than that? I don't know. Something just . . . weird."

"Then we're still sitting here," Bose said. "Doing what we're doing."

The woman behind the restaurant counter, the one who had invited Bose to make himself comfortable, left for the day. Sandra caught a glimpse of her as she drove off in a ten-year-old blue Honda. She was replaced by a teenage boy with facial eczema and a nervous tic. The night manager poked his head out of his office a couple of times, eyeing them, until Bose got up and said something reassuring. He bought a couple of doughnuts, which neither of them touched.

The next bus arrived on schedule. The rain was still gushing down, overflowing the gutters and rinsing the street of its sheen of oil. Four people got off this time. They all looked like shift workers to Sandra. None of them was Orrin Mather. Three of them ran to the left, hurrying toward shelter. One turned right and began walking at a casual pace, as if the rain didn't concern him.

She turned away from the window but found Bose still staring intently through the glass. "What is it?"

"The young guy. The one by himself."

Young, yes. A skinny young guy wearing a black poncho and carrying something bulky in a plastic bag.

"Shit," Bose said.

She leapt to the same absurd but unavoidable conclusion: "You think it's Findley's son? You think that's Turk Findley?" The boy reached the corner and then turned south, toward the warehouse. "What do we do?"

Bose stood up abruptly. "Stay here. Keep your phone handy. Call me if you see Orrin. Or anything else I need to know about. Otherwise sit tight until you hear from me."

"Bose!" she said.

"Love you," he said, maddeningly and for the first time.

He was out the door before she could close her mouth. She watched through the window as he cut through the restaurant parking lot, keeping to a fence line parallel to the street and ignoring the rain that instantly soaked him.

The counter clerk must have noticed her startled expression. "Ma'am?" he asked helpfully. "You want a coffee or something?"

"Crazy," she said aloud.

"Ma'am?"

"Not you."

CHAPTER TWENTY-SIX

ALLISON'S STORY

1.

I waited for Turk among the aircraft on the docking level high above the city.

I had taken a twisty route to get here, up the quiet starboard terraces and along the shaded parkland corridors Treya had loved as a child. Every garden and gateway along the way was freighted with memory (*her* memory). It was hard not to grieve. Vox was dying and there was nothing I could do about it— nothing I could do for lost friends or the family that had ostracized me or the city I had once loved. Nothing except carry my memories and misgivings to a safer place, worlds away.

The aircraft bay was an open terrace, protected from the toxic atmosphere by an electrostatic roof. Voxish aircraft were aligned across this vast flat acreage as if they had been planted there, silvery crops in a mechanical garden. The maintenance and flight crews had all gone home to be with their families. My footsteps sounded like water dripping in a vacant room.

I found an inconspicuous place at the base of a light tower and sat down and waited. An uncomfortable amount of time passed. I began to think Turk might not show up. That he might have been prevented from showing up. That he might have *chosen* not to show up. The node had finally infiltrated the parts of his brain that governed love, loyalty, needs, and desires, and with every passing moment the neural webwork grew more subtle and efficient. The Coryphaeus was singing a soft, sweet refrain in the echo chamber of his medial prefrontal cortex.

What if he didn't come? But it was an easy question to answer: I would die here. In all likelihood the Hypothetical machines would dismantle and consume Vox Core the way they had dismantled and consumed the vanguard expedition out on the Antarctic plain, and that would be the end of it. I felt an uncontrollable upwelling of fear. Not the predictable fear of dying but the special and very Voxish fear of dying *alone* . . .

Then I heard a door slide open in one of the transport pods some distance away. I hid myself and waited until I was sure it was Turk. He walked out of the vertical transport stiffly, maybe reluctantly. His expression was hollow and haggard. I called his name and ran to him.

Because Vox was a peaceful and crime-free community it had little use for internal security beyond the routine vigilance of the Network. But for much of its history Vox had been at war with external powers, chiefly the bionormative communities of the Middle and Elder Worlds. Our aircraft were weapons of war, and they were secured as weapons of war.

I chose us a large but lightly armed craft of the kind used to transport weapons or troops. The entry hatch was a Network-enabled interface like the ones Turk had lately taught himself to use. When I was Treya I could have opened it effortlessly just by putting my hand against the control surface and working the options in my head. But I had lost that ability when I lost my node. As Allison, I was locked out of all but the simplest Voxish appliances and applications. The problem was that Turk was a novice, and he was obviously having a hard time focusing his intentions. He may, at this point, have been uncertain about what he really wanted. A long breathless moment passed; then the hatch slid open.

We stepped into the vehicle as the interior lights winked on. I quickly checked to see that the aircraft had its full complement of supplies, including food and water to last us through the Arch to Equatoria. The stasis lockers were stocked and complete. There were no warning lights or sounds, which meant we were good to go. Turk took a seat in the forward compartment of the aircraft. It was possible to fly the vehicle from any of its control surfaces, and you didn't need visuals to know where you were going. But Turk had been a pilot in his past life, flying by eye and hand. The first thing he did after he established an interface was to create a window display in the front wall, as if he were sitting in an old-fashioned cockpit. Suddenly I could see the wide expanse of the hangar deck in front of us—it made me feel defenseless; I would have preferred a blank wall.

But if it helped Turk, so be it. I took a seat beside him and watched the deck for any sign that we'd been noticed. Which came immediately. Yellow lights blinked on over the transit pods. Company was coming. I was surprised it hadn't come sooner, but that might have been Isaac running interference for us. "We have to leave," I said, "now." The ship's controls couldn't be overridden from outside the vehicle . . . at least I didn't think so; but if a second vehicle came after us we could theoretically be intercepted or shot down.

The aircraft didn't move. "Having a hard time keeping the menu in front of me," Turk whispered, visualizing a display I couldn't see. Sweat beaded on his forehead.

"It's just like the training interfaces. All we need is to go *up*."

Outside, the nearest transit pod slid open and disgorged a company of soldiers.

"Now, Turk. Or else we stay."

He gave me a helpless look.

I said, "I don't want to die here."

He nodded. He closed his eyes and swallowed hard. Abruptly, the deck fell away beneath us.

2.

Our aircraft pushed through the electrostatic barrier into murky daylight.

Suddenly Vox was a dark patch on the surface of the Ross Sea far below us, the scuttled islands of the

Farmers surrounding it like a sunken reef. We rose at a vertiginous speed until the sea was lost in mist, rose until we soared above a deck of clouds that ran to every horizon.

Turk confirmed our destination with the aircraft's onboard protocols and managed to lock out any signals coming from Vox. Which also isolated his node from the activity of the Coryphaeus—he shuddered once, then shook his head as if to clear it. He instructed the vehicle to alert us in the event of pursuit (there was none, probably thanks to Isaac) and sat back, drained and pale, from the control surfaces. The clouds below us looked as forbidding as a range of wild mountains.

He looked at me with his eyes narrowed. I remembered that feeling—the way Treya had felt when the Network shut down, as if all the color and sense had been drained from the world. "Promise me something," he said.

"What?"

"The thing they attached to my spine—once we get where we're going, promise you'll cut it out of me."

Solemnly, I promised I would.

Once we get where we're going. We hadn't been able to talk much about that.

Back at Vox Core I had spent a lot of time viewing material from the Voxish archives (using only manual interfaces, a slow and frustrating process) and reading the histories that had been prepared for Turk. Vox had been persecuted for centuries by jealous cortical democracies, or so I had been taught. But without the cheerleading of the Coryphaeus, those familiar stories seemed ambiguous and even disturbing. The founders of Vox had been the activist wing of a radical belief system, ostracized by the bionormative majorities of the Middle Worlds for their experiments with banned Hypothetical biotechnology. In response the founders had chosen to create their own closed polity, a limbic democracy with built-in metaphysics.

Vox must have seemed, at least at first, just a slightly more eccentric example of the many artificial island communities that grew and thrived in the oceans of Ester, a watery Middle World. The founders had abandoned experiments with Hypothetical biotech in favor of their belief in an eventual human-Hypothetical union, which was why they made saints of everyone who had ever been touched by the Hypotheticals—beginning with Jason Lawton at the dawn of the Spin era and including countless longevity cultists, ancient Martian Fourths, and the reckless or unlucky souls who had been taken up by temporal Arches.

The bionormative majority was the recurring villain in Voxish history. Ester had banned limbic neural collectives soon after the tragedies of Hyum and Loi, and Vox had been forced to raise anchor and set off on its centuries-long pilgrimage to Old Earth. But today, on most planets up the Ring—Ester and Cloud Harbor, especially—the cortical democracies were still thriving. *Once we get where we're going* meant, in the long term, one of those prosperous, peaceful Middle Worlds.

I thought about that after sunset, as we traveled north. Turk ate listlessly, alternating his gaze between the barren moon above and the toxic clouds below.

His mind had wandered to old griefs. He said, "We fucked up this planet pretty good, didn't we?"

"Depends on what you mean by 'we.'"

"People in general. I guess, my generation in particular."

The view from the forward cabin was ample testimony to human failure. The clouds were oddly beautiful, but the moonlight that reflected from them was tinted a poisonous green. "Maybe so," I said. "But that's not the end of the story. What was the population of Earth when you left it? Six, seven billion people?"

"Something like that."

"But we don't just live on Earth anymore. We live on all the worlds of the Ring. You know how many people are alive in the Ring of Worlds right now? Almost *fifty* billion. And that's not a toxic bloom, like the population on Old Earth. That's fifty billion people living in a sustainable relationship with their environment—fifty billion reasonably happy human beings. We're not a failed species. We're a success story."

"That's what Vox was running from? A success story?"

"Well, Vox . . . Vox wasn't running away from the Middle Worlds. It was running toward the Hypotheticals."

"It wasn't the Hypotheticals who nuked Vox Core."

"The Middle Worlds aren't paradise. People are still people—greedy and shortsighted, often enough. But they've learned how to make better decisions."

"By putting wires in their heads?"

His hand stroked the lump at the back of his skull,

perhaps unconsciously. "Not exactly," I said. But it wasn't the concept of cortical democracy he was struggling with. "Turk—did something happen? After I left you, before you came up to the aircraft docks . . ."

"No . . . nothing important."

I didn't need to be Networked to know that for a lie. "Do you want to tell me about it?"

"Not now," he said. "Maybe when we get where we're going."

We were still a couple of hours away from the Indian Ocean when the aircraft's alarm sounded.

I had been asleep. Turk had insisted on standing watch in the forward compartment—he didn't trust the ship to pilot itself without supervision—but I was too exhausted to keep him company. So I had crawled into a crew cot and closed my eyes, and when I opened them again the alarm was chiming.

I hurried forward. Turk had already synced himself up with the ship's interface, and by the frustrated look on his face I could tell he was having trouble working the controls. The wall was still a window; the moon had set; the sky was dark except for the high tip of the Arch, close to zenith now, reflecting a reddish glow that in another couple of hours would be our sunrise.

I put my hand on his shoulder. He looked up and said, "I've got a warning display but I don't know how to read it."

"Okay. Can you put it into the wall so I can see it too?"

He managed to do that. The display appeared superimposed on the night sky. It was a radar signature with tracking details. Turk said, "It's seeing something, but I can't read range or trajectory."

Were we being chased? But no: the object the ship had detected was high and to the northeast. I said, "The ship pinged us because there shouldn't be anything in that airspace. Whatever it is, it looks like it's not on a controlled course. It's ballistic."

It was falling, in other words. Probably a natural phenomenon, some piece of ancient debris tumbling out of orbit. But then the alarm chimed and chimed again, and two more targets popped up on the display.

By the end of an hour we had detected five such falling objects, all traveling east to west and roughly parallel to the equator. They were impacting close enough to our charted course that Turk instructed the aircraft to hold and circle until we could figure out what was going on. There was a lull of twenty minutes or so, then the alarm chimed yet again. According to the vector display it had detected an even bigger target this time, maybe big enough to be visible to the naked eye. Turk instructed the ship to aim its window at the appropriate quadrant of the sky.

We looked out into darkness, a few stars beginning to dim behind the first light of the dawn. *"There,"* Turk said.

The object streaked across the horizon a couple of degrees above the cloud deck. It was as bright as burning phosphorous and it left a luminous trail that quickly faded. The glare of it tracked across the cloudscape and made hectic, moving shadows. Once it had passed out of sight darkness fell again, but only briefly. The next burst of light came from beyond the horizon. That was the impact.

"Ask the ship to calculate its trajectory backward," I said. "See where it came from."

Easier said than done, with only a rough estimate of the object's size and mass to work with. But the ship calculated a cone of possible trajectories and matched it against the other objects it had monitored, then superimposed the likely paths. The result was inconclusive, but Turk saw what I saw: the most likely trajectories all intersected at the Arch of the Hypotheticals.

"What's that mean?" Turk asked.

I didn't know. But the sun was coming up and the nearest leg of the Arch would soon be visible from where we hovered. Turk aimed the window so we could see it.

The Arch of the Hypotheticals had been and would forever be the largest artificial structure ever to contact the surface of the Earth. Its apex was higher than the atmosphere and the base of it was embedded deep in the planet's mantle. It straddled the Indian Ocean like a wedding band dropped edge-up into a shallow pond. The fraction of it we could see from where we circled above the clouds looked like a silver thread laced into the yellow fabric of the dawn. "Focus on the peak of it," I told Turk, "and amplify the image."

He struggled with the interface but eventually succeeded. Because he had configured the display as a window, we seemed to zoom suddenly and dangerously close to the upper reaches of the Arch. The image wavered, distorted by the intervening atmosphere; then the one-dimensional thread acquired width and became a ribbon. In reality it was many miles wide.

The most detailed telescopic images of the Arch, beginning back in Turk's day, had never revealed even the slightest imperfection in its surface. Until now. Now the ribbon was visibly flawed. The smoothly curving edge of it was ragged and sawtoothed. "Amplify it another times-ten," I said, though we were approaching the limits of the aircraft's optical functions.

Another vertiginous leap forward. The image writhed and twisted until the ship applied corrective algorithms.

And I gasped. The Arch was worse than merely imperfect. Visible cracks ran across it. There were gaps where immense pieces of it had calved away.

That was what had been coming out the sky: pieces of the Arch the size of small islands, some of them moving at only a little less than orbital velocity, burning on re-entry and spending their enormous kinetic energy in the Earth's dead oceans or on its lifeless continents.

It should have been impossible. But it happened again as we watched. A dark crack widened and expanded and intersected another, and suddenly a piece of the Arch separated and began to fall. It moved with the elephantine grace of its own inertia, and I guessed it might circle the planet a couple more times before it began its final burn and tumble.

I looked at Turk, he looked at me. We didn't have to say anything. We both knew what it meant. It meant the door to Equatoria had been closed forever. It meant our plan had failed. It meant we had nowhere to go.

CHAPTER TWENTY-SEVEN

SANDRA AND BOSE

Bose followed a line of hedges down the street, keeping low and hoping the rain would help disguise his presence. The kid with the plastic bag—Turk, presumably—strode down the sidewalk, out in the open and half a block ahead. Another couple of yards and he'd be within sight of one of the guard cars Bose had identified earlier, an anonymous-looking gray vehicle with two sullen and undoubtedly well-armed men inside it.

Bose recognized the moment the kid spotted the car by the hitch in his step, a momentary hesitation you'd never notice if you weren't looking for it. The kid gave no other indication. He kept walking, head down, rain running off his poncho. He walked straight past the car. The guards inside watched as he passed, their heads turning in unison as if they were attached to a string.

A left turn would have taken the kid down another block to the front entrance of the Findley warehouse, but he kept on going, sensibly. Bose took the opportunity to cut through the weedy lot in back of an industrial building, which shielded him from the guard car but also cut off his view of Turk. The rain was coming down so hard it felt like brusque hands trying to get his attention. His shoes were already saturated. At the next corner he caught sight of the kid again, still kept walking in the same direction, well past the warehouse now. *Just keep on going,* he thought. *Catch another bus. Make my life easier.*

But the kid turned left. He was circling the warehouse from a distance, Bose realized, looking for a way past the cordon.

Bose tried to put himself inside the kid's head, on the assumption that this really was Turk Findley, more or less as described in Orrin's notebook. It wasn't easy. Bose had worshipped his own father. Patricide—even symbolic patricide—was a foreign concept to him.

But he understood rage and impotence well enough. It was what he had felt when the thieves had broken down the door and come into his father's home in Madras. Bose's father had sent him to hide under the desk in his room, and Bose had stayed there, dutifully, his heart beating madly in his chest, his lungs starved for air because he kept trying to hold his breath. "I'll deal with this," his father had said, and Bose had believed him. He didn't come out until he heard his father's first and final scream. Which was followed, soon enough, by his own.

His father hadn't taken the Fourth treatment himself, though he had facilitated the treatment for many others. He had still been in the broad midstream of his life, not yet ready to assume the duties and obligations of longevity. Bose's mother had been less scrupulous: she arranged the treatment as a life-saving intervention for Bose himself. Bose was far too young for it, but Martian ethics made an exception for life-or-death cases. Typically, she had administered the treatment first and asked for her colleagues' approval only later. Bose had never been as grateful as he knew he should have been; often, when the memories of the Madras attack came back to torment him, he thought it wouldn't have been so bad if she had just let him die.

The kid in the rain kept walking at a steady pace. He passed a second guard car. The perimeter was even better defended than it had been when Bose did his first drive-around, hours earlier. So what was going on at the warehouse that required all this security? He guessed Findley had been alarmed by the news that Orrin had escaped from State Care. Probably he was afraid some federal agency might issue a warrant for the premises. But what he was doing to counter that threat remained an open question.

Bose hoped Turk would simply give up and go home; failing that, Bose might have to intercept him and warn him away. Too much time was passing and he still had Orrin Mather to worry about. He sped up a little, avoiding streetlights and keeping to the Dumpster-and-delivery lanes whenever possible.

The next time he came within sight of Turk the kid was only a dozen yards away, standing still. He was south of the Findley warehouse by a couple of blocks and there were no guards in sight. Bose ducked back as the kid surveyed the street in both directions, seeing nothing but locked doors, shabby sidewalks, the endlessly falling rain. The kid was nervous, shifting the heavy plastic bag he carried from hand to hand. Bose was about to step out, either to confront him or to scare him off, when the kid suddenly turned left, cradling the bag in his arms, and ran between two darkened buildings.

Shit, Bose thought. He followed quickly but cautiously, hoping the kid wouldn't be spotted and get them both killed.

But the kid was quick and, at least in the tactical sense, smart. He knew the neighborhood was riddled with alleys and laneways, many of them poorly lit, and he managed to make his way undetected to the street on which the warehouse had its front entrance. That street was well watched, but Turk sidled up between two empty parked cars, dashed across the open space in a particularly heavy gust of rain, and made it unseen to the mouth of another alley. It wasn't the front of the warehouse Turk wanted access to, Bose surmised. It was the back lane with the loading bays. Just like in Orrin's story.

Bose followed along the same route, feeling absurdly conspicuous. He reminded himself that his only objective was to keep the kid from making a huge mistake and getting himself or someone else hurt. The problem was, any attempt he made to approach Turk at this point might startle him into unpredictable action. Nevertheless, he had to make contact.

He was weaponless but he brought some skills of his own to the situation. Unlike the hacked pharmaceuticals the longevity-sellers traded in, the Martian treatment suppressed and enhanced certain neurological functions. It suppressed spontaneous aggression, which meant Bose was what people called "slow to anger." It enhanced empathy and it suppressed fear. It also improved visual acuity and reaction time, which had helped gain Bose his police academy reputation as a first-rate sharpshooter.

Turk moved up the laneway to the place where it intersected the alley behind the warehouse. He crouched down, almost invisible in his black poncho, darting his head out to see what was happening. Bose used the opportunity to move up behind him.

Now or never. "Hey," he said, keeping his voice low but just loud enough to be heard over the rattle of the rain.

The kid jerked out of his crouch and whirled around. Bose held his hands out, palms up. "I'm unarmed," he said, taking a couple of steps closer. "And I'm not one of *them*."

"Who are you, then?" the kid managed. He had the jug of methyl hydrate in his right hand, holding it so he could swing it like a mace.

"I used to be a cop," Bose said. "You're Turk Findley, right? The owner's son?" The kid said nothing, but his unsurprised silence served as confirmation. "All I want," Bose said, "is for us both to turn around and get out of here. Whatever you're thinking of doing, it's not practical. Not tonight."

Rain guttered down from the kid's sodden black

hair into the collar of his poncho. He looked at Bose through the downpour. Then he said in a small, flat voice, "Behind you."

"What?"

"They're behind you."

The kid crouched down hastily. So did Bose. He risked a look back. There were two men coming up the alley, wraithlike in the rain. They hadn't seen Bose or Turk yet—the angle of the wall had hidden them— but unless they turned around they surely would.

Turk seemed reassured by Bose's reaction. "This way," he said.

Bose had no choice but to follow him around the corner into the back lane, where they would almost certainly be spotted . . . but no, there was a narrow gap between a green steel Dumpster and the ledge of a loading bay, just big enough for the two of them to squeeze into. Bose tried to get a good look around during the brief moment he was exposed. The bays of the Findley warehouse were half a block to his left. Three cars were parked in the alley and a white un- marked van had pulled up to one of the bays. The loading bay door had been rolled up, spilling a rect- angle of light into the darkness. Bose tried to fix the scene in his mind, calculating relative distances and possible avenues of escape. Then he hunkered down next to Turk, who was shaking like a wet dog.

The two guards came up the alley and into the open. Bose caught a glimpse of their yellow rain jackets as they passed the Dumpster, heading back to the open loading dock. The presence of the van explained what was going on at the warehouse, Bose thought. Findley had gotten nervous and was cleansing the building of contraband. There were boxes stacked floor to ceiling in the back of the van—probably chemicals from Lebanon or Syria, bound for black-market bioreactors.

Bose decided he needed a better look. He went from a crouch to a kneeling position and then down onto his belly. The asphalt under him was wet but still warm from the heat of the day; it smelled like some kind of oil-drenched animal. He snaked forward and peered past the rim of the Dumpster. All he had for camouflage was his dark hair and dark skin.

He got a good look at the man supervising the loading, a middle-aged man with a haggard expression and a flashlight in his hand. Bose recognized him as the elder Findley. "Your father's here," he whispered.

After a pause the kid said, "You know my father?"

"I know him when I see him."

"Are you going to arrest him?"

"I wish I could. But I'm not a cop anymore. I can't arrest anybody."

"Then what are you *doing* here?"

"Helping out a friend. What are *you* doing here?"

No answer.

Bose was about to suggest that they attempt to head back the way they had come—dangerous though that might be—when a fourth car pulled up by the van. The driver got out and climbed onto the concrete loading bay and approached Findley, who gave him a *what now?* look. The driver said something inaudible, pointing back down the alley. Suddenly Findley clapped his hands and began to shout loud enough to be heard over the rattle of the rain, telling the loading crew to finish up and pull in the security perimeter.

Bose checked his watch. The next bus was past due: it would have arrived minutes ago. *Orrin,* he thought. His best guess was that one of Findley's security men had spotted Orrin Mather and brought the matter to the boss's attention.

The elder Findley climbed into a car with one of his security guys. The car rolled down the laneway, its wheels splashing Bose and Turk where they crouched in the shadows. Bose saw Turk blinking at the ripples left by the car in the pavement's skin of rainwater, aware that his father had passed within a few feet of him. Much of the rage that had carried him here seemed to have collapsed into confusion.

More footsteps down the alley behind them: the lookouts had been called in.

"We need to get out of here," Bose said. He added, "We might need a distraction."

The kid turned up a near-tearful face. "What are you talking about? What distraction?"

Bose said, "You happen to be carrying anything flammable?"

CHAPTER TWENTY-EIGHT

ALLISON'S STORY

Our aircraft could have flown days more without exhausting its supply of fuel, but there was no point in circling aimlessly. Turk found a small, steep island off the southern flank of what had once been the Indonesian archipelago and landed us there. The island was far enough south to be out of range of the falling fragments of the Arch and high enough to protect us from any resulting tsunami. The aircraft came to ground on a fairly gentle slope. The land around us was as blank and poisoned as any other part of the planet, but we could see the ocean to the southwest of us. We could have left the ship and gone outside— there were masks and protective gear in the storage lockers—but there was no reason to do so and it might have been dangerous to attempt it: gale-force winds were blowing steadily, maybe as a result of the monstrous impacts farther north.

We discussed the possibility that the Arch might still be functional, that even in its fractured condition it might still be able to detect Turk and allow us passage to Equatoria. That was almost certainly wishful thinking, however, and it would have been insanely risky to try an approach. As soon as we had landed, the ship detected two more fragments inbound from orbit. We couldn't see them through the cloud deck, but the impacts created a shock wave that rattled the vessel's hull even these many hundreds of miles away. An hour later the sea receded from the shore of the island, revealing ancient dead corals and black sand, then came rushing back in a surge that would have been catastrophic had there been any living thing in the path of it.

We could go back to Vox, I pointed out. The aircraft would do that anyway, automatically, once its fuel supply was nearly exhausted.

"There might be nothing left of Vox," Turk said. The Hypothetical machines would have reached it by now.

Maybe. Probably. But we didn't know what had caused the Arch to fail—maybe the same thing was happening to the Hypothetical machines; maybe they were disintegrating at the shore of the Ross Sea. If Vox was intact, it would still be capable of harvesting enough protein from the ocean's bacterial blooms to support a small population.

"In that case they'll be fighting each other for food," Turk said. "And if *all* the Hypothetical mechanisms are breaking down, that's still not good news."

He was right, of course. The one Hypothetical technology we all took for granted was the intangible barrier that protected Earth from her swollen, aging sun. If that failed, the oceans would boil, the atmosphere would cook off into space, and Vox would end up as a dispersed cloud of superheated molecules.

But I was still in favor of heading for Vox Core when the time came. It was where (as Treya) I had been born. It would be a suitable place to die.

That night we witnessed the biggest impact yet. The ship alerted us to a large incoming object, and Turk adjusted the window so we could monitor the northwest quadrant of the sky. Despite the heavy cloud cover we could see the fireball as a moving blur of red light, followed by a sunset glow on the horizon. A substantial shock wave was inevitable, so we instructed the ship to anchor itself to the island by means of high-tensile cables fired into the bedrock.

The shock arrived as a solid wall of wind and hot rain. Our aircraft was pressure-tight and well anchored, but I could hear it straining against its cables—an agonized groaning, as if the Earth itself were in pain.

I went to bed when the winds had calmed some, and that night I dreamed of Champlain—Allison's Champlain. In my dream I walked Allison's streets and I shopped at the mall where Allison had shopped and I made conversation with Allison's mother and Allison's father. All this seemed intimately real, but it took place in a world drained of color and texture. Allison's mother served chicken pot pie and baked beans for dinner and I was Allison and I loved chicken pot pie, but the meal she put in front of me was indistinct, a diagram of itself, and it tasted of nothing at all.

Because these weren't really memories. They were details extracted from a dead woman's diaries. I had learned a lot about myself and the world I lived in by masquerading as Allison, but in truth I had never stopped being Treya. Oscar had been right about that. Allison was simply the tool I had used to pry Treya away from the tyranny of Vox. For whatever that was now worth.

I climbed out of my cot and went forward. Turk was still awake, keeping a pointless vigil. The wind continued to rage but had lost some of its ferocity. According to our sensors, the rain beating against the hull was as hot as steam.

I told Turk about my dream and what it meant. I told him I was tired of pretending to be Allison. I didn't have a name worth wearing, I told him. I was going to die on an empty planet, and nobody would know who I was or had been.

He said, "I know who you are."

We sat together on a bench opposite the window-wall. He put his arms around me and held me until I was calm.

That was when he told me what had happened back at Vox Core before we escaped. He said he had talked to Oscar and, through Oscar, to the Coryphaeus. He had confessed a truth about himself.

"What truth?"

I thought I knew the answer. I thought he meant the truth he had been evading ever since we had plucked him out of the Equatorian desert, the terrible and obvious truth about himself.

But he told me a different story. He told me how he'd killed someone, back when he was a young man on the living Earth. He spoke stiffly and with a grim restraint, his face turned away and his fists clenched. I listened carefully and let him finish.

Maybe he didn't want me to say anything in response. Maybe silence would have served him better. But there was no real future ahead of us now and I didn't want to die with an important truth unspoken.

After he had composed himself I said, "Can I tell you a story in return?"

"I don't see why not."

"This is an Allison story," I said. "It happened back on Old Earth. Otherwise it's not much like your story at all. But it's something that weighed on her conscience for a long time."

He nodded, waited.

I said, "Allison's father was a soldier as a young man. He served overseas in the years before the Spin. He was forty years old when Allison was born, fifty the year she turned ten. On her tenth birthday, he gave her a present—a painting in a cheap wooden frame. She was disappointed when she unwrapped it—what had made him think she wanted an amateur oil-color portrait of a woman holding a baby? Then he told her, almost bashfully, that he'd painted it himself. He'd done it a few years ago, working nights in his study. He said the woman in the picture was Allison's mother and the child was Allison herself. Allison was surprised, because her father had never seemed artistic—he made a living managing a shoe store in a strip mall, and she'd never heard him mention literature or art. But having a baby daughter, he explained, was the best thing that had ever happened to him, and he had wanted to remember that feeling, so he'd made the painting to remind himself of it. Now he wanted Allison to have it. So Allison decided it was a pretty good gift after all, maybe the best she'd ever gotten.

"Eight years later he was diagnosed with lung cancer—no big surprise; he'd been a pack-a-day smoker since he was twelve years old. And for a few months he tried to behave as if nothing was wrong. But he got steadily weaker, and eventually he was spending most of the day in bed. When it got to be too hard for Allison's mother to look after him—when he couldn't eat, when he couldn't get up even to use the bathroom—he had to go to the hospital, and by then Allison understood he wouldn't be coming home. He was in for what they called palliative care. Basically, the doctors were helping him die. They gave him drugs for the pain, more every day, but he was pretty clear-headed up until the last week, although he cried a lot—the doctors said he was 'emotionally labile.' And one day when Allison was visiting he asked her to bring him that painting, so he could look at it and call back the old memories.

"But she couldn't do it. She didn't have the painting anymore. At first she had hung it on the wall above the headboard of her bed, but at some point it had begun to embarrass her—it seemed crude and sentimental, and she didn't want her friends to see it, so she put it in her closet, out of sight. If her father noticed, he never said a word. Then one day when she was cleaning out her old stuff—her baby things, dolls and toys she was never going to touch again—she put the painting in a box along with everything else and carried it down to the Goodwill store as a donation.

"But she couldn't bring herself to admit that, not

when her father was gaunt and yellow and breathing with the help of an oxygen tank. So she nodded and said she'd bring the painting next time she came to the hospital.

"Back home, she went through her closet as if she expected to find the painting still there, knowing all the time it was gone. She even went to the thrift shop and asked about it, but the painting must have been sold or recycled long since. So when she came to the hospital the next day her father was disappointed, and she made some excuse and promised she'd remember to bring it tomorrow, a lie that only compounded her shame. And she came back to the hospital room every day, day after day, and every day he was weaker and more frightened, and every day he asked about the painting, and every day she promised she'd bring it to him. Of course he died without seeing it."

There was no sound but the groaning of the ship's hull. Fragments of the Arch were coming in more often now, their radar tracks rolling across the display like bright blue raindrops. Turk was quiet for a long time. Finally he said, "That's Allison's grief—the original Allison. She lived and died with it. You don't need to carry it for her."

"No more than you need to carry the burden of that old killing."

"You don't see any difference?"

He was still avoiding the truth and he had missed the point of my story. So I tried to lead him to it more bluntly:

"Think about that temporal Arch, back in the Equatorian desert. It's not like the Arches that connect the worlds—the temporal Arches were never meant for human beings. They're a device the Hypotheticals use to preserve information over time. Preserve it by duplicating it. The Hypotheticals *took* you and they *remembered* you and eventually they *re-created* you, and that means the *real* Turk Findley is as dead and long-gone as the real Allison Pearl. You're a convincing replica, but you were born in a desert with another man's memories—you're no more responsible for that man's sins than I am for Allison's."

Turk stared at me. For a moment he looked violently angry. And for a moment I was afraid of him.

Then he stood and walked into the aft section of the aircraft, down among the shadows, leaving me alone with the roaring of the storm.

Debris impacts began to diminish over the following days, and after a week the ship's radar registered nothing above the atmosphere but a scattering of dust and fragments. All that remained of the Arch on Earth were two fractured stumps projecting from the Indian Ocean, the tallest rising five thousand feet above sea level. The Earth was entirely isolated now—as alone in the universe as it had been in the long millennia before the Spin.

Turk and I didn't talk about what we had said to each other that difficult night. Instead we took solace from simple words and simple warmth. We may have been false and inauthentic things, but at least we understood each other. Each of us made a presence for the other's vacancy. We tried to pretend time wasn't passing.

But it was. The ship's stores began to run low. And when it was impossible to delay any longer, Turk unmoored us from our rocky island and took us up above the highest clouds, up where we could see the stars.

I didn't want to stop there. I wanted to go where our airship couldn't take us. I wanted to range out among those distant suns and worlds. I wanted to take giant steps from star to star, the way the Hypotheticals did.

Of course I couldn't. We couldn't even go home. We had no home. All we had was Vox, if there was still a Vox. So we flew south, dawn to starboard and the ruins of history behind us and nothing ahead but strangeness and faint hope.

CHAPTER TWENTY-NINE

SANDRA AND BOSE

The minutes tracked past like boxcars in an endless train as Sandra sat at the restaurant window, waiting for Bose. Fifteen minutes. Then thirty. Then forty. *We're doing this insane thing,* she thought, *and now it's going wrong.* Outside, the storm eased and then gathered strength again. It was the price paid for all those weeks of remorseless dry heat, a terrible karmic balance being struck.

Across the street, a bus pulled up. It idled briefly, then cleared its throat and ambled off into the sheeting dark. At first Sandra thought no one had gotten off. Then she saw the figure standing outside the halo of the streetlight, dressed stupidly for the weather: a yellow short-sleeved shirt that stuck to his skin like a coat of paint. A skinny kid, all ribs. It was Orrin, of course.

She stood up without thinking and ran from the

restaurant, the counter clerk calling after her in alarm: *Ma'am? Ma'am?*

"Dr. Cole," Orrin said when she reached him. He didn't seem surprised to see her. His expression was mournful. "I got lost," he confessed. "I should have been here before now. I guess you know I mean to stop Turk Findley from doing what he means to do." His lip trembled. "But I think I'm too late."

"No, Orrin, listen, it's all right." The rain had gone through her clothes as if they didn't exist, and she hugged herself to keep from shivering. "I understand. Turk got here a little while ago, but Officer Bose went after him."

Orrin blinked. "Officer Bose is with him?"

"Officer Bose won't let him set that fire."

"You mean that?"

"It's the absolute truth. He ought to be back any minute."

Orrin's shoulders slumped with relief. "I thank you for coming here," he said, his voice barely audible over the hammering of the rain. "I really do. I suppose you read what I wrote in my notebooks?"

Sandra nodded.

"It's not happening the way it did. But I guess that's to be expected."

"How do you mean?"

"It's not just one thing," he said solemnly. "It's the sum of all paths."

Sandra wanted to ask what he was talking about, but not while they were standing exposed at the bus stop. "Come across the street with me, Orrin. We'll wait for Bose over there. He won't be long."

"I would like a cup of coffee," Orrin said.

Sandra turned, but drew back before she could step off the curb. A car pulled up, blocking her path. The passenger-side window rolled down and Sandra could see two men inside. The passenger was a middle-aged man, smiling tightly. The driver had a gun held loosely across his thigh.

"Hello, Dr. Cole," the passenger said. "Hello, Orrin."

Sandra recognized the voice. She felt numb. She wanted to run but she couldn't take her eyes from the car. She felt rooted in place.

"Hello, Mr. Findley," Orrin said sadly.

"I'm sorry to see you here, Orrin. That's not good news for either of us. Why don't you and Dr. Cole get in back, so we can talk."

The driver kept his engine idling but didn't drive away. Sandra prayed he wouldn't. As long as she was within sight of this ugly road, the bus stop, the coffee shop across the street with its yellow lighted windows, it was possible to believe she might still get away unhurt. But if the car began to move it would carry her out of the familiar world, into that unlit land where unspeakable things happen.

She knew about the unlit land. Often enough, at State, she had interviewed candidates who had been routinely beaten, abused, abandoned, or degraded. They were refugees from the land of unspeakable things, and through their eyes she had begun to sense the vastness and emptiness of its geography.

Findley looked at her from the front seat, his face lined and pockmarked, his eyes deceptively mild.

"First things first," he said. "One of you is missing. What happened to Officer Bose, Dr. Cole?"

She doubted she could have answered even had she wanted to. All the moisture in her mouth had dried up. The world was drenched in rain, and she couldn't even spit.

"Come on," Findley said impatiently.

She managed, "I don't know."

"Please."

"He's not with me. I don't know where he is."

Findley sighed. "You should have accepted the offer I made you, Dr. Cole. It was perfectly authentic. A second life for your brother, in exchange for nothing important. There was no downside to it. It was generous. You were stupid." He paused. "Over there across the street, parked in back, that's Bose's car. So where is he, Dr. Cole?"

She closed her mouth firmly and shook her head.

The driver—the gunman—turned in his seat to look at her. He didn't look like a criminal, Sandra thought. His face wasn't unpleasant. He looked like a high school English teacher, tired after a long day.

He showed her the gun. She didn't know anything about guns and she couldn't say what kind it was. It was as if he was saying, "Here is the source of my power over you." As if he wanted her to acknowledge and understand it. Then he struck her in the face with the grip clenched in his fist.

The blow glanced off her cheekbone and loosened a tooth. The pain was literally sickening. She wanted to vomit. Her eyes clenched shut and she felt tears leaking out of them.

"Don't do that," Orrin said.

Findley turned to face him. "Look at all this trouble you caused, Orrin. And why? What did I ever do to you but take you off the street and give you respectable work?"

"None of this is my fault, Mr. Findley."

"Whose fault is it, then? Tell me."

"Your own, I guess," Orrin said.

The gunman jacked his seat back so he could reach Orrin, but Findley raised a hand to stop him. Sandra watched through slit eyes, one hand clamped over her bleeding mouth. Everything looked watery, as if the rain had come inside the car.

"How do you figure that?" Findley asked.

"Your own son hates you," Orrin said calmly.

Findley reddened. "My *son*? What do you know about my family?"

"You shouldn't have done what you did about his friend Latisha. I don't believe he'll ever forgive you for that."

"Who have you been talking to?"

Orrin closed his mouth and looked away. Sandra cringed, waiting for the inevitable blow.

But the gunman was looking past her, down the street. He said, "Here it comes now, Mr. Findley."

Sandra risked a look. What was coming was a plain white van. Sandra couldn't begin to guess at its significance, but Findley was pleased to see it. He waved at the driver of the van as it passed. "All right then," he said. "We might as well get moving." *Into the land of unspeakable things.*

"One more chance to tell me about Bose," Findley

said. Sandra glanced at the gunman, who smiled hor-
ribly.

Orrin watched the van pull ahead. "Mr. Findley?"

"What do you imagine you have to say, Orrin?"

"Mr. Findley, I believe that truck's on fire."

Yellow flame guttered out of the van's loosely chained
rear doors. Smoke, too, though rain and mist concealed it. The driver of the van apparently hadn't yet
noticed.

Then something inside ignited with a visceral
thump. The rear doors flew open, feeding air to a
sudden inferno. The van swerved and came up hard
against the curb. Two men tumbled out of the cab,
looked back in horror, then ran into the darkness.

Findley and the gunman were still staring when
Bose's car barrelled out of the coffee shop parking
lot. Findley saw it first: "Go! *Drive* for fuck's sake!"
he shouted; but Bose braked directly in front of the
car, blocking it. The gunman put the car into reverse
but succeeded only in ramming his rear bumper into
the concrete bus bench. His last recourse was the
weapon in his hand. He raised the pistol, looking for
a target. Findley was still shouting, pointlessly.

Sandra saw Orrin lunge forward and grab the gunman's right arm. Orrin who wouldn't so much as step
on a bug, Sandra thought. Unless he was provoked.
He had wrenched the gun to a vertical angle when it
went off. The bullet cut a flanged hole in the roof of
the car, allowing in a fine spray of rain. Findley jerked
open the passenger-side door and threw himself out,

landing and rolling on the wet street. Sandra realized she should do the same. But she couldn't bring herself to move. She had become a still point around which the universe was revolving. Her body was leaden and her ears were ringing.

She wanted to help Orrin, who had one knee braced against the back of the driver's seat and was struggling to leverage the gunman's arm backward. The pistol looped around like a rattlesnake looking for something to bite. Orrin grunted and redoubled his effort, clutching the gunman's arm and pumping with both feet. The pistol went off again.

Then Bose pulled open the driver's-side door. He moved with a speed that took Sandra by surprise. His Fourth reflexes, maybe. He reached in and gripped the gunman's arm just as Orrin fell back, exhausted, letting it loose. Bose took the gun away and tucked it into his belt. He pulled out the gunman, who crouched in a pool of ponded rainwater like a cornered animal, clutching his wrist, teeth bared, looking at Bose and at the gun. Then he turned and ran. Bose let him go.

The burning van was the brightest light on the block, casting long and hectic shadows down the slick street. Sandra looked over at Orrin, who was slumped against the seat. He turned up his face, wincing with pain. "I'm all right, Dr. Cole," he said. But he wasn't. The second shot from the pistol had cut across his shoulder, furrowing a wound. Sandra looked at it professionally, as if she had been transported from this madness back to her internship. The med school basics. Apply pressure. The wound was bleeding, but not too badly.

She guided him out of Findley's car and into Bose's.

When she straightened up Bose put a hand on her arm to keep her still and examined her face where the gunman had hurt her. She said, "It looks worse than it is," then contradicted herself by spitting a wad of blood onto the wet sidewalk.

"We need to get away from here," Bose said.

Findley stood in the road, staring at a figure across the street.

The figure was his son, Turk. Sandra imagined she could see waves of surmise and dismay working their way into Findley's shocked consciousness.

"He knows what you are," she said—sternly and loudly, though the words were slurred by her loose tooth and swelling cheek. "He knows all about it, Mr. Findley."

Findley turned to her, his face a mask of rage and confusion.

Sandra ignored him. She was watching the boy now. The kid. Turk. The kid yanked the hood of his poncho up over his head and turned away from his father in a gesture that was eloquent with contempt. He was bound away from here, Sandra realized. She could read that in his body, the way he hunched his shoulders and straightened his spine. It wasn't the way it had happened in Orrin's story but it was the same, somehow. The boy was heading for his own unspeakable land . . . though perhaps not the one Orrin Mather had imagined for him.

Findley saw his son begin that long walk away from him. "Wait," he called out, weakly.

But Turk ignored him. He walked past the window

of the coffee shop, casting a reflection on the rain-slick, fire-bright asphalt. He turned a corner into darkness. Findley stared into the falling rain until there was nothing to see.

Sandra slid into the backseat of Bose's car, looking for something she could use to bandage Orrin's wound. Bose gave her a roll of cotton from the first-aid kit he kept in the glove compartment. Orrin had bled a lot—blood and rain had soaked the loose weave of his shirt—but a few sutures would close the wound. Sandra could do it herself, she supposed, if Bose decided they couldn't risk an emergency ward. "Hold this here," she told Orrin, putting his free hand on the cotton wad. "Can you do that?"

He nodded. "Thank you," he said, his voice unnaturally calm.

Bose drove past the burning van, a few barren blocks to the highway. The highway was almost empty of traffic and the storm was as dense as fog, a rain-slashed darkness. He drove at a steady pace toward the city he couldn't see.

CHAPTER THIRTY

TURK'S STORY

We flew to Vox under a crazed sky. External temperature readings rose so high that the ship's sensors began to sound intermittent alarms. Dawn was viciously bright, and the sun when it rose looked bloated and threatening. But it wasn't the sun that had changed; it was the protective barrier surrounding the Earth.

During the first uneasy years after the end of the Spin, people had speculated about what would happen if the Hypotheticals withdrew their protection. The answer was so appalling as to be unthinkable. And whatever their purposes, however obscure their motives, the Hypotheticals had seemed intent on preserving human life; so we had accepted the illusion of normalcy and even begun to believe in it, which was presumably what they wanted us to do.

But I remembered what the astrophysicists had

said. During the Spin the sun had aged almost four billion years. The sun was a star, and stars expand as they grow old, often swallowing the planets that surround them. Without the continuing intervention of the Hypotheticals, the atmosphere of the Earth would be scoured away, the seas would evaporate like puddles on a July afternoon, and the rocky mantle itself would begin to melt.

Now, at last, that protection had been withdrawn.

The influx of radiation was already driving the weather. We flew south to Antarctica at sixty thousand feet, dodging thunderheads that boiled into the stratosphere like black, fluid mountains. And as we approached Vox—as we dipped down into the buffeting winds and streaming rain—our aircraft informed us that it was pushing the limits of its performance envelope. A little more of this and it wouldn't be able to fly.

"Cut it out of me," I said to Allison.

We were in the forward cabin, watching the end of the world. She gave me a queasy look.

"I mean it," I said. "You told me this vehicle would fly back to Vox by itself if I wasn't controlling it."

"Yes, but—"

"Then cut the node out of me."

She thought about what I was asking her. "I'm not sure I can," she said. "I mean . . . cleanly."

"Then do it messy," I said. "You promised me as much."

She gave me a defiant stare, then dropped her head and nodded.

o   o   o

The man I had killed was not in any absolute sense an innocent man. Nor was my father, whose crimes were exposed by the killing.

The man I had killed (I learned) was a drifter by the name of Orrin Mather, who had robbed a half dozen liquor stores between Raleigh and Biloxi before he was hired by my father. In all of these robberies he had threatened to use a weapon (a secondhand .42 caliber pistol), and in three of them he had actually fired the gun. None of his victims died, but he left one paralyzed from the waist down. All these facts emerged during my father's trial.

My father may not have known the man he hired was a criminal, but it surely wouldn't have surprised him. It was his habit to recruit employees from among the casual and undocumented laborers who gathered around the Houston bus depot. He paid them in cash and asked only that they keep their mouths shut. If he happened to learn about a man's criminal record or uncertain immigration status, he used the knowledge to extort the man's loyalty. Generally he started such men as lifters and carriers in the warehouse, moving them into more sensitive positions if they demonstrated an acceptable combination of sobriety and servility. That had been Orrin Mather's career path.

I was never arrested for my crime. The fire was self-evidently an act of arson, but there were no witnesses. The subsequent investigation uncovered a cache of highly controlled substances in the warehouse, chemical compounds imported from the Middle East and marked for delivery to a longevity-drug ring operating out of New Mexico. By the time my father was remanded for trial I was on the road; by the time he was sentenced I was an ordinary seaman in the recently revived U.S. Merchant Marine, doing deck duty on a freighter bound for Venezuela. My father was found guilty on three counts including conspiracy to distribute, and he ultimately served five years of a ten-year sentence. I learned all that from the newscasts. I had no further contact with my family.

If Allison was correct, those things had happened not to me but to someone else—to the original and authentic Turk Findley, the long-extinct template from which I had been reconstructed.

And maybe that was true. Maybe I even wanted it to be true.

But if I wasn't the man who had started that fire, if I wasn't the man whose life had been shaped by it, if I wasn't the man who had carried his burden of guilt from an old world to a new one, if I wasn't the man who had second-guessed every opportunity and repented every pleasure, if I wasn't the man who had allowed a shamefaced sense of obligation to take him deep into the oil lands of Equatoria—if I wasn't that man, what was I?

Allison brought a med kit to the forward compartment and performed the surgery in view of the sky. Without moving my head I could see clouds the color of steel wool roiling against the aircraft's leading edge. "Stay still," she warned me.

She cut deep and fast. The blood covered her hands and clotted in my hair, and even after she packed the wound with gels, the pain was sickening. But she killed the limbic implant and extracted every part of it she could safely reach.

Our aircraft homed in on Vox, fighting turbulence so severe I could feel the deck bucking under me. According to its built-in protocols, it had been trying to contact Vox Core for landing instructions. I asked Allison whether there had been any response.

"Briefly," she said.

"Someone's alive down there?"

"Isaac," she said.

The clouds opened and we could see Vox Core a few hundred feet below us. There had been visible damage—the exposed surfaces of walls and towers looked eroded, almost melted—but most of the city was intact. Our aircraft banked unsteadily toward the nearest tower and landed on an open bay, along with a gust of toxic air.

Allison helped me to the hatch as soon as the air outside was clean enough to breathe.

Isaac had come up to meet us. He had left a trail of footprints on the deck, which was covered with floury white dust. The dust, he said, was what was left of the Hypothetical machines. They had come to consume Vox, to dismantle it, to catalog it, molecule by molecule, and Isaac had hacked their procedural protocols, broadcasting disruptive codes from deep in the Coryphaeus. But not soon enough.

"They took flesh first of all," he said.

There was no one left alive. No one but us, three bloodstained witnesses to the world's end. We went down into the ancient city to wait.

CHAPTER THIRTY-ONE

SANDRA

Sandra told her brother Kyle about the facility outside of Seattle. She thought he'd like it—it was a lot like Live Oaks, she said. Good doctors. Big rooms. Lots of green lawn and even a little bit of forest, that green wet West Coast forest. Seldom as hot as Houston.

Though even Houston was tolerably cool this morning. She had wheeled Kyle from his room at the residential complex to the mott of live oaks by the creek. The sky was blue. There was a breeze. The oaks bent together conspiratorially.

Kyle was looking skinny. The doctors had said they were adjusting his feeding regimen to deal with a minor but persistent digestive problem. But today his mood was benign. He registered his appreciation of the weather, or her presence, or the sound of her voice, or nothing at all, with a gentle *ah*.

The managers of Kyle's trust fund had given tentative approval to her plan to relocate him, and they were negotiating terms with the Seattle facility. As for herself . . . Bose had been patient and encouraging, but it was still a radically new life she was about to embark on. Certainly, she couldn't go back to the old one.

Nor could Bose. The investigation of the fire at the Findley warehouse had been appended to a federal investigation of the life-drug ring Findley had serviced. The FBI had cited Bose as a "person of interest," which meant he had to stay out of sight for a while, but that wasn't a problem: Bose's community of friends knew how to shield one of their own. He had asked her to join him, without preconditions, long-term or short-term, as a friend or a lover—or whatever she was comfortable with. His friends, he said, would help her find work.

She had met some of those friends of his, the ones who administered the Martian longevity treatment as the Martians had intended—the middle-aged couple who had driven Orrin and Ariel out of Houston, to begin with, and others when she visited Seattle.

They seemed like decent-enough people, earnest in their beliefs. The only hope of salvaging this overheated and heedless world, they believed, was to find a new way of being human. The Fourth treatment was a step in that direction. Or so they claimed, and Sandra wasn't sure they were wrong . . . though they might be naïve.

And there was Bose himself, a Fourth by default and at the wrong age. Some of the qualities she loved in Bose might have come out of that treatment—his easy calm, his generosity, his sense of justice. But most of Bose was just—Bose. She was certain of it. It was Bose she had fallen in love with, not his blood chemistry or his neurology.

But he had told her bluntly there was no hope of getting the Fourth treatment for Kyle. Bose had received it because it was the only way of saving his life; Kyle didn't qualify, mainly because the treatment wouldn't really cure him. As Bose had said, it would only render him an infant in a healthy man's body, perhaps permanently. And that was an outcome Bose's friends, after all their colloquies and ethical debates, couldn't countenance.

Kyle slumped in the wheelchair with his head inclined, his eyes tracking the swaying oaks.

"I got a letter from Orrin Mather yesterday." Bose's friends had been characteristically generous about helping Orrin and Ariel during the investigation that followed the fire, finding them a home where neither the law nor the criminals were likely to come looking. "Orrin's working part-time at a commercial nursery. His shoulder healed up nicely, he says. He says he hopes things are going well for me and Officer Bose. Which I guess they are. And he says he doesn't mind about me reading his notebooks."

(*I would of given you permission,* Orrin had written, *if you had asked,* and Sandra accepted the implied rebuke.)

"He says what I read was everything he ever wrote, except for a few pages he finished after he got to Laramie. He enclosed them with his letter. Look—I brought them with me."

You can keep these pages, Orrin had written. *I*

don't need them anymore. I believe I'm finished with all that business. Maybe you will understand it better than I do. It is all bewildering to me. To be honest I would rather just get on with things.

She listened to the creek as it rippled through the grove. Today the creek was running shallow, as clean and bright as glass. She guessed this water would eventually wend its way into the Gulf—or evaporate, perhaps, to fall as rain in some cornfield in Iowa, as snow in some wintery northern town.

The sum of all paths, Sandra thought.

Then she took up the pages Orrin had sent her and began to read them aloud.

CHAPTER THIRTY-TWO

ISAAC'S STORY / ORRIN'S STORY / THE SUM OF ALL PATHS

My name is Isaac Dvali, and this is what happened after the end of the world.

In the end, Vox was mine. Its people (whom I had hated) were dead (which I regretted), and there was no one left alive but Turk Findley and the impersona of Allison Pearl.

Do you blame me for hating Vox?

The people of Vox had resurrected me when all I wanted was to die. They had believed I was something more than human, when in fact I was something less. All I had ever received at their hands was pain and incomprehension.

I had been among the Hypotheticals, my captors insisted, the Hypotheticals had "touched" me; but that wasn't true. Because the Hypotheticals (as Vox imagined them) simply didn't exist.

My father had made me so that I could hear the Hypotheticals talking to themselves, the whispers they sent between stars and planets, and what I had learned was that the Hypotheticals were a *process*—an ecology, not an organism. I could have told my captors so ... but it was a truth they would have rejected, and it would have changed nothing.

The Hypotheticals were already billions of years old when they first intervened in human history.

They had originated with the first sentient biological civilizations to arise in the galaxy, long before the Earth and its sun condensed from interstellar dust. Like the first shoots rising from a wheat field in the spring, those forerunner civilizations were fragile, vulnerable, and alone. None of them survived the exhaustion and ecological collapse of their host planets.

But before they died they launched fleets of self-replicating machines into interstellar space. The machines were designed to explore nearby stars and broadcast home whatever data they acquired, and they did that, patiently and faithfully, long after their creators had ceased to exist. They moved from star to star, competing for scarce heavy elements, exchanging behavioral templates and fractions of operating code, changing and evolving over time. They were, in a sense, intelligent, but they were never (and would never become) self-aware.

What had been released into the desert vacuum

and starry oases of the galaxy was *the inexorable logic of reproduction and natural selection*. What followed was parasitism, predation, symbiosis, interdependency—chaos, complexity, life.

I hated the people of Vox—whom I could *hate* collectively, because they *behaved* collectively—for their deeply embedded limbic superstitions, and for calling me back from the indifference of death into the pain of my physical body. But I could not hate Turk Findley or the woman who had come to call herself Allison Pearl.

Turk and Allison were broken and imperfect things— like me. Like me, they had been created or summoned by the will of Vox. And, like me, they proved to be something more and less than Vox had anticipated.

I had first met Turk in the Equatorian desert, before he or I had passed through the temporal Arch. Out of ignorance or spite, and not quite by accident, Turk had once killed a man, and he had built a life on the foundation of that guilt. His best acts were acts of atonement. His failures he accepted as a kind of punishment. He craved a forgiveness he could never earn, and he was horrified when the Coryphaeus offered him that forgiveness. Accepting it would have dishonored the man Turk had killed (who was named Orrin Mather); and the people of Vox, by submerging all such feelings in their closed limbic collectivity, had made themselves monstrous in Turk's eyes.

Allison was a different case. She was a native of Vox whose artificial persona had allowed her a rare glimpse beyond the boundaries and limitations of her life. By adopting that persona as her own, she had successfully liberated herself from the Coryphaeus. The liberation had come at the expense of her family, her friends, and her faith.

It was a bargain I understood very well.

I wanted these two people to survive. That was why I abetted their escape. Even then, I had doubted they could successfully cross the failing Arch. But I made it possible for them to live a little longer, depending on how you measure time.

For more than a millennium the Hypothetical machines had been scouring the surface of the Earth, dismantling and interpreting and remembering the ruins of the civilization we had built on the planet that gave us birth.

There was no conscious will behind this act of scavenging, no thought, no *agency*. It was simply behavior that had evolved over time, like photosynthesis. The devices Turk had confronted on the Antarctic plain had accumulated a rich storehouse of data. Earth's tangible resources—rare elements that had been refined by human activity and concentrated in the wreckage of our cities—had already been extracted and transferred to orbit and beyond, where the space-faring elements of the Hypothetical ecology had feasted on them. The Hypotheticals were very nearly finished with the Earth.

But their sensors (orbital arrays of devices no bigger than grains of dust, complexly networked) had detected Vox as soon as it crossed the Arch and directed ground-based scavengers toward it. What the

Voxish prophecies had imagined as an apotheosis was just a mopping-up exercise: the last berry plucked from a barren, dying bush.

The Hypotheticals arrived not long after Turk and Allison had fled, as a cloud of insect-sized disassemblers. They were sharp-toothed and efficient. They exuded complex catalysts that unzipped chemical bonds; they came through the melting walls like smoke, followed by the toxic external atmosphere. Gusts of poison blew down the corridors and walkways of Vox Core. This was a mercy, in a way—most of the citizens succumbed to asphyxiation before they could be devoured alive.

Could I have saved them?

I hated the people of Vox for compounding my suffering by resurrecting me, but I wouldn't have wished such a fate on them. In fact I did what I could to protect them—which was nothing.

I was lucky to be able to save myself.

Of course I was protected in the most basic sense. Like Turk, I had passed through the temporal Arch. For ten thousand years I had been a memory in the archival functions of the Hypotheticals, and they had re-created me in the Equatorian desert because that was the business of the temporal Arches: to faithfully reconstruct certain information-dense structures so that the data they contained could be used to correct errors that might have crept into local systems. It was a homeostatic mechanism, nothing more.

The disassemblers wouldn't touch my body because I had been tagged as useful. But that protection would be worthless if Vox dissolved into its component molecules. I needed to be able to exercise conscious control over what the machines were doing.

My best opportunity lay with the Coryphaeus. The processors that constituted the Coryphaeus were heavily protected. Even the nuclear detonation that had brought down the Network had not destroyed these devices, only damaged their interface with the physical world. The disassemblers would surely devour them, but not until most of Vox Core had been pulled apart. Much of my consciousness was already embedded in these processors. The same inhibitions that prevented the disassemblers from dismantling my body might extend to the Coryphaeus's hardware, or could be made to—or so I hoped.

The Network began to fail as the citizens of Vox died in significant numbers, and I exploited that terrible opportunity. I used dormant processors to analyze the signaling protocols of the Hypothetical machines. I linked those protocols and signaling mechanisms into the deeply nested feedback cycles of the Coryphaeus, allowing me some measure of control.

And as Vox was sterilized of human life, the Coryphaeus became a chorus of one. I became the Coryphaeus.

Once I had decoded the procedural logic of the disassemblers, it became possible to feed them false recognition signals. They promptly abandoned the deconstruction of Vox Core. I used subtler and more potent instructions to reduce them to dormancy. They lost all organizing cohesion and fell from the air like dust.

But it was too late for the inhabitants, and nearly too late for the upper levels of Vox Core, which had been eroded to a skeletal framework of girders and fractured cladding. I was able to reseal the inner portions of the city and repair the relatively minor damage to the engine decks, using a combination of robotic devices and co-opted disassembler flocks. I allowed the disassemblers to dispose of all human remains, leaving nothing half consumed.

By the time I restored the city's lights, the corridors and tiers and plains of the city were as empty as if they had never been inhabited. The air-circulation system eventually seined away any remaining dust.

But that wasn't all I could do, I discovered.

As I waited for Turk and Allison to return—as I hoped they would—I began to explore the newly porous borderland between the Coryphaeus and the Hypotheticals. Before long I was tapping into systems larger than the Earth itself. All Hypothetical devices were interconnected, in nested hierarchies that reached from tiny disassemblers to archival machine flocks in translunar orbit, energy-mining mechanisms in the heliosphere of the sun, signal transducers in the outer solar system, transducers circling nearby stars. All these I could now perceive and influence.

I devised filters to compress this flood of information into intelligible packets, making the secrets of the Hypotheticals small enough that I could contain them. And making myself larger in the process.

My physical body began to seem redundant, and I thought about allowing it to die. But I would need it, I thought, to interact with Turk and Allison, if and when they came back. What they found here would be difficult for them to accept, and what I planned to do next would be difficult to explain.

Over the course of their multibillion-year evolution the Hypotheticals had learned to exploit a capability they had never acquired for themselves: *agency.*

Agency—that is, volitional action aimed at achieving conscious ends—had arisen only sporadically in the galaxy, mostly in the climax ecologies of biologically active planets orbiting hospitable stars. Species capable of agency seldom lasted longer than it took them to overload and overwhelm their planetary ecologies. They were, as the stars measure time, an unstable and ephemeral phenomenon.

But it was just such a species that had created the self-reproducing machines that were the first progenitors of the Hypotheticals. And these blooms of organic sentience were unfailingly useful: they generated unusual information; they concentrated valuable resources in their ruins; often they launched new waves of replicators, which could be harvested or absorbed into larger networks.

In time the Hypotheticals began to actively cultivate organic civilizations.

There was no *agency* in this, only a blind acquisitiveness. The Hypotheticals evolved in ways that maximized their exploitation of sentient organisms. Early in the history of the galaxy, an organic civilization had constructed twin Arches in order to colonize the marginally habitable planet of a neighboring star—the species suffered decline and extinction soon after, but its technology was analyzed and adopted by the Hypotheticals. In the same way the Hypotheticals had learned to extract energy from stellar cores and gravity gradients, to manipulate atomic and molecular bonds, to order and stabilize the exchange of information over distances of hundreds of light years. Eventually the Hypotheticals had developed a means of extending the useful life of such species. If a fecund mother planet was suspended inside a temporal distortion while a system of Arches was put in place—as the Earth had been suspended during the Spin—that planet's resource base could be expanded tenfold; its organic civilization would spill into new worlds and flourish on them, cycling through epochs of decline and expansion, reliably generating new and exploitable technologies.

Such organic species remained mortal and eventually died, of course. All biological species did. But the harvest of ruins increased exponentially.

Allison and Turk arrived at Vox Core in the storms that followed the collapse of the Arch and the dismantling of the systems that had for so many years protected Earth from its ancient, dying sun.

I welcomed them back and explained what had happened. I told them I could defend them even from the destruction of this superannuated planet—I had grown that powerful, and in a very short span of time.

But they were shocked by the deaths that had taken place. For days they wandered the empty corridors of the city. The rooms they once shared had been carved away in the initial attack of the disassemblers; they could have chosen any of tens of thousands of abandoned suites and rooms in which to make a home, but Allison told me she was unnerved by everything the dead had left behind them . . . the unsorted possessions, the place settings abandoned on tables, the nurseries without children. The city was full of ghosts, she said.

So I built them a new residence in a forested tier deep to starboard, using the city's fleet of robotic constructors. I chose a location far from the public corridors, accessible by footpath. The tier's artificial sunlight was bright and convincing, its ambient temperature consistently pleasant, its average humidity low. The recycling system stirred up gentle breezes every morning and evening, and rain fell every fifth day.

They agreed to live there until they found a better home.

I believed there might be a better home for them, though not on Vox, and certainly not on Earth. But most of my attention was occupied with the business of keeping Vox Core intact in an increasingly harsh environment.

At Earth's equator the oceans had begun to boil. Cyclonic winds scoured the lifeless continents, and the atmosphere grew thick with superheated water vapor.

Monstrous surge tides threatened to force what remained of Vox into the rocky Antarctic shelf. And it would only get worse.

I needed to manipulate very powerful Hypothetical technology, which meant extending and elaborating my control of it.

I was able to call down from orbit a small fleet of nanoscale devices—versions of the disassemblers that had first swarmed us—to encase and protect Vox Core. Scalding waves crashed over the rocky part of the island and broke against the city's jagged towers, but the city itself remained stable, temperate, and undisturbed. Preserving this equilibrium required gigajoules of energy, drawn directly from the heart of the sun.

It was still little more than a stopgap. Before long we would need to leave the planet altogether. I believed I could accomplish that, though it would necessitate an even greater disconnection between my mortal body and my mind.

Often during this time, walking through the passageways of Vox Core, I was startled by the sight of my reflection in a glassy surface—by the reminder that I was still a collation of blood and bone and tissue, bearing the scars of my forcible reconstruction. And the subtler scars of less visible injuries.

My father had made me what I was because he had believed in the power of the Hypotheticals to liberate humanity from death. The Voxish religion had fostered a similar belief, a programmed limbic rebellion against the tyranny of the grave.

And now the stone had rolled away, revealing only the weakling prophet of a mindless god. How disappointed my father would have been!

o   o   o

"I can control the passage of time," I told Turk and Allison. "Locally, I mean."

Although they were my friends, they were afraid of me and of what I was becoming. I didn't blame them for that.

I had come to visit them in their home in the forest. The house I had built for them was as pleasant as I had planned it to be. The trees beyond the windows were tall and graceful. The air that whispered through the portcullis smelled of living things. They asked me to sit down at their table. Allison offered me fruit from a bowl and Turk poured me a glass of water. I was too thin, Allison said. It was true that lately I had been forgetting to eat.

I told them about the world outside. The bloated sun was scouring away the Earth's atmosphere. Before long the crust of the planet itself would begin to melt, and Vox would be afloat on a sea of molten magma.

"But you can keep us alive," Turk said, repeating what I had told him weeks ago. "Right?"

"I believe I can, but I don't see the point in staying here."

"Where is there to go?"

The solar system wasn't entirely inhospitable, despite the swollen sun. The Jovian and Saturnian moons were relatively warm and stable. Vox could have sailed indefinitely on the blue-gray seas of Europa, for instance, under an atmosphere no more toxic than Earth's.

"Mars," Allison said suddenly. "If you're serious, I

mean if we can really travel between planets—there's an *Arch* on Mars—"

"No, not anymore." The Hypotheticals had protected Mars as long as there was a human presence there. But the last native Martians had died centuries ago and their ruins had been thoroughly scavenged; in recent decades the Arch had been allowed to decay and collapse. (I extracted this knowledge from the Hypotheticals' pool of data, which had become my second memory.) Mars was a closed door.

"But you're saying Vox Core can function as a kind of spaceship," Allison persisted. "How far can it go, how fast?"

"It can go almost any distance. But only at a very small fraction of the speed of light."

She didn't have to explain what she was thinking. The planets that comprised the Ring of Worlds were linked by Arches but separated by vast physical distances. Some of these distances had been calculated by astronomers even in Turk's time. The nearest human world was more than a hundred light-years from Earth. Reaching it would take several lifetimes. "But I can modify the passage of time so that it would seem like much less. A few hundred days, subjectively."

"But it won't be the same Ring of Worlds when we get there," Allison said.

"No. Thousands of years will have passed. It's impossible to predict what you might find."

She looked out at the forest. Beams of artificial sunlight raked through the trees like bright, vague fingers. The tier's high ceiling was the color of cobalt. No birds or insects lived here. There was no sound but the rustling of leaves.

After a while she turned back to Turk. He nodded once. "All right," she said. "Take us home."

I let my physical body sleep while I defined a sphere to contain Vox Core and part of the island beneath it. That sphere constituted our border with the exterior universe. Spacetime curved around us in a complex new geometry. Vox Core soared away from the dying Earth as if it had been fired from a gun, though we didn't feel it: I further modified the local curvature of space to create the illusion of gravity. After a few hours we had passed beyond the orbits of Uranus and Neptune.

Turk and Allison had expressed curiosity about the journey. I would have liked to show them where we were—show them directly, I mean, without mediation— but it was impossible to look at the exterior universe from inside Vox—to human eyes it would have appeared as a literally blinding cascade of blue-shifted energy, even the longest electromagnetic waves compressed to lethal potency. But I could sample that cascade at intervals and downshift it to visible wavelengths to create a series of representative images. I compiled these images and displayed them to Allison and Turk in their forest home. The result was spectacular but not soothing. The sun was a sullen ember against the darkness of space, the Earth already invisible at the edge of the heliosphere. Stars rolled past as Vox Core slowly rotated—a remnant motion I hadn't bothered to correct. "Lonesome," Allison remarked in a small voice.

To an outside observer we would have looked like

something paradoxical: an event horizon without a black hole, a lightless bubble from which nothing escaped but a few wisps of radiation.

In fact the barrier that enclosed us was more complex than any natural event horizon. There were no words in any human vocabulary to describe how it functioned, though I told Turk, when he asked, that it was both a barrier and a conduit. Through it, I maintained my contact with the Hypotheticals. And as we counted years for seconds I began to feel the long rhythms of the galactic ecology—the voids of abandoned or dying stars, the bright World Rings (only one of which was the familiar human one) thriving under Hypothetical cultivation, the intense activity that surrounded newly formed stars and emerging biologically active planets.

But there was no soul or agency in any of this, only the mindless pulse of replication and selection, unspeakably beautiful but as empty as a desert. The ecology of the Hypotheticals would churn on inexorably until it had depleted every heavy element, exhausted every source of energy within its reach. When the last star blinked into darkness, the Hypothetical machines would mine the gravity wells of ancient singularities; when those singularities evaporated and the universe grew dark and blank . . . well, then, I supposed the Hypotheticals would die, too. And unlike human beings, they would die without complaint. No one would mourn them, and nothing would inherit the ruins they left behind.

It became ever more difficult to remember to tend to the needs of my organic body. I lived in the quantum processors at the heart of Vox Core, and, increasingly, I lived in the cloud of Hypothetical devices that surrounded and followed us as we fell between the stars.

I allowed myself to wonder what would happen when Turk and Allison eventually left me. Where I would go. What I would become.

Allison had preserved, or perhaps inherited, her namesake's penchant for writing. I discovered she was setting down a narrative of everything she had experienced between the Equatorian desert and the holocaust of the Vox Archipelago, the words painstakingly hand-printed on crisp white paper. When I asked her who she was writing it for, she shrugged. "I don't know. Myself, I guess. Or maybe it's more like a message in a bottle."

And wasn't that what Vox Core had become? A bottle adrift and far from shore, its glass baked green by sun and starlight, bearing messages of bone and blood?

I encouraged her to keep writing and I memorized each page she showed me: that is, I committed it to every repository of memory available to me, not just my mortal brain but the processors of the Coryphaeus and the archival clouds of the Hypothetical entities surrounding us. One day these words might be all that remained of her.

I suggested to Turk that he might write his own story, but he didn't see the point of it. So I settled for conversation. We talked, often for hours, whenever I sent my mortal body to visit their forest home. I knew everything the Coryphaeus had once known about him, including what Turk had said to Oscar about the man he had killed, and he was able to speak freely.

"I made it my business to learn about Orrin Mather," he said. "He was born with some kind of brain damage. He lived most of his life with an older sister in North Carolina. He got into a lot of fights, drank some, eventually left home and made his way west. He held up a few stores when he ran out of cash and put a man in the hospital once. He wasn't a saint—far from it. But I didn't know any of that when I did what I did. Really he was just somebody who got dealt a bad hand at birth. Other circumstances, he might have been something else."

Which was true of all of us, of course.

I told Turk that if he wrote down what he remembered about Orrin Mather and Vox Core I would keep the words safe, along with Allison's, as long as Vox and the Hypothetical ecology survived.

"You think that'll make any kind of difference?"

"Not to anyone but us."

Turk said he would think it over.

These people, Allison and Turk, were my friends. They were the only real friends I had ever had, and I was sorry I would have to leave them. I wanted something of theirs to carry with me.

The Hypothetical ecology was a forest, lush and mindless, but that didn't mean it was uninhabited. You might say it was haunted.

I had had hints of this before. I wasn't the first human being to access the memory of the Hypotheticals, though my case was certainly unique. The Martians had attempted such connections, sporadically, in the years before the bionormative movement suppressed all such experiments. The first human being on Earth to make the link was Jason Lawton: he had survived his own death by colonizing the computation space of the Hypotheticals—still survived there, perhaps; but his capacity to act, his *agency,* had been very limited. (It occurs to me that this is almost the definition of a ghost.)

And many of the nonhuman civilizations that had come before us had found their own ways into the forest.

They remained there still, long after their physical civilizations had declined and vanished. They were difficult for me to detect, since their activity was disguised to prevent the Hypothetical host networks from identifying and deleting them. They existed as clusters of operative information—virtual worlds— running inside the data-gathering protocols of the galactic ecosystem.

I sensed their presence but could discern little else about them. The content of these clusters was fractally distributed and impenetrably complex. But there was genuine agency there—not just consciousness but deliberative action that affected external systems.

So I was not alone!—though these alien virtualities were so well defended that I couldn't contrive a way to contact them, and so ancient and inhuman that I probably wouldn't have understood anything they might have had to say.

o   o   o

Most of a year had passed since our initial conversation when Turk handed me, without comment, a sheaf of papers on which he had written the history of his experiences in Vox Core. (*My name is Turk Findley,* it began, *and this is the story of the life I lived long after everything I knew and loved was dead and gone.*) I thanked him gravely and said nothing further about it.

We were approaching one of the stars that hosted a planet in the Ring of Worlds. I decelerated Vox Core, dumping kinetic energy into this new system's energy mines (thus raising the temperature of its sun by some imperceptible fraction of a degree), and began to ramp down the time differential between Vox and the external universe. As we passed the orbit of the star's outermost planet I showed Turk and Allison an image I had captured: the host star, just beginning to show a discernible disc, seen past the rim of a cold gas giant orbiting far outside the habitable zone. Deep in this stellar system, but still too far away to be visible as anything but a pinprick of reflected light, was the planet its human occupants called (or had once called) Cloud Harbor (in a dozen languages, none of them English).

It was a watery world, laced with island chains where the tectonic plates of the planet's mantle ground against one another. It had once hosted a benign and relatively peaceful human society, occupying both the available dry land and a number of artificial archipelagos. Most of Cloud Harbor's polities had been cortical democracies, with a few settlements of radically bionormative Martians. But thousands of years had passed since then. We had to assume that any or all of this might have changed.

Allison asked me in a small voice whether I could tell anything about the planet as it was now.

In fact I had been trolling for stray signals. There had been none, or none that I could identify. But that might only mean that the resident civilization had adopted highly lossless modes of communication. Certainly the Hypotheticals were still active here. The icy planetesimals in the far reaches of the system swarmed with busily breeding machine entities.

I was with Allison and Turk as the time differential between Vox Core and the external environment counted down to 1:1. I had created a viewscreen which filled an entire wall of the largest room of their home—in effect, a window to the world beyond Vox. It had been blank. Suddenly it filled with stars.

Cloud Harbor swam into view, an amplified image; we were still light-minutes away.

"It's beautiful," Allison said. She had never seen a world like this from space—the people of Vox had never been very interested in space travel. But Cloud Harbor would have been beautiful even to a jaded eye. It was a swirled crescent of cobalt and turquoise, its icy white moon standing half a degree off the sunlit horizon.

"A lot like the way Earth used to be," Turk said.

He looked at me for a response. When I didn't speak he said, "Isaac? Are you all right?"

But I couldn't answer.

No, I wasn't all right. My body was numb. My mind

was full of inexplicable lights and motion. I tried to stand and toppled over.

Before my senses faded I heard the wail of a distant siren—it was the old autonomic defense system built into the city's deep infrastructure, warning of an invasion I couldn't see.

The people of Cloud Harbor had seen us coming. The warped spacetime around our temporal bubble, bleeding energy as it decelerated into the system, had broadcast easily detected bursts of Cherenkov radiation. So they had come to meet us.

They thought we might be hostile. They knew we weren't an ordinary Hypothetical machine—they had learned a great deal about the nature of the Hypotheticals in the centuries since Vox left Earth. As soon as we dropped our temporal barrier, they isolated Vox Core from local energy sources and infiltrated our processors with finely tuned suppressor protocols. The effect was that the Coryphaeus went to sleep. And since much of my awareness was embedded in the Coryphaeus, I promptly lost consciousness.

I was eventually able to reconstruct what followed. Spacecraft with human passengers swarmed through the disabled barriers and docked with Vox Core. Unopposed, they entered the city and tracked down Turk and Allison, who were able to explain—once linguistic difficulties had been sorted out—who they were and where they were from. They insisted that I was not dangerous and demanded that I be released from what amounted to an induced coma. The troops of Cloud Harbor declined to do that until they were certain I was harmless.

It was an inauspicious meeting, but by the time I came to myself again it had become a more or less friendly one. I woke in my mortal body, in a comfortable bed in a medical suite in Vox Core. My mental functions had been fully restored. A woman who claimed to represent "the combined polities of Cloud Harbor" entered the room, introduced herself, and apologized for the way I had been treated.

She was tall and dark-skinned. Her eyes were large and widely set. I asked her about Turk and Allison.

"They're waiting outside," she said. "They want to see you."

"They've come a long way, looking for a home. Do you have one to offer them?"

She smiled. "I believe we can make them welcome. If you're curious about our world, I've made public records from every polity available to your external memory. Judge for yourself what kind of people we are."

I accessed the records in an eyeblink and was reasonably satisfied, though I didn't tell her so.

She said, "You've come a great distance yourself, Isaac Dvali. We can make a place for you, too."

"Thank you," I said, "but no."

She frowned. "You're a unique individual."

"Too unique to leave this city." I repeated what she already knew, that I shared too much of my consciousness with the processors of the Coryphaeus to allow me to leave—my body would be little more than a drooling piece of meat if it was extracted from Vox Core.

"We can address that problem," she said confidently.

Humanity had learned a few things about the nature of the Hypotheticals, she explained. The polities of Cloud Harbor had already begun to establish virtual colonies inside the computational space of the local Hypothetical networks. Colonists were generally the elderly and infirm, who were eager to leave their physical bodies behind—I could do the same, she said.

"I'm happy enough here."

"Alone?"

"Alone, yes."

"Do you understand what you're sentencing yourself to? Solitary confinement—for eternity, or until your sense of self erodes and becomes chaotic."

"I can take precautions against that."

I could tell she didn't believe me. "What do you mean to do, then? Tumble through the galaxy until the end of time?"

Like a bottle on the sea.

"Long ago," I said, "my father owned a library of books. One of the authors I read there was a man named Rabelais. When he learned he was dying, Rabelais said, *Je m'en vais chercher un grand peut-être.* It means, *I go to seek a great perhaps.*"

"But all he found was death."

I smiled. *"Peut-être."*

She smiled in return, though I think she felt sorry for me.

I said good-bye to Allison and Turk. Allison begged me to take up the offer the ambassador had made and stay here, embodied or not. She wept when I refused, but I was adamant. I didn't want another incarnation. I hadn't sought or wanted this one.

Turk stayed a while after Allison left the room. He said, "I sometimes wonder whether something singled us out for all this—for everything that happened to us. It all seems so strange, doesn't it? Not like other people's lives."

Not much like, I agreed. But I didn't think we had been singled out. "It all could have happened countless other ways. There's nothing special about us."

"You think you'll find something at the end of it? Something that makes it all make sense?"

"I don't know." *Peut-être*. "We all fall. We all land somewhere."

"You have a long trip ahead of you."

"It won't seem long to me. I'm traveling light."

"You carry what you carry," Turk Findley said.

I enclosed the city in its bubble of slowtime and borrowed sunlight for acceleration. Vox Core soared beyond the orbit of the system's outermost planet, out into the interstellar vacuum and far from Cloud Harbor. From my vantage point this took only a moment. The city's clocks ticked seconds for centuries.

I had no destination. Occasional brushes with massive stars skewed my trajectory in unpredictable vectors, a drunkard's walk through the galaxy. Apart from avoiding obstacles, I did nothing to intervene.

In the physical body of Isaac Dvali I often wandered the tiers and passageways of Vox Core. The city persisted in its daily rhythms, regulating its atmosphere, tending its empty parks and gardens. On these walks I occasionally passed robotic maintenance machines as they rolled down public passageways, steel monks hurrying to their matins. They resembled people but they lacked moral agency, and I resisted the unreasonable urge to speak to them.

It was a pointless anachronism to preserve the cycle of day and night, but my mortal body preferred it. Days, I basked in artificial sunlight. Evenings, I read ancient books reproduced from the Voxish archives, or reread the memoirs Turk and Allison had left me.

Nights, while my body slept, I expanded my sense of self to include all of Vox Core. I modeled the aging galaxy and my place in it. I tapped trickles of information from the ever more complex skein of the Hypothetical ecology. Stars that had been young only moments ago exhausted their nuclear fuel and decayed into simmering embers: brown dwarfs, neutron stars, singularities in their bottomless graves. Compared to the passage of time in the exterior universe, my consciousness was vast and slow. This would have been the true viewpoint of the Hypotheticals, I imagined, had the Hypotheticals possessed a unitary consciousness.

Signals propagating at the speed of light passed between stars as quickly as one neuron communicated with the next in Isaac Dvali's mortal brain. I began to become aware of the galaxy as a whole form, not just a collation of stellar oases separated by light-years of emptiness. Hypothetical networks ran through it like fungal hyphae through a rotten tree. In my night vision I saw this activity as threads of multicolored light, revealing a complex and otherwise invisible galactic structure. Thriving world-rings stood out like the closed chains of carbon atoms in an organic molecule. Ancient, dead rings shimmered like pale ghosts as the Hypothetical machines associated with them died for lack of resources or scattered to nearby stellar nurseries.

The living galaxy pulsed with exhaustion and renewal. New technologies and energy sources were discovered, exploited, shared.

And as the universe aged and expanded, other galaxies, already immensely distant, fled toward the limits of perceptibility. But even these faint, far structures had begun to reveal a hidden life of their own, emissions of stray signals suggesting they had evolved their own Hypothetical-like networks. They sang like unintelligible voices in the darkness, fading.

It was inevitable that I would have to abandon my mortal body and live exclusively in the processors of the Coryphaeus and in the cloud of Hypothetical nanotechnology surrounding Vox Core. But I still wanted to be able to move about the city in a physical way. So—as I allowed the body of Isaac Dvali to lie in a self-induced coma, dying of starvation—I fashioned a more durable substitute, a robotic body equipped with equivalent senses, in which I could instantiate my consciousness. When this project was complete I gathered the remains of my organic self in my inorganic arms and carried the corpse to a recycling station, feeding its useful proteins into the closed biochemical loops of Vox Core. I felt no remorse or grief, and why should I? I was what I had become.

The fragile meat in which the message of myself had first traveled to the stars, the old somatic galaxy in its border of skin, I gladly fed to the city's forests.

Vox Core wasn't an entirely self-sufficient system. I was forced to harvest trace elements from stellar nebulae in order to replenish what couldn't be recycled. Of course, in the long run, Vox Core was as mortal as all baryonic matter, even inside its temporal fortress. It was only a question of time.

I courted the end of all things.

Vox Core fell into a long elliptical orbit of the galactic core. I began to divide my awareness into saccades, moments of perception separated by long periods of inactivity, so that experiential time passed more quickly, even inside the temporal bubble surrounding Vox Core.

Entropy—in the form of broken chemical bonds, irreparable system failures, radioactive decay—gnawed at the city's vitals. Blight and drought decimated the forests and rubble began to obstruct the public walkways. Maintenance robots expired for lack of maintenance. Atmospheric regulators—the city's lungs—gasped and finally failed. The air of Vox Core would have been toxic, had there been anyone alive to breathe it.

The quantum processors of the Coryphaeus continued to function, protected by multiple redundancies. But that, too, was only temporary.

The universe grew colder. The galaxy's stellar nurseries, the concentrations of dust and gas that gave birth to stars, had grown too thin to be fecund. Old stars guttered and died and were not replaced. The Hypothetical ecology retreated from this encroaching darkness to the galaxy's dense core, harvesting the gravitational gradients of massive dark holes for energy.

And something else happened to the Hypothetical ecology as it sheltered in the galaxy's still-beating heart: its information-processing mechanisms were co-opted and dominated by sentient species seeking to outlive their organic mortality. These rogue virtualities grew, encountered one another, and in some cases merged. (The human species was the source of one such sentient bloom, though its virtual descendents could hardly be called "human" in the classic sense.) Pools of post-mortal sentience began to cooperate in a collective decision-making process—a kind of cortical democracy, on a scale of light-years. The dying galaxy began to generate unitary thought.

None of these thoughts could be rendered in conventional language, though my larger self understood them, at least approximately.

I took a last walk in my robotic body through the ruins of Vox Core, its towers fractured and askew, its vast tiers dark or tremblingly half-lit. Vox had sailed the seas of several worlds, and was sailing now on the largest sea of all, but soon I would have to abandon it. I had already begun relocating my memories and identity to the cloud of Hypothetical nanodevices, which was linked in turn to the remaining Hypothetical networks, all powered by the dynamos of ancient singularities.

And even that last redoubt of order and meaning was doomed. Soon enough, the same phantom energy

that had inflated the universe would unravel matter
itself, leaving nothing but a dust of unbound sub-
atomic particles. Then, I thought, the darkness would
be absolute. And I could sleep.

But for now, Vox Core sailed on. Vacuum invaded
its faltering defenses. Empty, it succumbed to emptiness. In the absence of induced gravity, its contents
began to spill through breached walls into space.

Beyond it, outside of it, my somatic boundaries
expanded disconcertingly.

The Hypothetical network grew denser and more
complex as its virtual polities applied immense calculating power to the problem of survival. Gravitational
anomalies suggested the existence of megastructures
larger than the event horizon of the universe itself—
shallow gradients of ghostly energy that might serve
as a medium to carry organized intelligence out of the
entropic desert. But how, and at what cost?

I didn't participate in these debates. My own consciousness, though now totally incorporeal, was too
limited to fully comprehend them. In any case the arguments could never have been rendered in words—
the preamble to a single thought would have required
thousands of volumes, a legion of interpreters, a vocabulary that had never existed.

The three-dimensional macrostructure of the universe began its ultimate collapse. Collapsing, it revealed
new horizons. Hidden dimensions of space-time un-
furled as new particles and forces crystallized from
quantum foam. The ultimate darkness I had hoped
for never arrived. The entity that had been the Hy-

pothetical network—to which I was inextricably bound—expanded suddenly and exponentially.

But I can't describe the realm we entered. We were forced to invent new senses to perceive it, new modes of thought to comprehend it.

We emerged into a vast fractal space of many dimensions and discovered we were not alone there. Multidimensional structures hosted entities that had subsumed the four-dimensional space-time that once contained us. As old as we were, these entities were older. As large as we had become, they were larger. We passed among them unnoticed or ignored.

From this new point of view, the universe I had inhabited became an object I could perceive in its entirety. It was a hypersphere embedded in a cloud of alternative states—the sum of all possible quantum trajectories from the big bang to the decay of matter. "Reality"—history as we had known or inferred it— was only the most likely of these possible trajectories. There were countless others, real in a different sense: a vast but finite set of paths not taken, a ghostly forest of quantum alternatives, the shores of an unknown sea.

Putting a message in a bottle and setting it adrift is a quixotic act, sublimely human. What would you write, if you wanted to write such a message? An equation? A confession? A poem?

This is my confession. This is my poem.

Deep in that cloud of unlived histories were unlived lives, infinitesimally small, buried in eons of time and light-centuries of space, unreal only because

they had never been enacted or observed. I understood that it was within my power to touch them and
thus to realize them. What followed, if I made such
an intervention, would be a new and unpredictable
tributary of time: not obliterating the old history but
lying alongside it. The price would be my own awareness.

I could never *enter* that four-dimensional space-
time. Any intervention I made would create a new history from that point forward . . . at the expense of my
continued existence.

What is inevitable is not death but change. Change is
the only abiding reality. The metaverse evolves, fractally and forever. Saints become sinners, sinners become saints. Dust becomes men, men become gods,
gods become dust.

I wished I could say these things to Turk Findley.

I could have intervened in my own potential history, but I felt no urge or need to do so. I wanted my
last act to be a gift, even if I couldn't calculate its ultimate consequences.

Deep in the mirrored corridor of unenacted events, in
a motel room on the outskirts of Raleigh, North Carolina, a woman performs a sexual act in exchange for
a brown plastic vial containing what she believes to
be a gram of methamphetamine. Her partner is an
unemployed pneumatic drill operator on his way to
California, where he has been offered a job in his
cousin's construction business. He doesn't wear a con-

dom when he penetrates the woman, and he drives away shortly after the act is consummated. The taste of meth he gave her when he rented the room was authentic, but the vial he leaves on the dresser contains only powdered sugar.

Orrin Mather's existence is compromised from the moment of his inglorious conception. His anorexic mother delivers him prematurely. His infant body suffers the agonies of drug withdrawal. He survives, but his mother's malnutrition and multiple addictions have taken a toll. Orrin will never be able to make and enact plans as easily as others do. He will often be surprised—usually unpleasantly—by the consequences of his actions.

I cannot make him a more perfect human being. That isn't within my power. All I can give him are words. And by writing these words into the cerebellum of a child, I dissolve myself and make a shadow world real.

He lies sleeping on a mattress on the floor of a rented trailer home. His sister, Ariel, sits on a plastic chair a few feet away, eating cereal without milk from a chipped bowl, watching television with the sound turned down. Orrin dreams he is walking on a beach, though he has only seen beaches in movies. In his dream he sees something rolling in the surf—a bottle, its green glass faded by years of sunlight and salt water. He picks it up. The bottle is tightly sealed, but it opens, somehow, at his touch.

Papers tumble out and unfold themselves in his hand. Orrin hasn't yet learned to read, but, magically, he can read these words. He reads them all, page after page. What he reads here, he will never forget.

My name is Turk Findley, he reads.
And: *My name is Allison Pearl.*
And: *My name is Isaac Dvali.*

My name is Isaac Dvali and

I can't write this anymore.

My name is Orrin Mather. That's what my name is.

My name is Orrin Mather, and I work in a green-house in Laramie, Wyoming.

In the greenhouse at this nursery where I work, there are paths between the plants and the seedling tables. That's so you can get from one place to another. Also so you can work on the plants without stepping on them. Those paths all connect with one another. You can go this way or you can go that. It all has the same beginning and the same ending. Though you can only ever stand in one place at once.

I believe I was born with these dreams or memories about Turk Findley and Allison Pearl and Isaac Dvali. They troubled me much when I was younger. They came to me like visions. They blew through me like a wind, as my sister, Ariel, liked to say.

That's why I went to Houston on the bus so suddenly. That's why I wrote down my dreams in my notebooks.

Things in Houston didn't happen the way I expected. (As you know, Dr. Cole, and I expect you'll be the only one to read these pages . . . unless you show them to Officer Bose, which is all right with me if you do so.) I suppose I took a different path from how I dreamed it. I never robbed any stores, for instance. I guess I could have. God knows I was hungry and angry enough from time to time. But whenever I felt like hurting someone I thought about Turk Findley and the burning man (which was me!), and how terrible it would be to carry around the weight of another man's death.

I work in the greenhouse mainly at night but they keep the big lights on all the time. It's like a house where it's always noon on a sunny day. I like the wetness in the air and the smell of growing things, even the sharp smell of the chemical fertilizer. Do you remember those flowers outside my room at State Care, Dr. Cole? Bird of paradise you said they were called. They look like one thing but they're really another. But they didn't choose to look like that. They're just what time and nature made of them.

We don't grow that kind of flower in the greenhouse where I work. But I remember how pretty they were. They really do look like birds, don't they?

I don't believe I will write to you again, Dr. Cole. Please don't take that the wrong way. It's only that I want to put these troublesome things behind me.

The people Officer Bose introduced me to have been real kind. They found me this job, and a place for Ariel and me to live. They are good people, even if what they do is outside of the law. They are not criminals exactly. They just think they can invent a better way of living.

Maybe they will succeed at their work. If they do then maybe the world won't turn barren and poisonous, like in the dreams I wrote down. I hope that is the case.

I don't know, of course. But you can trust these people, Dr. Cole.

And I know you trust Officer Bose. He helped me when he didn't have to. He's a good man, I believe.

I thank him, and I thank you for the same reason.

Well, that is all I have to say. I have to go to work pretty soon.

Don't expect to hear from me again.

Ariel sends her kind regards, and asks me to tell you that Houston is too damn hot.

Orrin Mather
Laramie, Wyoming

ACKNOWLEDGMENTS

This book couldn't have been written without the help and patience of friends and family members too numerous to mention; needless to say, I thank them all. Thanks also to Glenn Harper, who generously answered a technical question (about the relative size of a human being vis-à-vis the Planck length and the limits of the observable universe)—the answer didn't make it into the final text of *Vortex,* at least not explicitly, but it helped clarify my thinking about the nature of "the Hypotheticals" and their intervention in human history. On the subject of oceanic eutrophication and the fate of the Earth, I drew on *Under a Green Sky* and *The Medea Hypothesis,* by the reliably pessimistic Peter Ward, and I commend both books to the attention of curious readers.